D1595598

WHEN I SLEEP, THEN I SEE CLEARLY

WHEN I SLEEP, THEN I SEE CLEARLY

Selected Poems of
J.V. Foix

Translated from the Catalan,
with an introduction by David H. Rosenthal

Persea Books / *New York*

Poems in this volume have appeared in *Catalan Review, International Poetry Review, New Directions 31, Seneca Review, World Literature Today,* Mr. Rosenthal's *Modern Catalan Poetry: An Anthology* (St. Paul: New Rivers Press, 1979), and his own book of poems *Eyes on the Street* (New York: Barlenmir House, 1974). The translator's introduction was originally published in somewhat different form in *World Literature Today.*

Translation copyright © 1988 by David H. Rosenthal
Original poems copyright © 1970, 1974, 1979, 1985 by J.V. Foix
All rights reserved.

For information, contact:

Persea Books
60 Madison Avenue
New York, New York 10010

Library of Congress Cataloging-in-Publication Data

Foix, J.V.
   [Poems. English. Selections]
   When I sleep, then I see clearly : selected poems of J.V. Foix ; translated from the Catalan, with an introduction by David H. Rosenthal.
      p.   cm.
   ISBN 0-89255-130-5 (pbk.) : $12.95
   1. Foix, J.V.—Translations, English.   I. Title.
PC3941.F57A27 1988   849'.9154—dc19   88-5786 CIP

The publication of this book was supported in part by a grant from the National Endowment for the Arts.

The publisher wishes to thank the Departament de Cultura de la Generalitat de Catalunya and Xavier Bru de Sala of Enciclopèdia Catalana for their interest and assistance.

Typeset in Galliard by Keystrokes, Lenox, Massachusetts
Printed and bound by Capital City Press, Montpelier, Vermont

First Edition

Let's write new verses with fossilized signs!
Let's paint immature nakedness on archaic sheets!

—J.V. Foix, "On a Lone Freshwater Boulder"

Contents

Introduction by David H. Rosenthal   ix

Letter to Clara Sobirós   *3*

Alone and dressed in mourning...   *6*

I like, at random...   *7*

Si pogués accordar Raó i Follia...   *8*
If I could reconcile Reason and Madness   *9*

Just as in my youth...   *10*

I fear the night...   *12*

Who lives me in you...   *13*

Bring on the oars...   *14*

When I spied my rival...   *15*

Les cases, de roure i de caoba...   *16*
The oak and ebony houses...   *17*

Practice   *18*

Last Sunday at three P.M....   *21*

Es feia fosc...   *22*
It Was Getting Dark...   *23*

Dead Faces Fell...   *25*

With Cold-Numbed Body...   *26*

We Would Have Split More Pines If the Oxen
Hadn't Stared at Us So Fixedly   *29*

Beyond the Centuries, Immobile   *31*

I Don't Know Where I've Come From   *33*

Al peu d'una muralla ciclòpia...   *34*
At the Foot of a Cyclopean Wall...   *35*

The Stroller and His Memory   *38*

At the Entrance to an Underground Station...   *39*

Frontiers   *41*

Es quan dormo que hi veig clar   *42*
When I Sleep, Then I See Clearly   *43*

The Other Landscape Foreshortened   *47*

The Difficult Encounter   *49*

El men país és un roc...   *50*
My Country's a Rock...   *51*

Vaig arribar en aquell poble...   *54*
I Arrived in That Town...   *55*

She Wanted to Stay Alone...   *58*

I Know a Town Far from Provence   *59*

We Were Three, We Were Two,
It Was Me Alone, We Were None...   *60*

Everything is Fenced-in and
Submissive Beyond the Segre   *62*

The ashes are hot, travelers...   *64*

A Rose with a Knife in its Breast Jumps,
Bleeding, from a Window   *65*

The Nunwatcher   *66*

At the hottest time of day...   *67*

Introduction

For almost seventy years, J.V. Foix (pronounced Foshe, 1894-1987), was the acknowledged master of avant-garde Catalan poetry. From 1917 on, he collaborated with his nation's artistic vanguard, including internationally known painters like Joan Miró and Salvador Dalí, both of whom he presented in their first one-man shows. In addition to his poetic and journalistic activities (he edited magazines like *Trossos [Pieces]*, *La Revista Catalana [The Catalan Review]*, and *Monitor*), Foix was also the prosperous owner of two fine pastry shops. His customers sometimes asked if by any chance he had a son who wrote those weird poems with the long titles.

Considering Foix's stature in Catalonia and in the Iberian peninsula as a whole, where his writing has been enthusiastically received in Castilian translation (he won Spain's highest literary honor, the National Prize for Literature, in 1985), it might seem strange that a book of his poetry in English has not appeared previously. In fact, he simply shared the fate of Catalan literature as a whole. Even such prose masterpieces as Joanot Martorell's classic fifteenth-century novel *Tirant lo Blanc*, described by Cervantes as "the best book in the world," and Mercè Rodoreda's *The Time of the Doves*, which Gabriel García Márquez called "the most beautiful novel published in Spain since the Civil War" were unavailable in English until recently. This situation, in turn, was partly caused by the Spanish Civil War, in which Catalans fought on the losing side. After Franco's victory in 1939, the Catalan language was banned from public use. Signs were hung in offices: *"No ladres. Habla el idioma del imperio."* ("Don't bark. Speak the imperial language.") Forgetful citizens were fined for speaking their native language in the streets, and books were burned. From the sixties on, the fascists' policy of frontal assault was softened to one of slow suffocation, but Catalan literature continued to lead a somewhat furtive underground existence, almost inaccessible to interested foreigners, until Franco's death in 1975.

I first met Foix, who had recently celebrated his ninetieth birthday, in 1984 at his summer home in Port de la Selva on the Costa Brava. Though he could no longer read, hike, or sail—three of his favorite activities—he remained entirely lucid and explained that although he had stopped writing poetry in the expectation that he would soon die, he had changed his mind, realizing that he might very well survive another five or ten years, and was about to publish a new volume of prose poems from which the last piece in this book is taken. My wife and I spent a long afternoon asking him questions about his work, consuming a first-rate paella, and listening to anecdotes involving close friends like Federico García Lorca, Salvador Dalí, and Joan Salvat-Papasseit. Not surprisingly, Foix said he sometimes thought life had been more interesting back in the 1920s. He also told us about the time, shortly after the Civil War, when the police had come to arrest him for his Catalan nationalist views. Covered with flour, Foix emerged from the back of his pastry shop and informed the cops that the proprietor had fled to France. On that visit and succeeding ones in Barcelona, I was struck by Foix's lively wit, his generous praise of younger writers and painters, and his utter lack of the vatic airs sometimes affected by aging "great authors." To the end, he delighted in life's poetic epiphanies and unexpectedly surrealistic moments, which he described as a major inspiration for his work.

Foix and Salvat-Papasseit, both of whom emerged in the 1910s, were the first truly modern Catalan poets. While Salvat died in 1924, Foix went on to forge a style and vision that made him a leading figure in modern European literature. In a fictitious "Letter from Italy" at the beginning of his book *Poems in Electric Waves* (1919), Salvat commented that "Here in Rome it's rumored that to understand Mr. Foix of Sarrià one should first read Sophocles." The choice of Sophocles is somewhat arbitrary, but Salvat's meaning is clear enough: part of Foix's subject matter is culture itself.

Foix was, indeed, far more cultured than Salvat. Like more traditional Catalan poets such as Carles Riba, Foix sought to establish direct links with the Catalan past, drawing into his work what he conceived to be an entire Mediterranean tradition. This synthetic effort is perhaps clearest in early sonnets like "If I could reconcile Reason and Madness . . ." At the time of its composition (between 1913 and 1927, according to an introductory note), Foix was also writing experimental prose poems, some of which are included here. Yet the form of "If I could reconcile Reason and Madness . . ." is classically Petrarchan and uses Ausiàs March's characteristic decasyllables. Broken into two sentences, the sonnet really makes one long, closely-knit period. The tone is meditative, philosophical, and suggestive of Ramon Llull's efforts to join intellect and feeling:

> Memory and desire came together and climbed the Beloved's [i.e. God's] mountain, so that understanding might increase and love be redoubled in loving the Beloved.

In this context, the word "Madness" also suggests Llull, who often appears in his own books under the *senhal* of Ramon the Mad.

Also evoked, however, are a series of "classical" equilibria—between Apollonian and Dionysiac principles, between transience and eternity, between imagination and reality. Thus, in the poem, the opposition of Reason and Madness is followed by a subtler dichotomy: between the clear morning air and Mediterranean Sea, symbolic of Greek rationality, and Foix's own individual sensibility "that lusts for joy." These dichotomies are joined together by the creative act itself. The Eternal can be made concrete through the poet's "fantasy . . . of words, sounds, and tones."

So explained, the argument sounds rather dry. In the poem itself, however, Foix imparts a deeply involving sense of breathless intellectual adventure. He does so, in part, by constantly linking abstractions with emotionally-charged language. Two examples would be "My mind, that lusts for joy" and "with fantasy/ That the heart inflames." Another instance is the fascinating shift from the abstract "O sweet ponderings!" to the vividly sensory "Sweetness in mouth!" The poem's syntactical structure—the way it slowly builds toward its final "light and dancing!"—also contributes to the emotional impact.

A glance at the epigraphs Foix chooses for his early sonnet sequences—quotations from Guido Cavalcanti and Dante, Ausiàs March and Llull, Bernart de Ventadorn and Jordi de Sant Jordi—will suggest some of his poetic models and give a more precise idea of what "Mediterranean tradition" means here. The link to the *stilnovisti* and to March and Llull is particularly evident in the densely speculative and passionate texture of Foix's poetry. He seeks what T. S. Eliot, speaking of the English metaphysical poets, called "a direct sensuous apprehension of thought, or a recreation of thought into feeling." In addition to Foix's medieval and early Renaissance sources, there is also a strong effort to reach back toward classical antiquity. This aspect is most obvious in the juggling of opposites ("make the Eternal present," "make today permanent," "and that strange shadow . . . be good sense and guide") that in the sonnet's final tercet are linked and brought into a kind of Platonic tension by the imagination:

> Bring alive sleep's eye-evoked images;
> And time might not be; and the hope
> Of Absent Immortals, light and dancing!

In these final three lines, Foix condenses a tremendous amount of thought and feeling. The imagination, conceived of here as closely akin to dreams, can make the transient permanent and turn the idea of the gods into a concrete ritual of artistic celebration.

Foix's sonnet-writing period ended in the late 1920s. From then on most of his work was unrhymed, more structurally open, and often enriched by long explanatory or scene-setting titles that are poems in themselves. When the poetry has a specific historical context, these titles—together with the dates at the end—can be very useful. One poem, dated September 1936, opens with a scene from the outbreak of the Spanish Civil War:

AT THE ENTRANCE TO AN UNDERGROUND STATION, BOUND HAND AND FOOT BY BEARDED CUSTOMS OFFICIALS, I SAW MARTA SET OFF IN A TRAIN FOR THE FRONTIER. I WANTED TO SMILE AT

HER, BUT A POLYCEPHALOUS MILITIA-MAN CARRIED ME OFF WITH HIS MEN AND SET FIRE TO THE WOODS

In other cases the titles may be more complicated, but they usually attempt to orient the reader. "At the Foot of a Cyclopean Wall . . ." opens with a clearly etched scene involving two figures: a pulley-adjusting mechanic and an uneasy observer, perhaps the poet himself, "watching the sea with an old book in my hand."

It is helpful to know here that Foix was an aficionado of amateur aviation and a member of the Catalan Aviation Circle. "At the Foot of a Cyclopean Wall . . ." opens in a mood of mystical adulation for the mechanic. Foix knows him "in fable and sleep," describes him in terms suggesting Poseidon ("regal, in a cave by the sea") and Hephaestus ("humming and surrounded by tools,/ Measuring stellar chasms and their foliage"), and even follows him "torch in hand." In the poem's first section, the realistically presented mechanic in his overalls gradually evolves into a god of airplanes who "anoints their gears/ In elliptical hangars and sacred watch posts."

At the same time, Foix develops a strain of natural imagery centered on the sea. This imagery is woven into the portrait of the mechanic ("as if dressed in moss") and is played off against the artificial world of tools and planes just as the clear sea, tamarisks, and sheltered inlets interact with Platonic ideas in "If I could reconcile Reason and Madness . . ." The mechanic is slowly enveloped in a nimbus of magic and ancient Mediterranean myth.

The second stanza continues and deepens this pattern, with natural and sexual imagery gradually gaining dominance over the mechanical. The mechanic disappears and we are left with the plane, which by now is as much a sexual presence as a machine:

> Night's androgyne, generous with seed,
> Darkening the solitudes of primitive meadows,
> Present wherever we covet the body

The plane itself has become alive, a "bird of the afternoon" as well as a divine presence, beautiful and frightening, an "ancestral form" or "menhir."

This series of mystical parallels and correspondences is reinforced by the poem's incantatory quality. Though there is no rhyme scheme, the meter (decasyllables and Alexandrines) is regular within each stanza and underlines the mysterious prayerlike intonation. Another element in this atmosphere is the series of syntactically parallel lines beginning with nouns:

> Flama perenne...
> Brisca cantaire...
> Forma ancestral...
> Claror de freixe...

These nouns are then linked to another series of nouns that locate them in imaginative space:

> ...als merlets de les calmes,
> ...a les blavors boscoses,
> ...als nocturns de les cales,
> ...en el congost del somni.

A final element—the most obvious but the most important of all—is Foix's intensely lyrical imagery in lines like "darkening the solitudes of primitive meadows" or "a singing breeze in the leafy blueness." Such lines are at once literal descriptions of a plane and magical interpenetrations among mechanical, natural, and emotional worlds.

The poem's last stanza introduces still another element: the Eternal Ungraspable. With this transcendent abstraction, another speaking voice also enters the poem, first addressing the poet and then gradually merging with him in a final chant. Here images of the sea mingle with images of fertility and birth ("when joy runs to seed," "It hatches secret creatures") and with the repetitive songs of night fishermen. The result is a sense both of the oneness of everything and the miraculous possibilities of each individual object.

Though "At the Foot of a Cyclopean Wall..." is formally quite distinct from "If I could reconcile Reason and Madness...," the two poems do have a number of interesting similarities—in particular their effort to bind together such opposites as imagination and reality, concrete and abstract, old and new. The effort, in both poems, ends in Platonic unity and in the synthesizing nature of art, an art that makes the intangible specific and brings together all of man's experience. In an often-quoted "Letter to Clara Sobirós," Foix describes the poet as a "magician, word-speculator, pilgrim of the invisible, unsatisfied, adventurer or researcher on the border of sleep." Though the word "magician" seems to emphasize the poet's role as inventor, the succeeding terms suggest that he is the revealer of a world that already exists, independent of his verse. This conviction of a prior poetic reality is even more explicitly stated in an earlier paragraph:

If you read me—and I'm afraid you're thinking of it like someone determined to cross against a traffic light—always remember that I'm a witness to what I tell of, and that the real, from which I depart and live, with my insides burning as you know, and the unreal you think you'll find there, are the same.

To achieve this synthesis, Foix relies heavily on the Catalan physical, cultural, and historical landscape, one aspect of which is the Hellenic and Renaissance tradition that I have already discussed in some detail. Another aspect is the world of Pyrenean shepherds from which Foix's own ancestors came. This world forms the focal point of "My Country's a Rock...," a poem dedicated to his family line and to Catalonia's rough mountain folk in general:

> Freedmen, tough, with freeheld land
> In a circle of rhumbs their slingshot
> Smote the centuries' menhir
> In an autumn of oxen.
> O, the pure honeys of that spot!
> To rediscover my people's image
> Water beyond the furtive garden,
> Wet with dew from the cavern,
> Eternal night's heirs
> With the stars for glowing ashes!

As is often the case with Foix, the date at the end— August 1939, immediately after the Spanish Civil War—is significant. The poem's last four lines, coming after the celebration of a heritage that seemed mortally threatened, are among the most poignant expressions of Catalan post-war sensibility:

> I come and go from rock to rock
> —Or pasture shaved pebbles

In a grove of wild cries—
And when it's dark, I fan the fire.

The end of the war evoked some of Foix's very best work. Prior to 1939, he had been an ardent Catalanist and one of the leaders of Catalan Action, a conservative nationalist group that included a number of prominent intellectuals. An admirer of the French reactionary Charles Maurras, Foix had denounced the Catalan anarchists. He accused them, both in poetry and in prose, of destroying the nation's classically balanced heritage and replacing it with Iberian fanaticism. Despite his often conservative positions, Foix was a highly respected figure during the 1930s. He led the separate Catalan delegation at the 1934 PEN Club Conference in Dubrovnik. He was also the literary director and a frequent columnist for *La Publicitat (Publicity)*, a Barcelona newspaper.

With Franco's victory, of course, all this came to an end. For a time, the future of Catalan literature itself seemed in doubt. It might appear that Foix, whose verse had been so allusive and philosophical, would have been among those least equipped to express the mood of the postwar period. But in fact he did it better than virtually anyone else. Perhaps his outstanding poem of this period is "I Arrived in That Town..." Once again, the date (1942) situates it historically and the title establishes the tone of disorientation and nightmare:

I ARRIVED IN THAT TOWN, EVERYONE GREETED ME AND I RECOGNIZED NO ONE. WHEN I WAS GOING TO READ MY VERSES, THE DEVIL, HIDDEN BEHIND A TREE, CALLED OUT TO ME SARCASTI-

CALLY AND FILLED MY HANDS WITH
NEWSPAPER CLIPPINGS

The clear, simple images that follow, and the innocent speaking voice, help create a mood of childlike bewil-
derment. Beneath this mood, there is also Foix's condition
as a poet suddenly deprived of his audience:

> Just look at that crowd in the square!
> They must be waiting for me;
> I, who read them verses;
> They're laughing as they leave.

It is not just poetry, however, but an entire culture that
has been dislocated. Foix's portrait flutters on a scrap of
newspaper, perhaps symbolizing the end of the Catalan
press and of his position as a public figure. An entire
national identity—and with it memory itself—has been
obliterated. And Foix, who had striven to reconcile
Reason and Madness, has now become a madman, a mem-
oryless imbecile wandering through a town he does not
recognize.

This atmosphere of disorientation is made grim-
mer by lines hinting at the poverty and bloodshed that
followed the war:

> I look at my bare foot;
> In the shadow of a barrel
> A puddle of blood is shining.

In general Foix plays down this element, allowing the
panic to build as the half-naked speaker is mocked by the
townspeople and cannot find his way home. Only in the
penultimate stanza do public events suddenly burst into
the open: "What do they say on the radio?/I'm cold, I'm

scared, I'm hungry." And in the final lines the Devil, whom we had met in the title, reappears. He awaits the amnesiac speaker, consummating the feeling of infantile terror.

"I Arrived in That Town . . ." is one of Foix's most famous poems. In it, surrealistic imagery is played off against a colloquially direct tone in the same way that it was earlier against accumulated literary tradition. Whether Foix really *is* a surrealist has been debated among Catalan critics, but the poet himself always denied it. Though in isolation some of his images may seem rationally inexplicable, they usually do fit into a coherent system of ideas, conceits, and personal myths. In an excellent study of Foix's work, the poet Pere Gimferrer describes his poems as transposing "into metaphorical or visionary terms data from the poet's individual or social experience."

The best explanations, however, come from the poet's own writings. Foix describes himself as a "poetic researcher," one who "rediscovers, by means of new symbols, the permanent." For him, the experimental verse of the 1920s was not so much a new form of consciousness as a new set of genres in which he could work. These genres demand the same poetic discipline and craft as any other kind of verse. Thus Foix admonishes his fellow avant-gardists: "in your verses be hard and precise."

The language here is similar to much of Ezra Pound's criticism. Though it seems improbable that either poet influenced the other, there are a number of parallels between them. Both writers drew on the Mediterranean Middle Ages and Renaissance for inspiration, while using experimental techniques in highly individual ways. Both attempted—Foix more responsibly, I think—to reunite a Western culture they saw as fragmented and decaying, and brought together art and social reality partly by applying artistic standards to the latter. But above all, the two poets both possessed a kind of literary perfect pitch: an ability to write verse at once lyrical and precise, intellectually demanding yet dense with feeling.

Beyond certain superficialities (such as his famous long titles), Foix has had no imitators in Catalonia. His poetry is perhaps both too rigorous and too idiosyncratic to form the center of a school. Nonetheless, he is recognized by young poets and by the reading public as a monumental figure. Appearing early in this century, he—along with Salvat—marked off a broad area of sensibility that Catalan poets have been exploring ever since. This area, which ranges from the most immediate daily impressions to intricate philosophical speculation, is partly responsible for Catalan poetry's rich diversity in the last sixty years.

The prose poems in this selection (with the exceptions of "A Rose with a Knife in Its Breast Jumps, Bleeding, from a Window" from Foix's *Allò que no diu "La Vanguardia,"* Barcelona: Proa, 1970 and "At the hottest time of day..." from *Cròniques de l'ultrason,* Barcelona: Quaderns Crema, 1985) can be found in his *Obres completes II* (Barcelona: Edicions 62, 1979). The remaining poems are collected in his *Obres completes I* (Barcelona: Edicions 62, 1974). I would like to thank Pasqual Maragall (a graduate student in New York at the time he helped me with my translations, and currently mayor of Barcelona), Josep Pujol, Lourdes Beneria, and Josep-Lluís Urpinell for their useful comments and suggestions—and to express my special gratitude to Frederic Amat, Foix's friend and neighbor and one of Catalonia's most talented young painters, for his marvelous illustrations. When I first met Foix in 1984, his face lit up at the news that I brought regards from Amat, whom he described as "a young man who paints with faith, love, and hope!" In addition to my translations, I have included seven poems in the original Catalan. Anyone with a reading knowledge of a Romance language should be able to grasp their texture and sonority, thereby penetrating more deeply into Foix's world and also gaining a sense of the Catalan language's particular sound—a rougher, brusquer sound than one usually finds in Latin-derived tongues.

DAVID H. ROSENTHAL
NEW YORK CITY, 1987

WHEN I SLEEP, THEN I SEE CLEARLY

LETTER TO CLARA SOBIRÓS

Dear and beloved friend,
You wanted me to tell you what I think of poets and poetry.
You didn't dare to ask what I thought of my verses or what I expect
from them. We were returning to Rozesbruck, climbing the road
that runs by where those feverish men hole up in their clamorous
shells, and where the stupidest throw themselves off. But the heart
burned the first ashes and, in brilliant sunlight, at a turning
surrounded by wooded darknesses, I only remembered the night of
your body, and so many unwonted stars that are born and die there.
You urged me to clarify the meaning of some expressions that at-
tracted you by their arrangement, and the sense of several words
that suggested other realities, by no means immediate for everyone.
I, almost out of the game by that time, rejoiced in naming the
clear—or cloudy!—seas reflected in your eyes, or in accelerating
madly to lose myself in a jungle of forms, colors, and sounds, where
you, the other, also were.

What shall I tell you, now that I live by evoking the fennel's
scent in a twilight of forest fires and open fields? I'd like to reply as
though you weren't yet entirely present for me. I move among
appearances, and yours, multiple, dominates. But perhaps you, who
are many, will quickly understand if I tell you that at my age I
find it difficult to define a poet—the world is full of them, but they
don't write—or to clarify what a versifier is. There are also lots of
them. They move through wastelands reading poetic precepts, not
always written with sufficient wit, and copying, clumsily, everything
poets have said through the centuries.

You, when you read, go straight to the meaning of what
writers say or wish to say. If you read me—and I'm afraid you're
thinking of it like someone determined to cross against a traffic
light—always remember that I'm a witness to what I tell of, and

that the real, from which I depart and live, with my insides burning as you know, and the unreal you think you'll find there, are the same. Just as you are another and there are two of you—or more— and you have and are known by a single name: Clara.

I write, when I write, and I wish I had more time for it, beyond precepts, never taking into account, as is the custom nowadays and so many young people die of it, how Teutons, Yankees, Frogs, or Soviets write. The tone of others, and their rhetorical criteria, almost never help me, since it seems to me—I told you this when, amused by my words, you led me further toward where the olive tree glows at night—that I'm one of those who believe that every poet is him. Him alone, face to face with the poem he's written, not to amuse himself or others, or to save himself, but to express himself.

The poet, magician, word-speculator, pilgrim of the invisible, unsatisfied, adventurer or researcher on the border of sleep, expects nothing for himself. Not even redemption. He doesn't florify, or competitionify, or try to please little old ladies. If he were brave enough, and if the bourgeois self-satisfaction of all strata with their extreme vanity hadn't infected him with certain diseases, he wouldn't sign his works. He'd paste up his poems at dawn, like anonymous posters on the walls, or fling them off rooftops. He'd freely show his displeasure with the great, the satisfied, the settled, the contented, at widows chaste and resigned. The poet knows every poem is a cry of liberty.

I already know you'll make me realize, Clara, that in many of my lines I try out ancient rhymes and centuries–old rhythms. It has been—and kiss me before I tell you this—a servitude to the language and the community. Who would dare to encrust invisible walls in a hostile area?

You, who enjoy the unknown and the new—though, from time to time, you bedeck and bejewel yourself with tasteful out-of- fashion cast-offs—can't be totally displeased by the play of images, or by what to others might seem mysterious and even strange in my books. I know by now that you rave with me when the forest

4

raves and the vines burn brightly. But there's lots of sun, as you know, and if I don't speak or sing of you when you take a flying leap and lean your skis against the wall to dry, and savage that you are, you deliberately dishevel your hair, comb it, and laugh as you call my name—the other—it's because my poems always tend to fall short of or go beyond the ground I tread.

Not long ago when you were in Naples, you wrote that I preferred living to writing. As though you were complaining. But I don't think you were frank enough. Or would you rather see me in a bathrobe and house slippers like any decorated writer, and furthermore "Goncourt"?

Alone and dressed in mourning, in an ancient tunic,
I often find myself in dark solitudes,
In unknown meadows and heaps of slate,
And fathomless whirlpools that cunningly halt me.

And I say: Where am I? For what old land,
—What dead sea—or mute pastures
Do you yearn like a madman? Toward what miraculous
Unknown star do I wearily plod?

Alone, I'm eternal. The landscape of a thousand years ago
For me is present, the strange isn't strange.
There I feel born, and in arid desert

Or on some snowy peak, rediscover the place
Where I'd already wandered, and God's trap
To catch me whole. Or the Devil's deceit.

I LIKE, AT RANDOM...

I like, at random, to wander among walls
Of ancient times, and as darkness thickens,
Beneath a laurel tree by a rough fountain,
To remember, with heavy eyelids, sieges and battles.

In the morning I like, with iron tongs
And socket wrenches, to seek the tight-fitting piece
Where gears engage, or the bearing that jams
The axle, and take off smoothly down the highway.

And climb mountain passes, follow shady valleys,
Furiously conquer fords. Oh new-born world!
I also like a linden tree's soft shadow,

The ancient museum, the faded madonnas,
And today's extreme painting! A naive sudden impulse;
The new inflames me and I'm in love with the old.

SI POGUÉS ACORDAR...

Si pogués acordar Raó i Follia,
I en clar matí, no lluny de la mar clara,
La meva ment, que de goig és avara,
Em fes present l'Etern. I amb fantasia

—Que el cor encén i el meu neguit desvia—
De mots, de sons i tons, adesiara
Fes permanent l'avui, i l'ombra rara
Que m'estrafà pels murs, fos seny i guia

Del meu errar per tamarius i lloses;
—Oh dolços pensaments!, dolçors en boca!—
Tornessin ver l'Abscon, i en cales closes,

Les imatges del son que l'ull evoca,
Vivents; i el Temps no fos; i l'esperança
En Immortals Absents, fos llum i dansa!

IF I COULD RECONCILE...

If I could reconcile Reason and Madness
And on clear morning, not far from clear sea
My mind, which lusts for joy,
Could make the Eternal present. And with fantasy

—That the heart inflames and my uneasiness turns aside—
Of words, sounds, and tones, could
Occasionally make today permanent, and that strange shadow
That mimics me on walls, be good sense and guide

For my wanderings among tamarisks and tombstones;
—O sweet ponderings! Sweetness in mouth!—
They might make the Secret true, and in sheltered inlets

Bring alive sleep's eye-evoked images;
And Time might not be; and the hope
Of Absent Immortals, light and dancing!

JUST AS IN MY YOUTH...

Just as in my youth, I delighted in paintings
Fabling the sea and its somber abysses,
Its waves, dark and lofty; and angry
Fictions in black and white, of nature

Cruel and stormy, gave nourishment to
My mind and spirit, at the harsh dawn
Of manly clamor, twilight and the mystery-divulged
Fairy have also brought me cheer and good luck.

Now, at the hour of overcast waters
And lighthouses on lost rocks, or at day's end
Amid ephemeral purples, I delight in the setting

Sun's uncertain light, the melancholy
Of a pine alone between two mountains, or a
Watchdog's sudden bark outside a dark farmhouse.

I FEAR THE NIGHT...

I fear the night, yet night transports me,
Rigid, down lanes past the sooty sea;
In the dying light the street band is heard, discordant.
I'm alone with myself, and this comforts me.

Black coals ring the dead sea,
The low hill and pine slope,
But in them I see a dense jungle
And imagine a door in the barren desert.

The dark night seems a blackboard
And like a child, I draw strange heads on it,
A brand-new world and the land that desire foretells.

I marvel, and am afraid—o night that sharpens
Stars and wisdom!—You fill the sea with clothes,
And a voice says: "It's raining blood in the cisterns."

WHO LIVES ME IN YOU...

Who lives me in you with inseparable joy
That finds me most alone when, a slave to your form
Of sea, light, and azure, I construct the palace
That everyone thinks is a pallet and stable?

Who enjoys you in me, drawing close to your mystery
As though I were, absent, the shell and the skin
Of a secret fruit in a golden husk
Or flimsy rags on a body without hope?

We're a warm bud sprouting in a frost-covered field,
A granary trod by an evident god,
Immortal furrow sown with mysterious seed;

And when my flesh overcomes your desire
We are, in the game, the astral presentiment
That we are free from the Eternal Permanent.

BRING ON THE OARS...

Bring on the oars, my family's always been wanderers,
The sun hangs on my chest amid coral beads
And I say, on board, that I long for peaks and valleys,
For cows milked in a barn while snow falls outside.

Wolves have never scared me; at home
I chase warlocks by torchlight
And, covered with sacks, I sleep beside horses
Or knead, with dead arms, unleavenable bread.

It is I who trod the young vine and stared at that old lady,
And I dive into cold gorges if the lad splits asunder
Or embrace the moon in its difficult meanderings.

One must take risks on land and sea, and in new art,
Kiss a soaked body beneath cinnamon trees
And drop dead at thirty-three, just like Alexander!

When I spied my rival in the distance, motionlessly awaiting me on the beach, I wondered if it was him, my horse, or Gertrude. As I approached, I realized it was a stone phallus, gigantic, erected in the far-off past. Its shadow covered half the sea and an indecipherable legend was inscribed at the base. I went closer so I could copy it, but before me, lying open on the burning sand, was only my umbrella. Upon the sea, without shadow of ships or clouds, floated those enormous gloves worn by the mysterious monster who chased you toward evening beneath the Ribera's plane trees.

Per a Joan Miró

Les cases, de roure i de caoba, s'enfilaven turó amunt i formaven una piràmide caprici d'un artifex ebenista. Aquell era el poble on, sota el signe d'Escorpió, sojornava Gertrudis. Eren tan drets els carrers, que em creia, abans d'ésser al cim, defallir. De l'interior de les cases sortien rares músiques com d'un estoig de cigars harmònic. El cel, de pur cristall, es podia tocar amb les mans. Blava, vermella, verda o groga, cada casa tenia hissada la seva bandera. Si no hagués anat carregat d'un feixuc bidó de vernís, inelegant, m'hauria estret més el nus de la corbata. Al capdamunt del carrer més ample, al vèrtex mateix del turó, sota una cortina blau cel, seia, en un tron d'argent, Gertrudis. Totes vestides de blau cel també, les noies lliscaven, alades, amunt i avall dels carrers, i feien com si no em veiessin. Cenyien el cabell amb un llaç escocès i descobrien els portals i les finestres on vidrieres de fosques colors innombrables donaven al carrer el recolliment de l'interior d'una catedral submergida a la claror de les rosasses. El grinyol del calçat em semblava un cor dolcíssim, i la meva ombra esporuguia l'ombra dels ocells presoners de l'ampla claraboia celeste. Quan em creia d'atènyer el cim, dec haver errat la passa: em trobava en el tebi passadís interminable d'un vaixell transatlàntic. M'han mancat forces per a cridar i, en cloure'm la por els ulls, desplegada en ventall, una sèrie completa de cartes de joc em mostrava inimaginables paisatges desolats.

For Joan Miró

The oak and ebony houses were clustered on the hillside, form-
ing a pyramid, the whim of some cunning cabinetmaker. In
this town Gertrude dwelt beneath the sign of Scorpio. The
streets were so straight I thought I'd lose heart before reaching
the top. Strange music wafted from the houses' interiors, as
from a harmonious cigar box. The sky, pure glass, was within
arm's reach. Blue, red, green, or yellow, each house flew its
flag. If I hadn't been carrying a heavy, inelegant drum full of
varnish, I'd have straightened my necktie. At the end of the
widest street, at the hill's very apex, Gertrude sat on a silver
throne beneath a sky-blue curtain. Winged girls dressed in that
same sky blue slid up and down the streets, pretending not to
notice me. Their hair was gathered with plaid ribbons, and
they flung open doors and windows where innumerable dark
tinted panes made the street as cozy as the inside of a cathedral
submerged in rose-window luminescence. The squeaking of
my shoes seemed the sweetest of choirs, and my shadow startled
the shadow of birds imprisoned in that broad celestial skylight.
Just when I thought I'd reached the top, I must have taken a
wrong turn. I found myself in a warm and endless oceanliner
passageway. I couldn't summon the strength to shout, and as
fear shut my eyes a complete set of playing cards spread before
me in a fan, revealing unimaginable desolate landscapes.

PRACTICE

It's absurd: they said I had to address you, and that at the very hour when sun, sea, and flesh weave dense arborescences and our ghosts wander through this miraculous jungle, I had to deliver a monologue without noticing that there were just a few dozen mummies before me, tragically sentenced to withstand the termite forever. You are by no means unknown to me. I've seen you in funeral processions at the parish storm door and within your moldy chambers, lying on mysterious slipcovered sofas. But I can imitate your faces, if need be, and like yours, my tight-stretched skin is a mask that allows me to behave with the idiocy of one who speaks because his fellow listens. It's absurd, it's absurd. No matter what I might uselessly seek to tell you, a flash of eyes across the sky makes it intelligible to our joyous shadow, which it guides through the jungle our carnal figurations have deserted. My pedantry, then, will humbly recite another's texts. In the jagged blanks between paragraph and paragraph, between author and author, o sister mummies, perhaps you will find those footprints revealing which way my Philips went.

1

An outsize spool unwinds thousands and thousands of yards of black gauze before my eyes. That portrait on the wall I'll never get to hang straight again: Is it Blake? Is it Lenin? Is it my father at thirty-five?

2

After passing through a dense forest of deflated tires, I finally got to touch his shoulder. He has glass eyes and a curly beard like the one on that giant at Poldo's house in Solsona.

3

A sofa on a riverbank is truly a marvel. A man bowed beneath the weight of a huge R slowly advances. He places the initial on the sofa, which teeters and falls into the river. But the river's made of glass and splits in a jagged crack from one bank to the other. If I lie down to touch it and see how thick it is, my hand will start bleeding. A voice makes the poplars tremble deep inside like theater props, and it calls out: MARTA! I simultaneously repeat the name (Could I be the only one who shouted it?). That R must have been an M; it *is* an M; no, it's an R. If only the man who brought it would return! But he's ashamed to be seen in shirtsleeves now that the curtain's risen.

4

If it weren't in such bad shape, we'd take the Ford out of its corner and go for a spin. But it doesn't have wheels! Nonetheless, Ernest Maragall hangs a clay angel above the radiator, clutching a piece of paper in its outstretched hands: *Gloria in excelsis Deo*. That's no Ford, it's a Mathis 717171. If it runs smoothly we'll go pick up Feliça (?), Maria Pepa and Niup (?). There's a dance at the Sant Gervasi Atheneum. But we're all naked and Maragall, jerking my head as though he wanted to strangle me, keeps repeating: "I never wear sport jackets! I never wear sport jackets!"

5

"It's not a horse. Among the grapevines, you say? But with a sea this hairy, the moon's whinnies are only audible at midnight, beneath Garraf's tunnels."

6

The coconut-vendor put on a false mustache so big it made me weep with fear. He took my hand and led me to the back of the stable where the horses slept. To keep me quiet, he showed me, through a cobwebbed crack, the vague landscape where a thousand silver rivers die in the sea, and he filled my hands with olives.

Last Sunday, at three P.M. on the promenade bridge, a drunkard killed a woman for love of a rose, which the murderer then left floating in a pool of blood. The Sunday before that, an identical deed had been witnessed at the same time and place. Today I feel another comparable murder coming on. I should, therefore, warn the tavernkeeper and the police. But my God, what if I'm the murderer? Here's my glass dripping wine, the scarlet of your lips, your self, your sex reflected in the murky red beverage. Pour me another, Rafel! It's two-thirty. On the promenade bridge stands a woman clutching a rose, and my knife is as sharp as the edge of a star.

ES FEIA FOSC I MIRÀVEM L'ESTESA
DE PELLS A CAL BASTER

Ja els fumerols acotxen els jardins;
Les rels, per terra i murs, s'ajoquen al misteri.
Tots dos, efígies de cuir abandonades
A la fosca arenella de la nit,
Cedim, fraterns, a l'hora fraudulosa.
Abrivades, les egües, afolcades,
Nades a l'ombra i a l'ombra nodrides,
Assolen els poblats.
Damunt la pell d'elefant del cel
Els astres obren llurs camins airosos.

Abril de 1928

IT WAS GETTING DARK AND WE GAZED AT THE HIDES SCATTERED AROUND THE SADDLER'S HOUSE

Already vapors clothe the gardens;
The roots, in earth and walls, withdraw into mystery.
Both, discarded leather effigies
In the night's dark sandpit,
We yield, fraternal, to the fraudulent hour.
Emboldened, the mares in their herds,
Born in shadow and on shadow nourished,
Raze the hamlets.
Above the sky's elephant skin
Stars open their airy paths.

April 1928

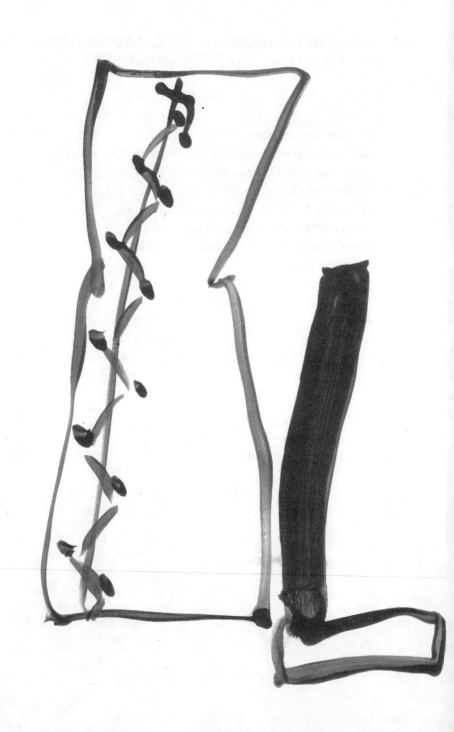

DEAD FACES FELL WITH A RUSTLING OF LEAVES, BUT THE FOREMEN ON THE BUILDING SITES DIDN'T STOP WORK

The sweetness of living conceals the Fact,
And moribund heads are twisted awry;
Firm arms raise up extravagant walls
—And we've ripped up the posters that covered celestial ceilings!
All of us peer through the skylight's eye.
We push down the head, with its dying face,
And your eyes, and my eyes, and all of your eyes
Now close, so tender and dreadful, in sleep.
If we all held hands we would no longer fear
The projection upon plaster
Of so many dead faces,
Nor the mirthless coming and going
Amid swamps, strands and ropes
Of impassive foremen on building sites.

April 1928

WITH COLD-NUMBED BODY, I OPENED DRAWERS
WHERE I KEPT THOUSAND OF POEMS I COULDN'T
REMEMBER WRITING. PILAR ASSURED ME—THE
LEAFY EVENING'S LOW SKY SPARKLED WITH
LIPS—THAT SHE HAD READ THEM. THE DRAWERS
WERE FULL OF HARD, COMPACT HANDS THAT
CLUTCHED MINE WITH STRANGE INTENTIONS

In what dark sea did a schooner sink
With birds deliriously wheeling above spars
And swooning sails that came to rest beneath moss

    —We pulled the petals from lilacs amid ashes.

In what blind grotto are there seashells
Where we hide treasures of roots and water
Eager for the dance, arming ourselves with reeds

    —Outside town we trod upon shadows.

In what unknown courtyard in a sealed home
Did we hear chants of celestial anguish,
Winged insects upon warm outstretched palms

    —Halfway down the gorge we doused our lanterns.

In the back of what tavern beyond the centuries
Did we taste new wines as we sat bewitched
By the sounds of archaic marble in fossil organs

    —We frightened each other with spectral masks.

In what ancient ravine, vital, did we dance
To the nocturnal plaints of swaying groves,
Lunar echo of voices and sea-chanteys

     —We hid our bodies beneath nets.

On what street did we hear rustling algae
When silent, we bade each other farewell,
Bathed in the light of sparkling predictions

     —Wearing new gloves, we scrutinized pearls.

In what hangar on ancient flatlands
In evening dress and crowned with roses
Did we stroke birds' feathers with trembling hands

     —We started hopeless engines.

At what fountain in lost shadow
One naked summer in open night
Were vestals weeping before gods of stone

     —Blindfolded eyes sang of misfortunes.

Above what wall in an hourless night
Did we write names we couldn't understand
And sketch, shame-facedly, lines that were dead

     —With mouths intact, we dulled lustrous laquers.

At what turning of a pale pathway
Did the girls fall from their bicycles,
Plummeting over the cliffs bright and airy

—We crossed ourselves with divining water.

In what fathomless drawers did I seek
Poems never written, that I recall
On crumpled paper and in forged handwriting

—I packed away china and ivory hands.

Cadaqués, September 1930

28

WE WOULD HAVE SPLIT MORE PINES IF THE OXEN HADN'T STARED AT US SO FIXEDLY

Hoist our anchors and gaze at the vaulting sky!
Butterflies sprout from your eyes
And altars branch from hermitage ceilings;
With palm leaves I imitate the beaks of birds.
Waters spray and reeds moan,
Ships hug the shore in the inlet's compass.

(This isn't the path;
                    nor the next one;
                                        there's a pool ahead.)

Hearts thirstily float upon gusty fields of grain.

(It's on the other side, where you'll see a footbridge.)

Blue petals sail upon an ocean of lifting fog,
The oxen's calm pupils mirror deep antediluvian seas,
Raised axes paint warlike symbols amid thick smoke
        shadowing bushes.

Solar poplars fan black windows.

Tell me who you are.
"I don't know where I am."
Tell me what you're doing.
"I don't know where I'm from."

Let's plunge dark carving knives into polyhedrons of lard.

August 1931

BEYOND THE CENTURIES, IMMOBILE

Walls of lime, inaccessible,
The insistent sea, inexorable turquoise
Filling the docile beach with day and night,
With setting suns and tree-trimmed moons;
And you, and I, immobile through the centuries
At the shadowy foot of an eternal column.
We no longer gaze at each other with fiery pupils,
Nor do we, absent, peer into others' eyes
—Permanent transients
Amid white adverse walls
And the nets that conceal abysses behind doors—.
They bear in their hands the most useless of tools,
And pass by, and return,
And strew black feathers upon the sand.
The aroma of fresh-baked bread drifts through caverns,
Our bodies' pink marble,
Far-off latent snow-capped peaks,
Tar's high-billowing fragrant smoke,
And sleepwalkers, present in their timeless passing,
Are the breath of all:
A school of fish bursts into sparks,
Then thrashes in the hollow left by receding waves
Or echoless pulsing in the One Supreme Beat,
Tossing our nets from the tip of the Cape.

El Port de la Selva, August 1931

I DON'T KNOW WHERE I'VE COME FROM

I don't know where I've come from, but light gathers
Beyond the port, with coolness of hawthorn berries
In a twilight of bells and voices
—When chants put forth shoots in the salt of doorways
And the unsubmissive unravels a book's linen.
A bright-eyed sailor leaps over sleep's
Shadowy wall, is lost amid lapping waters,
And plunges into an ancient city of emblems.
Nor do I know where I'm going. I'm neither Slav nor Semite;
On the other sea, stars elude
The utter night, and the desert shore's
Sole tree is a shout of naked whiteness.
Winds burn the hour's scrub
And now a voice shows me a vessel
On the very last pier, with Croatian silences
And forgetful farewells in a chasm of rigging
When we set sail and seabirds roost
In a holly grove of exiled twilights
—Alone and desired amid the straw heaped on our prow—
Fire and grain will make frontiers fertile.

Trieste, April 1933

AL PEU D'UNA MURALLA CICLÒPIA L'HOME DE LA GRANOTA BLAVA, MÉS ALT QUE TOTS, ENCERAVA CORRETGES I AJUSTAVA POLITGES. DE TANT EN TANT, DES DE LES PREGONESES D'UNA ESTRANYA VISERA, EM MIRAVA, SORRUT. JO FEIA EL DISTRET TOT MIRANT EL MAR, AMB UN LLIBRE VELL A LA MÀ

En faula i son conec aquell qui escampa
Vora la mar, pels rocs antics oberta,
Falsos estels, marcits, coberts amb fulls impresos.
Torxa en má l'he seguit entre avions bipètals
Quan, d'amagat, n'ungeix els engranatges
En el·líptics hangars i garites sagrades.
L'he vist, reial, en cova marinera,
Com si vestís draperies de molsa
A sol colgant
                    —quan les ombres palmades
S'ajoquen pels torrents i espien les naixences—,
O en clos murat
                    —quan les hores ancoren
Als ports mentals—
                                brogent i voltat d'eines
Mesurant els avencs estel·lars i llur fronda.

És el menhir de l'alba selvatana,
Remorós de flors d'aigua i llum flairosa,
El muscle adolescent i sangós de migdia,
L'ocella de la tarda, exiliada
Entre hèlices romeves, moridores,
I evanescents motors, a la pista captiva,
L'androgin de la nit, generós de semences,

AT THE FOOT OF A CYCLOPEAN WALL, THE MAN IN
BLUE OVERALLS, TALLEST OF ALL, WAS POLISHING
LEATHER STRAPS AND ADJUSTING PULLEYS. FROM
TIME TO TIME HE LOOKED AT ME FROM BENEATH
HIS STRANGE VISOR, TACITURN. I PRETENDED NOT
TO NOTICE, WHILE WATCHING THE SEA WITH AN
OLD BOOK IN MY HAND

In fable and sleep I know that man who,
Among ancient rocks near the open sea,
Scatters fake faded kites covered with printed sheets.
Torch in hand, I've followed him among twin-engine planes
When in secret he anoints their gears
In elliptical hangars and sacred watch-posts.
I've seen him, regal, in a cave by the sea
As if dressed in moss
Beneath a setting sun
                —when the hand-shaped shadows
Retire into streams and see births—
Or within a closed wall
                —when the hours anchor
In mental harbors—
                humming and surrounded by tools,
Measuring stellar chasms and their foliage.

It's the menhir of forested dawn
Rustling with waterflowers and scented light,
Muscle, adolescent and bloody, of midday,
Bird of the afternoon, exiled
Among wandering mortal propellers
And evanescent motors on the captive runway.
Night's androgyne, generous with seed,

Ombrant les solituds de prades primitives,
Present pertot on cobegem els cossos,
Flama perenne als merlets de les calmes,
Brisca cantaire a les blavors boscoses,
Forma ancestral als nocturns de les cales,
Claror de freixe en el congost del somni.

És l'Etern Inconcret que vaga per les dunes:
—*Llum en ta faç quan em mires i calles*—
O forada els penyals amb punxons impalpables:
—*Obre esguards infinits damunt la mar vermella,*
quan surten fora port les barques de l'encesa
i modulen llurs cants veus pregones i humides.—
Invoca déus novells per les platges abstractes:
—*El teu nom exaltat per gaies tramuntanes,*
quan grana el goig, defalleixes i pregues.—
Crema brossa immortal en els barrancs maresos:
—*Floreix ton cos amb fulla i flor ignorades.*—
Cova obscurs animals en imminents boscatges:
—*Quan l'ombra de tots dos és la Sola Ombra.*

1935

Darkening the solitudes of primitive meadows,
Present wherever we covet the body,
Perennial flame on the battlements of calm,
A singing breeze in the leafy blueness,
Ancestral form in the nocturnes of inlets,
Brightness of ash trees in the canyons of dreams.

It's the Eternal Ungraspable wandering through dunes:
"Light on your face when you see me and grow silent."
Or it pierces boulders with impalpable drills:
"It opens vast vistas above scarlet seas
when fishermen's boats set sail in the darkness
and deep humid voices modulate their chants."
It invokes new gods on the abstract beaches:
"Your name exalted by gay northwinds
when joy runs to seed you faint and you pray."
Immortal burning speck in the ocean's ravines:
"Your body bursts forth in unseen leaves and flowers."
It hatches obscure creatures in immanent groves:
"When the shadow of both is the Single Shadow."

1935

THE STROLLER AND HIS MEMORY

Rose half open in darkness,
Palm by a deserted roadside,
Sea in captive horizon;
Turning will into usury,
I again think the figure:
If you were, then I am.
Burning scrub in dead evening,
A drunken knock at the door,
Love's cries in the night;
I want to speak again,
But the word becomes fable
And my empty chest resounds.
Vanquished star at crack of dawn,
Infants' chorus in purple dusk,
Cuttings from violets;
Forgetting name and chamber
I follow routes of amber
And am unknown to myself.

May 1936

AT THE ENTRANCE TO AN UNDERGROUND STATION, BOUND HAND AND FOOT BY BEARDED CUSTOMS OF-FICIALS, I SAW MARTA SET OFF IN A TRAIN FOR THE FRONTIER. I WANTED TO SMILE AT HER, BUT A POLY-CEPHALOUS MILITIAMAN CARRIED ME OFF WITH HIS MEN AND SET FIRE TO THE WOODS

Stairs of glass on the solar platform
Where trains of light leave for open beaches
Among transparent walls and branching corals
And bright-eyed birds in branches' buzzing.

Is it you, white in the white of this insular dawn,
—Liquid of gaze, hearing inner music—
Do you write wet goodbyes on a forest of windowpanes,
With seed of night for an open dream?

You go beyond joy toward enchanted shores
With gigantic drunks in the thorny cove
And stuffed falcons on rocks marked with crosses,
To a sea where gods walk at night's furtive onset.

I can't reach you, sleeping, blind to light and in mind,
Dressed like a child, without voice or luggage,
Guarded among hoes by double-formed innkeepers;
The passports are old and bloody the hearts.

You take mountains and rivers and stellar lakes
And fountains in cool shadows within deep mailsacks;
A shadowy watch on the flaming peak
Calls to me with strange names and says no with his hands.

In the open they wave torn flags.

1936

FRONTIERS

Down a path, amid inky flames
    I sense nothingness ahead;
A doused lantern flickers in old skies
    And a shadow upon the wall.

I still advance, but a hand bars my way
    And, hard, a voice
Soaked in ancient dew rings out:
    "You're guilty of all murders."

As I shut my eyes, gazing at the landscape
    Of my body's death,
I leave my native country's baggage
    Abandoned upon the ice.

Sant Quirze Safaja, September 1937

ÉS QUAN DORMO QUE HI VEIG CLAR

A Joana Givanel

És quan plou que ballo sol
Vestit d'algues, or i escata,
Hi ha un pany de mar al revolt
I un tros de cel escarlata,
Un ocell fa un giravolt
I treu branques una mata,
El casalot del pirata
És un ample gira-sol.
És quan plou que ballo sol
Vestit d'algues, or i escata.

És quan ric que em veig gepic
Al bassal de sota l'era,
Em vesteixo d'home antic
I empaito la masovera,
I entre pineda i garric
Planto la meva bandera;
Amb una agulla saquera
Mato el monstre que no dic.
És quan ric que em veig gepic
Al bassal de sota l'era.

És quan dormo qui hi veig clar
Foll d'una dolça metzina,
Amb perles a cada mà
Visc al cor d'una petxina,
Só la font del comellar
I el jaç de la salvatgina,

WHEN I SLEEP, THEN I SEE CLEARLY

To Joana Givanel

When it rains I dance alone
Dressed in algae, gold, and fishscales.
There's a stretch of sea at the turning
And a patch of scarlet sky,
A bird whirls in flight
And a bush brings forth branches,
The pirate's old mansion
Is a broad sunflower.
When it rains I dance alone
Dressed in algae, gold, and fishscales.

When I laugh I look hunchbacked
In the pool beneath the threshing floor.
I dress like an old gentleman,
I chase the custodian's wife,
And between pinegrove and kermes oak
I plant my banner.
With a sack-needle I kill
The monster I never name.
When I laugh I look hunchbacked
In the pool beneath the threshing floor.

When I sleep, then I see clearly
Crazed by a sweet poison
With pearls in both hands
I live in a seashell's heart,
I'm a fountain on the canyon floor
And a wild beast's lair,

—O la lluna que s'afina
En morir carena enllà.
És quan dormo que hi veig clar
Foll d'una dolça metzina.

Abril de 1939

—Or the waning moon
As it dies beyond the ridge.
When I sleep, then I see clearly
Crazed by a sweet poison.

April 1939

THE OTHER LANDSCAPE FORESHORTENED

In deep islands I seek the no-thing
Without profiles or marshaled miles,
And between shadow and nacre the new style;
In celestial sea I open shells
    Of dew and light.

From rainbows and knots I shape images,
And in the light of white places
I heed sounds and voices from Nowhere;
The lost trunks are characters
    And I move among them.

I gather sapphires from the haughty sea
When in sunlight the north wind
Languishes on enclosed plateaus;
Amid a hut's straw-colored gold
    A body germinates.

Will I be a shepherd in a vast meadow
Or a sailor in the fiery night?
What goddess fills the valley?
Her ivy and coral nakedness
    Throbs everywhere.

O eternal day, eternal calm:
In bright vineyard and dark grotto

I bump against my absent self:
From algae and salt, palms and blueness
I make my thought.

Calella de Palafrugell, June 1939

THE DIFFICULT ENCOUNTER

You are and are not, and I thrive on deception.
I am and am not, and touch useless fluff.
I watch the impossible flowering stump
And the name you bear above endless beaches.

      In lost ghettos and steep watchtowers
      I seek the lighthouse of absurd milestones.

Like a giant in forgotten lands
I cry out for combat and beseech a foe,
And in dry fountains yearn for birds and fairies
Or man's works bewitch me with their own enchantment.

      In a stormy valley, among fossils and nacre
      I multiply myself into meek simulacra.

Who, of the two, is carnal? Who quickens
The other, and isn't? Where's the Eternal Present?
Oh burning flame along the shore!
Oh sweet blaze of mind and spirit!

      In night's rustlings upon beaches
      I worship the Thing in myriad images.

Calella de Palafrugell, June 1939

EL MEU PAÍS ÉS UN ROC...

A l'estirp dels Foix,
dels Torrents

El meu país és un roc
Que fulla, floreix i grana,
Franc de caça hi tinc cabana
Sense pallera ni soc.
No hi ha omeda, ni pineda,
I la nit s'ajoca, freda,
Sense brossalla ni bruc,
El cel hi venç la fatiga
I si la lluna hi espiga,
Jo peixo, dòcil, el duc.

De silencis faig el jaç
Amb boires per capçalera,
Entre els brancs de la tartera
M'acotxen vents de mal pas.
Tot aleja, pur, i avança
Per camins de deslliurança
Quan el son llumeja el cim:
Só el pastor d'una contrada
On el temps no té plomada
Ni l'home dards per al crim.

No em cal cleda, ni paranys,
Ni freturo l'orriaire;
Sota arbrats de glaç i aire
Bec a la sal dels estanys.
Pel solell i per l'obaga

MY COUNTRY'S A ROCK...

To the family line of the
Foixes and the Torrents

My country's a rock,
Bearing leaves, flowering, seeding.
Freed from hunting, I keep a shed there
Without hayloft or logs.
There are neither elms nor pine groves,
And the night goes to roost cold
Without heather or scrub,
The sky conquers weariness,
And if the moon grows slender
I meekly pasture the eagle owl.

I make my bed of silence
With a headboard of fog.
Winds from high passes tuck me
Among rock-slope branches.
Everything wings, advancing pure
Down paths of liberation
And when sleep lights the summit
I'm the shepherd in a place
Where time has no plumb lines
Nor man darts for murder.

I don't need folds or snares,
And I've got a milking shed;
Beneath groves of ice and air
I drink the ponds' salt.
On sunny and shady slopes

Só el darrer d'una nissaga
Amb erols a tots els vents:
Tots hi són, sense misteri,
Sota creus en captiveri
En un delta de torrents.

Lliberts, i durs, amb alous,
Llur fona en rosa de cercles
Colpia el menhir dels segles
En una tardor de bous.
Oh mels pures del paratge!
Recobrar, dels meus, la imatge,
Aigua enllà de l'hort furtiu,
Molls de rou de la caverna,
Hereus de la nit eterna
Amb els astres per caliu!

Si entre els pics em puny la ment,
La flor de l'alba m'aroma
Amb clarors de l'ampla coma:
Só la pedra en calm clement
Fita en un coll de miracle,
De tots, i de mi, l'oracle;
Vaig i vinc de roc a roc
—O pasturo palets tosos
En un bosc de crits confosos—
I, en ser fosc, hi vento foc.

Els Torrents, de Lladurs,
agost de 1939

I'm the last of a race
With gardens to every wind.
They're all there, without mystery,
Beneath captive crosses
In a delta of streams.

Freedmen, tough, with freeheld land
In a circle of rhumbs their slingshot
Smote the centuries' menhir
In an autumn of oxen.
O, the pure honeys of that spot!
To rediscover my people's image
Water beyond the furtive garden,
Wet with dew from the cavern,
Eternal night's heirs
With the stars for glowing ashes!

If among peaks my mind is troubled
Dawn's flowers perfume me
With broad dells' brightnesses.
I'm a stone in forgiving calm
Marking a wondrous pass,
Everyone's oracle, and my own.
I come and go from rock to rock
—Or pasture shaved pebbles
In a grove of wild cries—
And when it's dark, I fan the fire.

Els Torrents, de Lladurs,
August 1939

VAIG ARRIBAR EN AQUELL POBLE, TOTHOM ME SALUDAVA I JO NO CONEIXIA NINGÚ; QUAN ANAVA A LLEGIR ELS MEUS VERSOS, EL DIMONI, AMAGAT DARRERE UN ARBRE, EM VA CRIDAR, SARCÀSTIC, I EM VA OMPLIR LES MANS DE RETALLS DE DIARIS

Com se diu aquest poble
Amb flors al campanar
I un riu amb arbres foscos?
On he deixat les claus...

Tothom me diu: —Bon dia!
Jo vaig mig despullat;
N'hi ha que s'agenollen,
L'altre em dóna la mà.

—Com me dic!, els pregunto.
Em miro el peu descalç;
A l'ombra d'una bóta
Clareja un toll de sang.

El vaquer em deixa un llibre,
Em veig en un vitrall;
Porto la barba llarga,
—Què he fet del davantal?

Que gent que hi ha a la plaça!
Em deuen esperar;
Jo que els llegeixo els versos;
Tots riuen, i se'n van.

I ARRIVED IN THAT TOWN, EVERYONE GREETED ME
AND I RECOGNIZED NO ONE. WHEN I WAS GOING
TO READ MY VERSES, THE DEVIL, HIDDEN BEHIND
A TREE, CALLED OUT TO ME SARCASTICALLY AND
FILLED MY HANDS WITH NEWSPAPER CLIPPINGS

What's the name of this town
With flowers on the steeple
And a river with dark trees?
Where did I leave my keys?

Everyone says "Good morning!"
I go around half-dressed;
Some people are kneeling,
Another offers me his hand.

"What's my name?" I ask them.
I look at my bare foot;
In the shadow of a barrel
A puddle of blood is shining.

A cowherd lends me a book,
I see myself in a window;
My beard has gotten long.
—What's become of my apron?

Just look at that crowd in the square!
They must be waiting for me;
I, who read them verses;
They're laughing as they leave.

El bisbe em condecora,
Ja els músics han plegat,
Voldria tornar a casa
Però no en sé els topants.

Si una noia em besava...
De quin ofici faig?
Ara tanquen les portes:
Qui sap on és l'hostal!

En un tros de diari
Rumbeja el meu retrat;
Els arbres de la plaça
Em fan adéu-siau.

—Què diuen per la ràdio?
Tinc fred, tinc por, tinc fam;
Li compraré un rellotge:
Quin dia deu fer el Sant?

Me'n vaig a la Font Vella:
N'han arrencat els bancs;
Ara veig el diable
Que m'espera al tombant.

Setembre de 1942

The bishop decorates me,
The musicians have stopped.
I'd like to go home
But I don't know the side streets.

If a girl kissed me...
What would my job be then?
Now the doors close.
Who knows where the pension is?

On a bit of newspaper
My photograph flutters;
The trees in the square
Wave goodbye to me.

What do they say on the radio?
I'm cold, I'm scared, I'm hungry.
I'll buy him a watch.
What's his Saint's Day?

I'm going to Font Vella.
They've pulled up the benches;
Now I see the Devil
Who awaits me at the corner.

September 1942

SHE WANTED TO STAY ALONE IN THE MANSION OF TREELESS PLAINS WHEN THE HOURS ARE NETTED AND BLOOD TRICKLES FROM SLEEP

You entered that mansion with inflatable pen
Full of yourself, by the light of darkness
   —When she-wolves sniff trails
   And waters are becalmed on plains—.
You threw open the window to rustling stars,
Naked of mind, where shadows flow together
   —Where rocks bud upon cliffs—,
Gifted with prophesy, you inhaled the scent of juniper
And rubbed out the Sign with thick flannel cloths.
Taciturn, I've seen you in a room full of deserts,
Dressed in gold, squeezing wax
   —When blood trickles from sleep, time is netted,
   And the miracle-worker walks upon kindly lakes—.
All alone by yourself, in the frost of treeless plains
   —When oils fill the circle
   And invoked flowers open behind turreted walls—,
You live on the deaths of those who run to seed, singing.

Ull de Ter, 1943

I KNOW A TOWN FAR FROM PROVENCE

To Concepció Martí

I know a town far from Provence
White with morning petals,
With no towers for defense
Or estates tilled by serfs
Without houses or mills
Or longing or fear
Or birds perched on sea rocks.
Grapevines smile everywhere
And in swooning wastelands
Sprouts the ever-nourished grain.
All is light at the tense hour
With monastery coolness.
By Lofty Grace
The sun draws forth seed
In the stubble of good passage.
All is gift, reward,
And Ultimate Knowledge
For those who find the way.
In the Dawn of Birth
You and I wish to die there.

May 1952

WE WERE THREE, WE WERE TWO, IT WAS ME ALONE, WE WERE NONE...

To Rosa Leveroni

We were three, heads down in the darkness of vintages,
With the sea in our eyes and wine-dregs on our hands,
When the canal starts smoking in the forest's salt
And a child's cry sparkles upon the mountain.

We were two, standing on the rock of stars,
Our hearts bloody, without darts or sling,
When the wasteland starts burning and the tar begins to sob
In the latent deeps of lighthouse furrows.

It was me alone, a shade among old shadows,
Representing another shadow, on the beach
Where, among scattered nets, the sleep of all
Signs on in the feverish darkness.

We were none, robed in leaves of darkness
When fear rains on the marsh petals
And the other, the Pure, freed from rudder and sails
Sets out, watchfully, toward the brilliant Instant.

Port Lligat,
August 1953

EVERYTHING IS FENCED-IN AND SUBMISSIVE
BEYOND THE SEGRE

There are neither paths, nor turnings, nor footbridges:
Everything is fenced-in and submissive beyond the Segre
—In a draught of mouths
And feudal exile of gazes
With nuptial languours—
When the mist's torso lengthens
And we burn stellar foliage for charcoal.

She isn't there; nor are those other women.
They aren't there, branching beneath the ceilings
Of a ruined house close by the French border
Where the merchant, selling on credit, squeezes ice
And where he who deserts his flock and fold must fan ashes.
—*Break the ugly windows on those ancient barracks!*
Erase the times from those farmhouse sundials!

Follow me, pitchfork in hand,
Prisoner of a smokeless, flameless fire,
Amid the cloister's chilly haystacks,
Attentive to furrows where silence sprouts
Full of hidden forests and confidential fountains.
A star sinks behind the mountain range
With pure reds and greens, sparkling fiercely.

How scary to be alone, by the river, at open midnight;
How scary to be alone together

If they knock at the waters' door
And we slip sticks of dynamite into our cartridge belts,
While ravens soar high above the plain
And we must die together, witnessing the Other.

Cervera de la Segarra,
1955

"*The ashes are hot, travelers!*" said the voice guiding those winterers through the forest's depths. No one could explain the meaning of that cry. Some feared a spell and longed for their country's springtime shadows. Others feared a meeting with the great beast. As we were going through a pass, the skeleton of an ox struck by lightning one windy autumn had already given them pause, and they hadn't even noticed that burning purple in the west from which happy dreams emerge. The night air's cold wing again sheltered their thoughts when the same voice, with a gentle splash of fountains, repeated: "*The ashes are hot!*" At the foot of a burnt pine stump lay the recently-stabbed corpse of a young man. The pious travelers covered him with dry branches and went down to take refuge in the village. Everyone glowered at them like bandits as they entered the hotel. Someone cried: "*Profaners!*" and they marveled at the word. But early the next morning, they went drowsily through the streets, writing long chains of verses dripping blood and dew on the walls. I don't know who rang so early and asked my mother if I was home.

A ROSE WITH A KNIFE IN ITS BREAST JUMPS, BLEEDING, FROM A WINDOW

Stabbed by a warm, realistic, and expert hand, an authentic rose, thanks to its remarkable powers of endurance, kept its form despite the hemorrhage. With beating petals, it crossed plains, forests, rivers, mountains, islands, and harbors, letting its wound's red moss fall everywhere. It halted on the peaks to contemplate pallidly shadowy antarctic glacial deserts, the petrified forests and fossil fish of three million years ago. It fell to earth in New Zealand, where it died beneath the wheels of a shameful tricycle. The courts have ordered an autopsy to determine the cause of such irreparable defoliation.

THE NUNWATCHER

That the man who kneads dough every night at Pió's bakery on Main Street should be the same one who pours sacks of pastry flour into puddles of his own creation when he fills buckets at Christina's Well, already surprises me; that this same man should serve as altar boy at the five o'clock parish Mass, and that the rector should let him—Mother and I saw it!—dress in red without a surplice, with three pointed horns on his forehead and a long burning tail that leaves a mark wherever he goes, intrigues me; but that he should don a wig and beard on his nights off and keep watch outside the convent, spying on the drowsy nuns as they sniff the early morning air with lifted veils, while he stands at the garden gate with sweet words and muffled laughter and then carries them off in a sack like proud cauliflowers wet with dew, loads them in a pushcart, and sets out for market, baffles and astounds me.

AT THE HOTTEST TIME OF DAY...

At the hottest time of day, when clocks are most distressing, I make my way along hilltop paths to the densest olive groves. Sometimes I veer off, heading down through clumps of pines that hide the villas of those who love solitude. One rarely sees many people; an occasional indigenous swimmer dressed in ritual vestments, or a few daring, scantily-clad foreigners on their way to almost-secret beaches where they seek out sunny spots or cool nooks. Today I changed my route. I went through the center of town and, as I passed the church, I noticed a semi-stately home surely built at the turn of the century and legendary for the ghosts that, according to the townspeople, appear whenever the moon wanes behind the cypresses. Pensive, pondering these nocturnal apparitions, I saw one of the windows—which I had thought was shut like the others—pushed open by a pair of delicate hands. An old lady stuck her head out and shouted: "No, not Maria Dolors's hair!" I stopped, startled by her presence, and recalled that the lady's words came from a poem I had written long ago. The old lady closed the window and opened the front door, repeating the same words in a loud and crusty voice: "No, not Maria Dolors's hair!" She descended the three steps leading down to the front yard and approached me. White of hair and withered of visage, she stretched out her hands, repeated the line, and said: "I was fifteen years old." More than sixty years, then, had passed since I last had seen her. I didn't know what to say. I started running, as though I were a child again, up the street. At the corner, an unaccustomed mirror absorbed my image: with white beard and close-cropped hair, I was pulling the petals from a fresh and sparkling rose. Closing my eyes, I saw an old sea with ancient boats and limping fishermen. I remem-

bered my first poems all over again, and the old lady's words.
I stopped, not sure where I was.

D1478804

PRAISE FOR

THE NECESSITY OF LAVENDER TEA

"In the world of magical realism, Jennifer Moorman is an important new voice. She is a sensitive, engaging, quirky, and soulful storyteller. Her characters speak their truths only to inspire us, the reader, to embrace and respect our own true gifts. As a lifelong fan of Alice Hoffman, I am adding Jennifer to a short list of writers who can carry the torch forward to a new generation."

—JANE UBELL-MEYER, *FOUNDER OF BEDSIDE READING*

"A delicate magical allure and heartwarming storyline that make a truly memorable coming-of-age classic. In this inspiring tale, Jennifer takes us on a tender journey through profound loss and budding love and the transforming power of choices. Readers looking for a vibrant splash of Southern charm will fall in love with the vividly painted Mystic Water and the wise, whispering nature and compelling characters who inhabit it."

—JEANNE ARNOLD, *BESTSELLING AUTHOR OF THE YOUNG ADULT STUBBORN SERIES*

"A sweet, magical coming-of-age tale about the best and hardest parts of love and friendship and family."

—AMY IMPELLIZZERI, *AWARD-WINNING AUTHOR OF LEMONGRASS HOPE AND I KNOW HOW THIS ENDS*

"Jennifer writes so beautifully about life and love, growing up and trying to fit in. Sprinkled with just the right amount of magic, this heartwarming book will bring you to tears as you become one with Kate as she struggles through hiding her ability, the pain of wanting to belong, love, and the awkwardness of being different. The book leaves you wanting to visit Mystic Water again and again."

—ELISA FERSHTADT, *HOSPITALITY PUBLIC RELATIONS CONSULTANT*

THE
NECESSITY
OF
LAVENDER
TEA

THE
NECESSITY
OF
LAVENDER
TEA

A NOVEL

JENNIFER MOORMAN

Full Moon Press

The Necessity of Lavender Tea

Copyright © 2023 Jennifer Moorman

All rights reserved. No portion of this book may be reproduced, stored in a retrieval system, or transmitted in any form or by any means—electronic, mechanical, photocopy, recording, scanning, or other—except for brief quotations in critical reviews or articles, without the prior written permission of the publisher.

Published by Full Moon Press, Inc.

This book is a work of fiction. The characters, incidents, and dialogue are drawn from the author's imagination and are not to be construed as real. Any resemblance to actual events or persons, living or dead, is entirely coincidental.

Any internet addresses (websites, blogs, etc.) in this book are offered as a resource. They are not intended in any way to be or imply an endorsement by Full Moon Press, Inc., nor does Full Moon Press, Inc. vouch for the content of these sites for the life of this book.

Library of Congress Cataloging-in-Publication Data is on File

ISBN 978-1-7347395-1-0
ISBN 978-1-7347395-6-5 (eBook)

Printed in the United States of America
23 24 25 26 27 FMP 5 4 3 2 1

*To everyone and anyone who has struggled to be
normal in order to fit in. You are unrepeatable.
Let the world see how extraordinary you are.*

To be yourself in a world that is constantly trying to make you something else is the greatest accomplishment.

—Ralph Waldo Emerson

CHAPTER 1

KATE MUIR COULDN'T STOP THE INEVITABLE. COULDN'T STOP dragging around a worthless, damaged ability that would, year after year, destroy her. She hated her cursed fate. She would give anything to sever the curse, hack it away like a toxic poison ivy vine. But that wasn't an option, not according to her mama, who assured her this ability would make Kate's life a tragedy, trapping her forever inside her mind with no escape. No redemption.

Kate kicked her sandaled feet through fresh pine needles and bright-green sycamore leaves that had only yesterday been part of the forest canopy above her. Last night's storm—in its desperate madness—had stripped trees of their summer growth and coated the forest floor like a crisp, verdant blanket, potent with scents of sweet sap and rain-soaked earth.

Midsummer storms blown in by east winds brought mischief and rebellion. The oppressive summer heat had been replaced with a cool breeze, making it feel as though autumn crept in early and without permission, like the weather was up to something.

Gentle breezes in July could never be trusted. July was anything but gentle; July was intense, sweltering, burning. July made people in Mystic Water want to live in the water like mermaids. A few dozen people would dive into Jordan Pond in July and not emerge until Labor Day.

Normally, Kate loved summer vacation, the days that stretched out long and free. During the summer, she didn't worry about whether or not her classmates liked her or if they would avoid her during group activities. She wouldn't have to suffocate beneath their pity, wouldn't have to hear anyone whisper the name Evan. It didn't matter if she was the darkest face in the woods or if she was so skinny that her sixteen-year-old body still resembled a boy's. She could just be. Outside among the flowers and the wildness of the forest, Kate felt free.

But today the world around her seemed to be plotting for a surprise attack, tugging her into a false sense of security, cooling her with its whispery breeze, coaxing her to relax. But she couldn't. Her fingers tingled, and she felt as unsettled as a caged canary in a coal mine. The periwinkle-blue sky stretched like a bowl over the too-quiet woodlands.

The silence reminded Kate of the caves upriver, where the deeper you ventured, the stiller and more extreme the darkness became—a silence so profound that you could hear the heartbeats of those around you. Now in this wooded hush, she heard nothing but her own breath, which unnerved her. Where were the birds, the chittering squirrels? The breeze died, further dampening life. Kate started humming one of her mama's Cherokee songs, trying to settle her anxiety. It didn't help.

Ahead, the pine trees became sparse, leaving an open space covered in juvenile ferns and mats of soft ocher and blue-green

moss. A cluster of mauve flower heads stretched their blooms above darker foliage, testing the afternoon sunlight. *Eupatorium purpureum*, Kate thought. Joe-Pye weed to everyone else. July was too early for blooming Joe-Pye weed, but the plants boasted their blood-red stalks and deep-pink buds. A harbinger that something was definitely out of sync.

Monarch butterflies darted in and out of the flowers, acting just as surprised as Kate was to see the plants. Kate knelt in front of the blooms. The storm had not snatched the vibrant petals from their delicate stalks. An orange-and-yellow butterfly fluttered above her, and she reached out her hand like a damsel asking a prince for the honor of kissing her hand. The monarch landed on her knuckle and shivered against her skin.

Almost instantly, a dark veil dropped over Kate's vision, graying the colors and creating a world that was clouded and out of focus. She recognized the rush of icy prickles across her taut skin. A sickly sensation gathered in her stomach, causing heat to rise inside her like a stoked fire. Instinctively, she lay flat on her back, spreading her arms out as though she might create an angel in the pine needles. The butterfly flapped its wings above her, sending sighs of air across her cheeks. Before the darkness overtook her, Kate breathed in the scents of burning rubber, sour breath, and men's cologne.

When Kate was five years old, she experienced her first premonition. She'd woken up disoriented on the floor of her bedroom, drooling on the threadbare rug, arms and legs crumpled beneath her. Broken images of her parents, a man with blue

eyes, and a semitruck with shattered headlights lingered in her mind for a few seconds, but the vision soon burned away like fog in sunlight. She didn't tell her parents what happened, mostly because she didn't understand it herself. Kate didn't have another vision for five years.

On her tenth birthday, Kate watched her older brother, Evan, swim through the gentle currents of the Red River, which snaked behind their house. During heavy spring rains, the river swelled and flooded the banks like the Nile, leaving behind fertile soil where cattails and American lotus thrived. When the summer heat parched the land and the thin blue skies withheld rain for weeks, the river turned into a rock-filled creek where tadpoles flailed in tiny puddles.

"Hey, birthday, girl!" Evan climbed onto a water-slicked rock and called her to join him, motioning enthusiastically as the sunlight turned his skin to the color of caramel.

The heavy rains had swollen the river to twice its summertime size, and swirls of water churned and gurgled as it rushed by. Kate shook her head, but Evan's laugh could persuade a recluse to rejoin society, and she knew she wouldn't stay on the riverbank. Not with his attention so focused on her, knowing he wanted to spend time with her.

Kate put one foot into the water, but her vision tunneled, her legs buckled at the knees, and she fell sideways like a discarded doll. She knocked her head on the smooth stones and succumbed to the persistent darkness.

When Kate awoke, her clothes were soaked. She blinked up at her mama whose dark eyes were as large as walnuts and lips were taut and trembling; her sharp cheekbones angled and gleamed like polished obsidian. Evan hovered nearby; his grass-green eyes

were overly bright, and the muscles in his neck strained against his skin.

"What happened?" Kate mumbled, her voice thick and unsure.

"You fell in," Evan said. "The current dragged you downstream about fifty yards. I didn't think I could get to you before you rounded the bend—"

"But you did," her mama interrupted. "Help me get her inside."

Once inside the house, her mama forced Kate to stay awake and sit at the kitchen table. Her head throbbed like an intruder was trying to push its way out of her skull, and she couldn't stop shivering. Something was different inside her; her bones ached with the awareness. Kate's mama wrapped her in a wool blanket like a swaddled baby to help battle the October chill.

"What did you see?" her mama asked as she busied herself in the kitchen, staring at the kettle as if willing it to whistle. Her pacing caused pots to rattle in the cabinets.

Kate's insides clenched. "What do you mean?" But Kate knew what her mama meant.

"She was out cold," Evan said. "She didn't see anything."

Kate shuddered and avoided her mama's intense gaze. Images surfaced in her mind: blue eyes and fingers linked with hers, an upside-down car. She kept seeing a man with dark hair, laughing, picking daisies from the forest and then headlights shining through the fog straight into her eyes, blinding her, and her heartbeat exploded. She tried to remember what happened, how the images might be connected, but her thoughts muddied as the seconds ticked.

Dissatisfied with her answer, her mama sent her daddy and

Evan to the store for traditional remedies—Tylenol—but Kate knew Evan had disobeyed. She felt her brother's presence in the hallway, just out of her mama's sight in the kitchen.

Her mama poured boiling water into a teacup. She placed a tea infuser stuffed full of dried lavender into the steaming liquid and set the cup in front of Kate. She motioned for Kate to swirl the infuser around through the liquid. The clinking of metal against porcelain exaggerated how silent the rest of the house was, as if everything else had stopped and waited for what was coming. Kate's body started trembling.

"Little Blackbird," her mama said, "it's time you know the truth. You are cursed."

"What?" Kate asked, dropping the tea infuser. Her fingers itched, and she reached up to touch the darkening bruise on her forehead.

"My grandmother had premonitions too. Her life was a tragedy because of it. You will see slivers of the future. Both your own and futures belonging to others. You cannot change them. You cannot interfere with what you see. That alone will drive you crazy."

Her mama walked to the suncatcher hanging above the kitchen window. She lifted the colorful glass in her fingers, tracing the bronze welding lines connecting the fragments together. Vibrant flashes of light danced across the kitchen floor. "Sometimes you will see the future in broken pieces. It will be like trying to make complete pictures out of the shattered glass in a suncatcher. Impossible. Other times the future will be a clear path, but you cannot change it. You can only see and know—but never act."

Kate grasped the teacup to hide her unsteady hands. The

words *tragedy* and *broken* joined the ache in her head, hammering away like a woodpecker on a mature pine. Her tongue tasted like dry earth and bitter leaves.

Her mama walked to her and stood beside the table. Her strong gaze locked onto Kate's face. "No matter what you see, you cannot try to alter it. Interfering with the future is forbidden. There are no exceptions."

"Forbidden?" Kate asked. The word sounded archaic, plucked from a fairy tale. "By who? What if I see something bad happening to someone else?"

Her mama shook her head. "No exceptions. Changing the future could have terrible consequences."

"But what if I could help—"

Her mama stamped her foot. "No exceptions. Now, drink your tea."

Kate glanced up and caught Evan's eyes in his hiding place just inside the shadowed hallway. His brow wrinkled when he frowned.

"Can I control when these visions happen?"

"No." Her mama returned to the stove. "They will come whenever they want to, even at the most inconvenient times. But the tea will help. It helped my grandmother not lose control as often. The lavender soothes, and a calm mind does not receive as many visions."

What if she had a vision in school? She grimaced. "But I don't want to be different. I want to fit in."

"Fit in with whom?" her mama asked.

Kate shrugged and looked away from her mama's knowing gaze. "Other kids? The kids in town?" Anyone.

Evan waved at her from the hallway. When she looked at

him, he mouthed, "You fit in with me."

"Little Blackbird," her mama asked, "why do assume you don't fit in?"

She looked at her mama, but she had already turned away. "What happened to your grandmother?"

"She lost her mind," her mama said matter-of-factly. "Ended up ranting and blubbering like a child." Her mama's sigh caused the dishtowel to shudder on the counter. "There was too much in her head, too much that wouldn't leave. Trapped there by the curse." Only then did her mama turn to her and offer a comforting smile. "Drink your tea."

Later that night Kate sat cross-legged on the floor with her back propped against her bed. Her birthday joy curdled like buttermilk. She forced herself to eat cake after dinner, but now her growing despair caused her stomach to respond like she'd eaten hemlock flowers.

"Hey," Evan said, pushing open her bedroom door and walking in. He sat beside her, stretching out his long muscular legs beside hers. "Not quite the birthday you imagined."

Kate mimed handing Evan a box. "You'll never guess what your gift is—a curse."

Evan leaned his shoulder against hers. Her trembling lip stopped his teasing. "Hey, I'm sorry. Mama . . . well, she's like the *rosa rugosa*." When Kate looked at him, he added, "Beautiful and hardy but with great, big thorns."

"I'm not sure what's worse, that she told me I'm cursed or that she said her grandma went insane." Kate stared at her open palms. "Here's to the future."

"What I meant was," Evan said, "it might not be as bad as she says. Maybe it will be cool to see things, to know what's

happening."

Kate half-smiled at him. Evan, the relentless optimist.

"Maybe you could get a second opinion," he offered.

"From a doctor?"

He shook his head. "I was thinking about one of Mama's people. Aurora Catawnee—"

"The crazy lady?" Kate balked. "No way. Everyone knows she's kooky."

Evan's eyebrows raised. "Have you ever met her?"

"No."

"So you're basing your judgment of her on someone else's opinion?" he asked. "That's shaky ground, Little Blackbird. I've met her a few times. She's wise and has a way of speaking that makes you feel calm. If Mama's grandma had what you have, Aurora Catawnee will know all about it. Maybe it's worth learning what she knows, hear another perspective."

Kate shrugged. She wasn't ready to talk about the curse with anyone yet, and what could a kooky old Cherokee woman possibly know anyway?

After her birthday, Kate had premonitions at least once a month, sometimes as often as once a week if she forgot to drink lavender tea daily. Her mama explained how the tea would slow the premonitions, perhaps even put them to sleep for a while. Kate fretted about having an episode—as she'd named them—during school. Wasn't it bad enough that she was already physically different with her too-black eyes, hair as dark as ravens, and skin the color of Georgia clay? Now her insides were jumbled, broken, and manic. Now she saw familiar faces in her visions—her schoolmate Sally's blue eyes haunted and lost, a schoolmate Mikey skipping rocks across the river, her daddy's tears on his fingers.

None of her visions made sense. Most of them frightened her. Sometimes she'd wake in the middle of the night and eat dried lavender by the handfuls just to stop seeing anything at all.

Kate never had the same vision twice, and she never had premonitions that followed a chronological timeline. Not until three months after Evan turned eighteen and he left for college.

She'd been dreading his departure for college like someone walking a pirate ship plank. She'd never known life in Mystic Water without Evan. He was a shield, a first line of protection between her and the whole world. Most days Kate felt Evan was the only person who really saw her. Saw her and loved her just as she was. What would life be like without him singing "Chattanoogie Shoe Shine Boy" through the garden? Who would make her laugh at the dinner table when Mama was discussing her midwifery and Daddy's mind was preoccupied with work, imagining architectural designs, mm-hmming and saying, "Yes, love" in all the right spaces?

The state university offered Evan a football and an academic scholarship. Everyone in town overflowed with excitement for him, slapping his back and telling him they couldn't wait to see all he would accomplish. No one doubted he would succeed, because Evan had remarkable talent. There didn't seem to be anything he couldn't master. Many believed Evan's athletic prowess was his greatest talent; others said it was his uncanny ability to remember everything he read. Kate believed his greatest talent was making her feel like she belonged somewhere, which was a feat no one else in town had even attempted.

So while the town couldn't stop talking about Evan's future after Mystic Water, Kate obstinately denied he was leaving until she stood in the front yard that fall, staring as his car bounced up

the dirt driveaway toward new beginnings. With his arm hanging out the window, Evan waved enthusiastically, happy to be spreading his wings and flying away.

That night, Kate had a vision that dropped her like a mayfly. She saw a man with heavy eyelids wearing a cowboy hat, hands loosened on a faded-leather steering wheel, headlights veering across solid yellow lines on a blacktop. When she awoke in her bedroom, a pool of tears stained the hardwood floor the color of drying blood.

Two weeks later, Kate blacked out while planting yellow roses in the backyard and saw wheels spinning on a car that was crushed like an accordion. A blurry face stared at her through the shattered windshield. Without his cowboy hat, the man's bald head shined like a polished pearl in the moonlight as he staggered away from a tractor trailer and across the road, blubbering sloppy, broken prayers.

Then, a week later, Kate stumbled into her bedroom, dizzy and sweating profusely, and collapsed. That night she saw the color of the car—thistle green—with a spot of paint chipped away in the shape of Texas above the front right wheelhouse. Kate knew that car. She had traced that flaked paint outline a dozen times on Evan's car. When she emerged from the vision, her face was wet with tears, and she lay curled on her bedroom floor, wrapping her arms around her knees, pulling them to her chest. She wanted to tell Evan immediately. She wanted to tell him to never drive home or to come home in someone else's car or to ride the bus, but she did none of those things.

You can't change the future. You can't interfere. She repeated her mama's words over and over again.

As silvery moonlight turned her tears to glitter, she prayed

that her vision wasn't the future. She prayed Evan would be safe and not trapped inside his busted-up car, but it seemed that nobody was listening to her prayers.

On this July afternoon when Kate awoke in the forest, she blinked up at the cloudless sky and pushed herself into a sitting position. Her heart pounded an unnatural rhythm against her ribcage. A memory of blue streaking across pavement and the stench of blood hung in the air for seconds before fading. Butterflies flitted around her cheeks, and she waved them away before standing on quivering legs. How had she been stupid enough to forget to drink her tea? She rubbed her fingers across her collarbone, trying to smooth away the ache in her chest. Her temples pulsed as though her heart had grown tired of its placement in her chest and risen to her skull instead.

Kate wandered down to the river and removed her sandals. She stepped barefoot into the tepid water and followed the current toward home. Her steps were sluggish, and she tried to grab hold of one thread of the vision. A sense of urgency, a whisper of importance, attached to the vision, but its misty images followed her like a cloud of dust. What good were premonitions? Weren't they meant to tell the seer something? And even if the visions did reveal a truth, Kate could only watch the world unfold around her. She couldn't stop the inevitable or alter someone's steps. She was useless, dragging around a worthless ability that would, year after year, destroy her more—if her fate were to be the same as her great-grandmother's.

Squealing tires and the crunch of metal caused birds to burst

from the tall pines. Kate stopped. She watched the birds fly over-head, blocking out the sun in groups of twos and threes, creating pulsing shadows across her face. Evan's name struck her heart like a lightning bolt. Without thinking, she dropped her sandals and ran in the direction of the sound.

CHAPTER 2

KATE CRASHED THROUGH THE FOREST, IMAGINING HERSELF AS A deer escaping her predator. Why did she feel as though she were running toward the hunter? Wind whipped her hair behind her like a black satin ribbon. Squirrels leaped from branch to branch, barking questions.

Kate smelled gasoline and slowed to a jog and then to a walk. Up the steep embankment in front of her, a royal-blue convertible lay on its side, crashed into the stand of trees. A splintered pine tree had fallen down the slope.

The acrid stench of burned rubber caused her stomach to churn. When she closed her eyes, she imagined Evan behind a windshield that spiderwebbed, creating a thousand separate broken versions of his face. The cool breeze blew across her cheeks, and she exhaled a shuddering breath.

Kate used the tangle of kudzu and ivy to scale the slope. Her pulse throbbed in her neck, and she wiped her clammy, dirty hands on her shirt when she reached the top. The loose gravel scattered across the road dug into her bare feet.

She approached the overturned car, hesitant, blinking

rapidly. The silver underbelly of the car faced her, and oil leaked onto the road and formed an inky misshapen stain. She held her breath as she peered around the front bumper now marred by deep gauges that ripped through the once-shiny metal. Broken glass glittered on the road. There were no bodies in the car, beneath the car, or around the car. It was as though the driver had disappeared.

Her gaze fell upon a smear of blood leading to the opposite side of the road and into the weedy grass. A young man slumped against the trunk of a pine. Kate avoided the glass and darted across the road before considering whether or not it was a bad idea. As soon as her feet hit the high grass on the other side, she recognized his bruised face. Geoffrey Hamilton, the eighteen-year-old son of the wealthiest man in Mystic Water and probably the state.

How many times had she watched Geoffrey from across the schoolyard while he joked around with Evan? How many times had she wondered what it would be like to be a part of his world? Hundreds of times. She'd long ago memorized the way one corner of his mouth lifted into a smirk just before he laughed. She could recognize his gangly stride from across the baseball field. But she'd never been close enough to him to see the dusty shadow of stubble on his face.

Kate dropped down beside him. His head sagged toward his right shoulder. A gash on his high forehead spilled blood into his thick eyebrows and dripped a crimson river down the crooked bridge of his nose. His curly brown hair was plastered to his head in sweaty, dark patches like swirls of mud.

Kate reached out a hesitant hand and poked her finger into his shoulder. "Are you dead?" No answer. She pressed two fingers

against the vein in his neck. A slow, steady beat pulsed against her fingertips.

Someone had once pressed fingers to Evan's neck too, but the heart had already given out, and the blood had stilled.

Geoffrey lifted his head. Hazel eyes with dilated pupils gazed at her. "I dunno," he slurred.

Kate exhaled in relief and pressed a shaky hand to her chest. Specks of gold flecked the thin line of hunter green circling his irises. She looked over her shoulder at the wrecked convertible. "How did you get over here?"

"Where am I?" he asked. He tried to shift his weight to see around her, but he groaned and reached for his leg. Losing his balance, he slid from the tree and collapsed onto his side.

Kate gasped, reaching for him. "Are you okay?"

Geoffrey whimpered and rolled onto his back. Blood seeped through a rip in his striped button-down shirt. A tremor rippled through his body, and his eyelids fluttered closed. Was he going into shock? What would her mama do? Kate slapped lightly at Geoffrey's face.

"Hey," she said. "Hey, Geoffrey. Wake up. Don't leave me. Stay here. Focus."

She leaned over him. His eyes opened, and he moaned. Kate straightened and grimaced. He smelled sweaty and sour, like the alley behind the bar on the edge of town. Kate had been there only once when she'd gone with her daddy on a job to see if he could help redesign the interior layout. She'd made the mistake of sneaking out the bar's back door and nearly suffocated from the stench of regret and fermented drink.

Kate tapped his cheek again, gentler this time. "I need you to stay awake, and that would be simpler if you were sober."

JENNIFER MOORMAN

Geoffrey reached one hand toward his head. Kate grabbed it and shook her head. "Your hands are disgusting. You'll likely infect the wound if you touch it." She needed to get help. But how? This dead-end gravel road led to only two places—Look-Off Pointe and her home. Her daddy was working, and her mama was in town helping Mrs. Tyler deliver her fourth child.

Geoffrey's head lolled to the side, and his eyes focused on the car. "Oh, God."

"Were you driving alone?"

"No," he said, "Ben was driving."

His oldest brother. The Hamilton son with the wild eyes and reckless spirit.

Geoffrey tried to sit up, but Kate pressed her hand against his shoulder. "Stay down. Ben isn't here."

"I know." He swallowed. Tears leaked down the sides of his face. "God, it hurts to think. Dad's car. He's going to kill us."

"You and your brother were drinking and driving?"

His glassy gaze met hers. "God, I don't need a lecture from Sacagawea."

Kate narrowed her eyes. "I'm half Cherokee."

"So?"

"Sacagawea was a Shoshone, you rude imbecile. I ought to leave you here on the side of the road." Kate tried to stand, but Geoffrey grabbed her wrist. His fingers were thin and long, looping around her narrow wrist and folding over themselves.

"Don't leave me," he said, pathetic and rasping, before releasing her. "I think my ankle is broken."

"It might be," she said. "And you have gashes on your forehead and chest." Not to mention the bruising. "Let me check your ankle." Both of his shoes were missing. "Where are your shoes?"

18

"I know *you're* not judging me for going barefoot. We were just going for a quick spin."

Kate scooted down toward Geoffrey's bare feet. They were scraped and bloody, but most of the blood looked to be from topical scratches. "I'm going to check for a pulse."

"In my foot?"

"Yes, so don't kick me." Kate checked for a posterior tibial pulse and found one. She told him to wiggle his toes, and she nodded when he did. His toes were long and thin, causing her to wonder if he could hold a pencil and write his name with his feet. She grabbed hold of his smallest toe. "What am I doing?"

"Squeezing my baby toe?" he asked, as though his answer might not be correct.

She grinned at him.

"What?" he asked, sounding defensive. "My toes are certainly not my good parts."

She caught his gaze and blushed so hard that the tops of her ears burned.

"Well, that was inappropriate. Just slipped right out." Geoffrey's grimace turned into a smile, and he chuckled. "God, it hurts to laugh. It hurts to breathe."

Then Kate laughed just to release the awkwardness constricting her throat. The limbs of the pine trees swayed around them. "You might have bruised or cracked ribs. Where is your brother? Why would he leave you?"

"He went to get Matt. Or Mom and Dad. Or anyone."

"Your house is more than five miles away from here. He's not likely to pass anyone on this road." Unless someone was going to Look-Off Pointe in daylight, which was doubtful even for the bolder townsfolk.

"I'm going to help you, but I need to run home first. I can get back faster than Benjamin can walk home, and we need to stanch this bleeding. Probably need to splint your ankle too."

"You're a kid," Geoffrey said, shuddering when he tried to move.

"I know *you're* not judging *me*, and I'm all you have right now." She stood, and he reached for her. His pupils dilated, causing his pale irises to swell. Was he . . . afraid? On impulse, she grabbed his outstretched hand. His skin felt clammy against her own.

"You're coming back, right?" he asked.

"Promise."

"I trust you." His fingers squeezed hers. "I trusted your brother. He was a good guy. I liked him."

Kate nodded and dropped Geoffrey's hand. "Everybody did."

When she returned half an hour later, she was thankful to find Geoffrey still conscious, even if his mood had soured more than his breath. Sweat saturated his ruined clothes, and his pallid skin had lost some of its youthful color. A flutter of pleasure rose within her at the sight of his relieved smile to see her return. Kate laid out her supplies beside them and started administering to his wounds.

"God, that hurts," Geoffrey complained. His jaw clenched, and his sweat stunk of whiskey and smoke. "I thought you were going to bring back bandages and antiseptic, not flowers and spit."

"Stop whining. The yarrow will numb the pain." Kate pressed the yarrow poultice into the wound on his forehead. "And stop blaspheming, or I'll tell your mama. I can't imagine she's going to be too pleased to find out you were drinking and wrecked your

daddy's car. She doesn't need to know you're a blasphemer too."

He opened his eyes and looked at her. "You don't even know my mom."

Kate rubbed the yarrow into the jagged cut on Geoffrey's chest. Her cheeks burned at the intimate contact, but he didn't seem to care. His mouth contorted, revealing two crooked bottom teeth that were slightly out of line with the rest.

"I know she volunteers at the Baptist church during the weekdays, and she sings in the choir every Sunday," Kate said. "She thinks her boys are the best behaved in town."

"Listening to gossip about my mom doesn't make you an expert," he snapped. "You don't know anything."

Kate's skin prickled. The grass around his body browned in his anger, and she moved her hands away. His gaze couldn't seem to settle on anything, and his eyes sluggishly moved from one spot to another. His anger didn't feel intentionally directed toward her. No one really knew what happened behind closed doors, and people often pretended to be one version of themselves in public and something else entirely in private. Maybe the Hamilton family had its own closet of secrets.

Kate didn't know much about Geoffrey's mom, Doreen Hamilton. He was right about that. Kate had only gathered information based on what she'd seen or heard around town. Mrs. Hamilton didn't appear to do anything but brag about her sons and her volunteer work. Her outfits were always pressed so severely that she reminded Kate of a paper doll come to life—perfection in an angular form with sharp edges. Even her smile was rigid and perfectly drawn. She looked like the kind of woman who never laughed.

"I'll tell you what I do know. I know how to splint an ankle,"

Kate said. "But you're going to have to stay still."

"Pretty sure I couldn't move far if I tried." Geoffrey's voice had grown thicker, slower, spilling heavy over the grass like turpentine. His arms splayed out beside him, palms facing up as though he were lying in a meadow soaking up the sunlight.

Kate grabbed the short boards and scarves. She tucked an aqua scarf beneath his calf and wrapped it around to the other side. Then she slid the purple scarf below his ankle. She propped the boards on either side of his leg before she lifted the scarves around the boards and tied knots, creating a tight bond around his leg.

"That should keep you from hurting yourself further," she said. "Don't put any weight on it. The splint will hinder movement until they come back for you."

Geoffrey's eyes were closed, and his chin rested against his shoulder. Her heart slapped against her ribcage. She pressed her fingers against his throat.

He reached up a lazy hand and touched hers. "I'm not dead," he mumbled.

She exhaled. The sound of a car engine rumbled up the street. Kate pulled her hand away and leaped to her feet. She couldn't be with Geoffrey when they found him. What would people say? She could already hear their voices. *What did she do to him? What was she doing out there alone? She's crazy, you know, especially after they lost Evan.* Kate glanced down at Geoffrey, feeling guilty for leaving him alone, but still she shot off through the woods and hid herself behind a fat pine.

The car neared, and as soon as she heard voices and car doors slamming, she took off running toward home. She didn't stop running until she reached her backyard. For the rest of the

day, she couldn't stop thinking about Geoffrey Hamilton. Was he okay? Had he been grounded to infinity? Did he tell anyone about her? Two nights later, her questions were answered.

CHAPTER 3

SOMETHING WOKE KATE IN THE DARKNESS OF HER ROOM. A FAR-away sound. She focused all of her concentration on heightening her sense of hearing. The cuckoo clock in the kitchen ticked with each swing of its pendulum. A whippoorwill called from its nest in a nearby tree. The steady rise and fall of her daddy's snores crept out from beneath her parents' closed bedroom door. She heard nothing strange or jarring. But something felt out of place.

Kate sensed the intruder before she saw him. Her eyes darted toward the window. A shadow stretched from the glass, across her floor, and over her blankets. She thought of Peter Pan coming to the Darlings' window, but the man at her window was tall and thin and too old to be called a boy. She sat up and pulled the cotton blankets against her, pressing fisted hands of fabric against her chest.

The young man outside the window rapped his knuckles against the glass, a gentle *tap, tap, tap*. A tentative sound beat to the rhythm of "Shave and a Haircut." Kate cut her eyes to her open bedroom door. Any good daughter who awoke to find a young man at her window would have gone straight to her parents, but Kate didn't. Instead, she tugged the quilt off her bed and

wrapped it around her body to conceal her nightgown. She closed her bedroom door and tiptoed toward the window because she recognized the dark silhouette—Geoffrey Hamilton.

Her fingers trembled as she reached for the window latch. She slid up the sash. Nighttime sounds pushed inside her bedroom on humid summertime air. Crickets chirped and the river gurgled. Kate couldn't get her mouth to form words, so she stood and waited for whatever happened next. In all of her imaginings, she'd never once pictured Geoffrey Hamilton outside her window.

"Finally," he whispered. "You sleep like the dead. I've been knocking for ages."

Her eyes widened. "How did you know I was here?"

"In the middle of the night? In your house? Lucky guess," he said, and he smiled at her for the first time ever.

Kate leaned away from the shine of a smile directed at only her. It pulled all the air from her lungs and caused a ringing in her right ear. She looked over her shoulder at her bed to see if her body was still tucked beneath the covers. Could this be a vivid premonition? Why else would Geoffrey Hamilton, Mr. Popularity, be standing outside her house? But her bed was empty, and a summer breeze slipped into her room, shivered across her skin, and threaded itself through her hair, calling her attention back to Geoffrey.

She placed her hands on the windowsill, draping her fingers across the wooden frame. "What are you doing here? It's not a common practice to visit strangers in the middle of the night."

He chuckled. "You're not a stranger. I know who you are."

She shook her head, and pieces of hair tumbled from her loose braid. "You know nothing about me."

Lightning bugs flickered messages in the trees behind Geoffrey. Kate glanced at them quickly, trying to interpret the pulsing messages but unable to concentrate because of the way her heartbeat quickened.

"I know you live here," he said, smiling again, causing the air around him to feel charged with electricity.

"The amount of information you know about me is staggering."

Geoffrey burst out laughing, and Kate immediately shushed him. He slapped a hand over his mouth, but she almost wished he hadn't. She wanted to scoop up his laughter and hide it beneath her pillow like a good-luck charm. She wanted to bring it out on those nights when she lay awake eating lavender.

"Come outside," he whispered.

"What? No," she said, looking at her bedroom door. It was still closed, but the hairs on the back of her neck prickled. She sensed her mama turning over in her sleep down the hallway. She looked back at Geoffrey and startled at the sincerity in his eyes. He wanted her to come outside with him.

Alarms should have been going off in her mind—the kind of sirens that activated when a bank was being robbed of its valuables. Or the kind her Sunday school teacher said should be triggered when someone tempted you to sin. But Kate didn't hear any warning bells. Maybe having a late-night conversation with a young man wasn't that big of a deal.

Everybody had a different opinion on what was acceptable versus shameful. And they weren't shy about telling you all the rules you needed to follow to live a virtuous, upstanding life. Those rules sometimes felt more constricting than a straitjacket and were about as clear as a smoke-filled room. Kate found most

people cherry picked the rules that applied to them and broke the rest. A small-eyed sphinx moth flew near Geoffrey's head and flapped in an arch over him, sending ripples of temptation on fluttery wings. Kate never believed she would have been given a chance to cherry pick this moment.

"Come on," he begged. "Just for a minute. I didn't get to thank you properly for helping me."

Oh, how temptation swelled inside her. She could imagine herself scrambling out the window like someone was offering free orange Creamsicles, but she located her good-daughter response. "You're welcome. Now go before my parents wake up."

Geoffrey leaned one arm on the windowsill. His skin touched hers. "Come outside and have a proper conversation with me." When he smiled again, the moon drew nearer and brightened. His face illuminated like carved Italian marble. Kate felt herself leaning toward him, drawn in by the pull of his gravity.

Her mama's voice crackled to life in a distant part of her mind. Kate forced herself away from the window. "There is nothing proper about a conversation in the middle of the night with a young man and no chaperones."

Geoffrey laughed again. "Oh, come on. Cool it. I just want to talk. No one will even know."

She knew she should slam her window shut, jump into her bed, and cover her head until the morning. But she wanted to go outside. She wanted to be near Geoffrey. Should she risk it? Her curiosity was momentarily quelled by doubt. "Is this some sort of trick?" Were there others waiting outside just to laugh at her for thinking someone like Geoffrey Hamilton would want her to sneak out of her house with him?

He frowned. "Why would I trick you?"

"Are you alone?" Kate asked.

"Yeah."

"How did you get here?"

"I rode a horse."

Kate's brow furrowed, and he smiled again. At her.

"I drove, of course, and it wasn't easy. Are you coming out or not?"

Lightness filled her chest as though a balloon had expanded and lifted her onto her tiptoes. Her mouth formed the word *yes*, but she immediately shook her head. Then she closed the window.

Geoffrey's shadow lingered outside. He didn't move. They stood in a silence so profound, with Kate on one side of the glass and Geoffrey on the other, that she heard her heartbeat thundering around the room sounding like a freight train barreling through Mystic Water.

Geoffrey tapped the glass. Moonlight reflected off his dark hair. He tapped again.

Kate bit her bottom lip and raised the window a few inches. She squatted down, propped her fingers on the sill, and whispered through the crack. "You said thank you. Now go away."

Geoffrey's long fingers stretched through the narrow opening and touched hers. "I can't."

"Why not?"

"Not until you come outside. Are you going to make me beg again?" His voice slipped through the opening and warmed her cheeks, circled her chest, and squeezed. "Please?"

Without a doubt, Kate knew she should say no again, but instead, she said, "Let me change. Go down to the river and take a left. I'll meet you beside the magnolia tree."

"Sounds like you give these directions often. How many men come to your window at night?" he asked.

Her chin dipped down, and she wondered if there was such a thing as a negative number of people who wanted to spend time with her. "Go." She closed the sash.

As soon as his shadow moved away from the window, she tossed off the quilt and stared around her room. Was this what people would say was an out-of-body experience? Like they're watching their lives from somewhere up above? Kate's bones vibrated with excitement and apprehension. Thoughts immediately formed in her mind, questioning her sanity and her morals. Geoffrey Hamilton was just another boy, so why was her body responding like she'd been eating fireworks instead of lavender?

She shushed her mind because it was making her temples throb, and she pulled on a light cotton shirt and a pair of capris she usually wore for gardening. Halfway down to the river, Kate began to think meeting Geoffrey was a terrible idea. She slowed her pace as she approached the tree because she didn't see him anywhere. Had he changed his mind and run off? Had it really been a trick? The river babbled, and fireflies blinked across the water, looking like shooting stars dancing across the rocks.

"Psst."

Kate looked into the shadowy stand of trees nearby. Her heart slammed so hard against her ribcage that her body lurched forward.

"I'm over here," Geoffrey said. "I can't get my leg wet."

His leg? Kate followed the sound of his voice and found him sitting on a boulder, stretching out his long legs. That's when she saw the short, white cast glowing in the darkness like a snow boot. A pair of crutches lay across the ground beside him.

"Broken?" she asked.

"Fractured my fibula, but you knew that didn't you?" he said. "You're a regular Florence Nightingale."

"That's an exaggeration."

He pointed toward a spot by the river. "You know there's a bench over there."

Kate glanced over her shoulder. Her daddy had handcrafted the bench for her and Evan when they were younger. Evan called it the Magic Bench. He said when they were sitting there together, no one could see them, nothing could harm them, and everything would be okay. No matter what was happening around them, the Magic Bench would set everything right again. And he'd been right; anytime she'd sat with him on the bench, she felt instantly better. But maybe that had been Evan and not the bench. Maybe his special gift had been to make everyone feel loved, cared for, and seen. Kate hadn't sat on the bench since Evan died; she didn't want to give her assumptions the opportunity to be the heartbreaking, dreadful truth. The bench wasn't magic; Evan was, and when he left, he took all the magic with him.

Kate cleared her throat. "It's a . . . special bench."

Geoffrey grinned. "I see. Not meant for strangers in the night?" He patted the boulder with his hand. "Won't you sit down?"

She clutched her hands together in front of her. "I'm comfortable standing, but thank you." She knew she'd come apart at the seams if she sat near him. Her body was already humming with frenetic energy. In the moonlight, his bruises looked like ink smears across his pale face. "You look better."

He smirked. "Get outta here. I look like I got in a fight with Sugar Ray Robinson."

JENNIFER MOORMAN

Kate allowed herself to smile. "Okay, so maybe you look worse, but the cut on your forehead is healing."

"Because of your Indian magic," he said with a smile. He touched his forehead with his fingertips. "It stopped bleeding and hurting, and my dad couldn't believe it was already healing without stitches."

Indian magic? Kate's brows drew together. The differences between her and Geoffrey glowed like the fireflies in the trees. Even in the darkness, she couldn't hide the fact that she wasn't like Geoffrey. Geoffrey's family heritage probably descended from some highfalutin British bloodline. She wouldn't be surprised if the Hamiltons could trace their ancestry back to the monarchy, especially with the way his mother carried herself. Did she drink tea with her pinky finger raised?

Kate's family, by contrast, was anything but light skinned and regal. Her daddy, Sean Muir, was a second-generation American born to Scottish parents who emigrated from the small seaside village of Dunbar. His parents and his three siblings uprooted their lives in hopes for a better future during difficult economic times in Scotland. Kate's grandfather, who died before she was born, was a professionally trained doctor. Not long after arriving in the US, he was fortunate enough to find someone who hired him as a medical assistant. Then a local hospital sponsored him as a resident so he could be qualified to practice full time, but it hadn't been an easy journey for any of them. Diversity wasn't always welcome, and more often than not, people refused to see how they were alike, choosing to focus only on the minor things that made them different.

To add more to her mixed family ancestry, Kate's mama, Ama Alunahaka, was from the Cherokee Nation. Her family, 100

32

percent indigenous people, had been living in the area for more than a hundred years. When others had been forced—or strongly coerced—to leave Georgia, Ama's family group had resisted. Because of their determination to stay on their land combined with the compassion of those around them, her family had stayed with little to no conflict. That didn't mean the Cherokee in the area were openly accepted by everyone. Ama often described people as "tolerating" the Cherokee presence.

Most of the Cherokee stuck close to their homes and worked with other members of the tribe, but growing up, her mama had a rebellious streak and wanted to move around and through any town however she pleased. She wasn't always welcomed with open arms, but Mystic Water had a way of bringing together all sorts of people with myriad backgrounds and giving them all a place to call home.

Having been taught ways to use nature to heal, support, and comfort people, Ama was not only a sought-after healer but also a reputable midwife. She'd been helping deliver babies in Mystic Water long before her own children were born.

Even with mixed ancestry, Evan always had a way of fitting in with everyone around him. He inherited the best qualities of both their parents. Tall, athletic, and dark skinned with high cheekbones and a wide smile, he was distractingly handsome. People found ways to be near him, ways to make him laugh just so they could hear it. No one seemed to care that he was half-Indian because he was friendly, well-mannered, and charismatic—the opposite of Kate.

"It wasn't Indian magic. I used plants that grow around here. If people took any time to study herbs, they'd find there are hundreds of ways the earth can help them heal."

Geoffrey held up his hands and chuckled. "Okay, okay, don't have a cow. I was trying to say that whatever you did worked well. And thank you."

"You're welcome." Looking at his cast, she asked, "How's Benjamin?"

"Ben? He's fine," Geoffrey huffed. "A few bruises and a busted lip, but he got off easy compared to me." Geoffrey rapped his knuckles against the cast in a one-two beat.

"And the car?" she asked. She wondered how his father had reacted to learning his convertible was wrecked. Based on Geoffrey's words, if he hadn't been delirious, he acted like his dad was going to go ape.

Geoffrey grimaced and tugged a blade of grass growing between the rocks. "The car is totaled," he admitted. "Dad yelled a lot, but after Benjamin explained a family of deer ran across the road and he tried to avoid them, he calmed down."

Kate's mouth dropped open. "Did that really happen?" She assumed they'd been drinking alcohol and Benjamin had lost control of the car.

Geoffrey's cynical laugh answered the question before he did. "Nope, but we do what we have to do to keep the peace."

Meaning Geoffrey lied to get what he wanted. "I should get back inside."

"You just got out here." The moonlight reflected in his pale eyes, and Kate knew she had to look away. She had to turn around and march herself home, close her bedroom door, and forget about Geoffrey Hamilton.

"You wanted to express your appreciation, and you have. Good night."

Geoffrey leaned over and grabbed his crutches. He hoisted

himself from the boulder and wobbled for a moment. He tipped an imaginary hat. "Good night, Miss Muir."

Kate made a noise in her throat. "'Miss Muir' sounds like you're talking to my mama. 'Kate' is good enough for me."

Geoffrey grinned. "Then, good night, Miss Kate. I hope to see you again soon."

Did she want to see him again, outside the safety of school walls and dozens of people separating them? Perhaps seeing him this way once—alone, without barriers between them—was enough. Because already her heartbeat was erratic, and her fingers twitched. Seeing him a second time felt like a dangerous idea, a fuse already burning toward a stick of dynamite. She turned and fled toward her house without looking back at Geoffrey.

CHAPTER 4

SUMMERTIME MEANT FREEDOM TO KATE, BUT IT ALSO MEANT chores around the house. Her mama kept busy most days supplying Mystic Water's townsfolk with natural healing remedies and traveling to the village outside of town where a group of Cherokee lived and worked. The local Cherokee mostly raised crops, primarily corn, beans, squash, and tobacco planted along the creeks and lowlands. During different seasons, they also raised sunflowers, sumpweed, *Chenopodium*, pigweed, giant ragweed, amaranth, canary grass, and melons.

Ama assisted during planting, growing, and harvesting seasons. She'd taken Kate and Evan with her when they were younger, but as they grew, she stopped. Kate didn't know why Ama quit bringing them to the village, and she'd never had the courage to ask.

These days, with her mama gone from the early morning to late afternoon, Kate's main chore was maintaining the thriving garden behind their cottage. Caring for a garden might sound like an easy job to someone with no experience, but the upkeep needed to produce a healthy garden was an everyday affair. Kate loved it, though. She loved everything about gardening—the way

it demanded all of her attention, the way it depended on her, the way it thanked her with brilliant blooms and impressive growth.

Kate had to inspect plants for pests and rot. One diseased plant could harm the whole lot. Eliminating destructive bugs like aphids, gnats, and whiteflies required vigilance and organic ways to exterminate them. The garden required proper watering. Too much water caused fungi growth, leaf spots, and water-logged plants. Underwatering led to a suffering, shriveled mess. It was also important to treat the soil because over time, topsoil degraded and needed to be refreshed. Kate used a combination of mulch and compost to keep the garden thriving.

Plant maintenance required pruning, deadheading, and culling plants as needed. While these methods appeared brutal to Kate at first, she learned that they helped clean away unhealthy bits, created more space for the garden to flourish, and encouraged new growth. Once the garden was cleaned up, it heightened her ability to spot weeds. Weeds could choke a healthy area quickly because they suffocated plant roots, harbored pests, and took up space that could be used by the plants. Although Kate didn't like to "kill" any kind of living thing, she understood the importance of removing the weeds because the alternative meant her beloved garden would greatly suffer.

Ama taught Kate how to add companion plants throughout the garden. There were certain herbs and flowers that, when grown together, encouraged growth with each other, like how best friends might inspire each other to flourish. Companion plants brought in pollinators, warded off pests, and controlled the habitat for beneficial insects, like ladybugs and bees.

Kate also kept the garden tools cleaned and in the best condition possible. Clean tools controlled disease and prevented bacteria

from entering the garden. Even though it wasn't a requirement or anything Ama taught her, Kate held long conversations with the flowers and plants. She believed they were as interested in her chattering as she was in their health, and because of their enduring friendship, Kate felt the garden prospered even more.

A few days after Geoffrey's unexpected nightly visit, Kate was strolling through the garden, inspecting the basil, and replaying that night over again in her mind. The more time that passed, the more she wondered if she'd dreamed it instead of lived it. Her daddy came out the back door and called to her.

"I need to run these plans by the bank," he said, holding up a rolled cylinder of designs. "Want to ride with me? I can drop you off at Sweet Stop."

Half an hour later Kate wandered up and down the aisles of Sweet Stop, the downtown candy shop. She knew she'd end up with a bag full of Bonomo's strawberry taffy, but part of the experience was looking at the wonderland of colorful sweets nestled in their jars and packed into bins, imagining how each would taste. Finally, after circling the store three times, she grabbed a pink paper bag meant for filling with candies and stopped in front of a bin of her favorite taffy.

Kate shoveled in half a bag before returning the scoop to the bin. As she folded down the top of the bag, the door opened and jingled the shop's bell. Geoffrey Hamilton and one of his older brothers, Matthias, walked in. Matthias held open the door while Geoffrey maneuvered inside with his crutches. In a moment of panic, Kate bent down to pretend to retie her shoelaces, but she'd worn sandals. She rose slowly and peeked over the tops of the candy bins.

Matthias and Geoffrey stopped by the checkout counter and

spoke to the young blond cashier, Sally Rensforth, who was a rising sophomore like Kate. Sally's hair was curled and held back with bobby pins, leaving fat, smooth curls to frame her heart-shaped face. She wore fire engine–red lipstick and black mascara.

Kate envied girls like Sally. Those girls fit right in with people like the Hamiltons. Sally, with her blue eyes and blond hair, looked exactly like the kind of girl every guy dreamed about, the kind of girl boys wanted to show off. Sally's laugh came out high pitched and nasal and maybe a tad too forced, but when Kate glanced over at her, the air around Sally looked shimmery and dreamlike. From his profile, Kate could see Geoffrey's smile, and even from across the room, it coaxed her toward him. She blinked rapidly and instead plotted an escape route.

Everyone in town knew the Hamilton men, which included the patriarch, Alfred, and his four sons, Benjamin, Richard, Matthias, and Geoffrey. Their smiles could enchant anyone. Daughters were warned to avoid looking directly into the face of a Hamilton man because if he smiled, then all would be lost—mostly hearts. Kate had never believed the nonsense until Geoffrey stood outside her window and she was the object of his attention. Now she felt her pulse beating through her entire body as though her heart might try to escape from the weakest point. She pressed her hands against her chest. She needed to get out of the shop without him seeing her. Bending down again, she inhaled three deep breaths and devised a plan. She would leave behind her candy bag, which was incredibly disappointing, and wait for Geoffrey and Matthias to start up one of the far aisles. Then, when she was certain they were looking away from the door, she'd scoot out as fast as possible. Even if they saw her, she wouldn't stop if they called out to her. She'd pretend she hadn't heard, but all of that hinged on them actually noticing

her and caring that she was nearby. What if Geoffrey saw her and completely ignored her like he'd been doing her entire life?

When she stood, she saw Matthias grab a pink bag and walk to the opposite corner where rainbow-colored candies sparkled, but Geoffrey was gone. She stopped breathing.

"Hello, Miss Kate," Geoffrey said.

Kate gasped and spun around. Geoffrey stood behind her, leaning on his crutches. She crushed her candy bag against her chest.

"Whoa, sorry. I didn't mean to scare you," he said.

So much for getting out unnoticed. "You shouldn't sneak up behind people."

"I wouldn't if they weren't trying to avoid me." His lips lifted in one corner.

"I hope you aren't referring to me. I'm not trying to avoid you." Her voice trembled like struck glass.

His dark eyebrows rose on his high forehead, his expression revealing his doubt.

She heaved a sigh. "Trying to leave unnoticed is not the same."

Geoffrey laughed, and Kate looked into his hazel eyes. His bruises had faded into faint yellow shadows. He studied her, and Kate felt Sally's eyes on them too.

"I noticed you," Geoffrey said.

"It's a small shop."

Geoffrey readjusted on his crutches. "No, I mean. I noticed you before. Anywhere really. You stand out."

Kate exhaled, and the jars around them vibrated on the shelves. She smoothed her hands down her lilac-colored, ruffled skirt. "Because I'm different and because of my brother."

Geoffrey looked taken aback by her words. "No, because you're

. . . well, you're a knockout."

A laugh burst unexpectedly from Kate's mouth. No one, other than her parents—and they definitely didn't count—had ever even hinted that she was beautiful. The most creative words anyone had ever used to describe her were *exotic but strange*.

She pushed past Geoffrey because she couldn't stand still any longer. Her heart hiccupped in her chest before gaining momentum in a way that made her feel faint. Her lungs pulled in shallow breaths. Geoffrey grabbed her wrist with a grasp that wasn't meant to hurt, only to make her pause. She looked down at his thin fingers wrapped around her tiny wrist.

"I'm serious," he whispered. "Can I come see you again?"

Kate's brow wrinkled. "Why?"

Geoffrey chuckled and released her. He stared down at his cast and then smirked at her. "You don't make this easy, do you? Because I want to talk to you. Get to know you. Like normal people do."

"Are you assuming you're normal?" she asked. Because she definitely wasn't. Kate felt more like someone in the circus freak exhibit where people could pay ten cents to watch the odd, sad half-Indian girl black out while having a worthless premonition.

Geoffrey's smile proved the stories about the Hamilton men were true. Her grip on the candy bag loosened, and an outrageous thought entered her mind. *I'd follow him anywhere.*

"So?" he asked.

In her mind she saw a burning fuse racing toward dynamite again, and she wondered who held the lit match. Her or him? "When?"

"Tonight?"

She glanced out the windows, looking for her daddy. His

errand at the bank must have finished because he stood by their car talking to a hefty man wearing denim overalls with an oil-stained rag hanging out of his back pocket. "After eleven. My parents will be asleep by then." When she looked back at Geoffrey, his pale eyes were full of mischief. She almost changed her mind. "This is a rotten idea."

"The worst," he agreed.

Her lips parted in question, and her heart stalled for a few breathless seconds. "Really?"

"I'll see you tonight."

Kate walked away from him, quickly putting distance between them and questioning her lack of propriety. As she rounded the last aisle to pay for her candy, Matthias stepped toward her. Kate inhaled the scent of peppermint.

"Good afternoon, Kate," he said.

Like all the Hamilton boys, Matthias was striking with dark hair, pale eyes, and a defined jawline that cast a perfect silhouette. He reminded Kate of a film star, exuding confidence and charisma. Where Geoffrey was comparable to a live wire, sparking with haste, Matthias gave the impression of steadiness and quiet calm. Matthias was just as tall as Geoffrey, but he lacked the lanky, loose limbs. Matthias was broader, less angular, and his eyes were as blue as a robin's egg.

Kate only saw Matthias occasionally during the summertime or around the holidays. He'd been away at college for at least three years. And in all the years she'd seen him in town, he'd never once spoken to her before. She had always been Evan's little sister, nothing more, and certainly not worth speaking to.

"Good afternoon, Matthias," she said politely after a long pause.

He stepped closer to her, and she loosened her grip on the candy bag. "I wanted to thank you for helping Geoffrey." Then his voice lowered and vibrated the air around them as he added, "The other day at the wreck."

Kate's eyes widened. "He—he told you?"

Matthias's smile was slow and dimpled his smooth cheek. "Not exactly. He said an angel helped him. Knowing that you lived up the road and that you were the most likely person who knew how to apply salves and splint his ankle, I put two and two together. My mom, well, she probably believes his angel story, but I'm not so easily fooled. Your assistance had a lot to do with his recovery. He would have been in worse shape without it."

The compliment caused a warm tingle to sweep up her neck and across her face, and she touched her cool fingertips to her cheek. "I would have done the same for anyone."

"I know," Matthias said.

When she met his gaze, he was smiling, and she wondered if the Hamilton men knew the power of the gesture. Her shoulders relaxed.

"And why couldn't it have been an angel who rescued him?" she asked, sliding the toe of her sandal against the floor.

Matthias chuckled. "My brother? Being visited by an angel? Highly improbable. But knowing it really was you, they could be one and the same."

His sincere words pulled a hesitant smile from Kate. Matthias wasn't trying to flatter her. She nodded good-bye. At the checkout counter, Kate saw curiosity in Sally's eyes, but Sally didn't ask Kate about her conversation with Geoffrey or with Matthias. After all, if she never spoke to Kate at school—not even to borrow a pencil—it was doubtful Sally would ask Kate about the Hamilton boys. What

would Kate have said to Sally anyway? Kate's shock over being acknowledged far surpassed Sally's nosiness. At the end of her work shift, Sally probably wouldn't even remember Kate being in her store and catching the attention of the Hamiltons. In contrast, Kate's mind replayed the conversations on a loop. Was Geoffrey really going to come over tonight? Did Matthias actually compare her to an angel? The world felt tilted off its axis. These kinds of things never happened to her, not even when Evan was alive.

Later that evening Kate stood in front of the narrow full-length mirror in her bedroom. She rolled long pieces of her fine black hair around a hairbrush handle. Then she tried to bobby pin the roll of hair to the top of her head. When she pulled out the hairbrush, her slick hair sagged against her head like a deflated balloon. Someone knocked on her bedroom door, and she snatched the bobby pin from her hair and raked her fingers through the strands.

"Come in," she called with a voice pitched too high.

Her mama pushed open the door and stepped inside. "What are you doing?"

Kate tossed the hairbrush on her bed and then fidgeted with the hem of her shirt. "Nothing."

Ama's coal-black eyes narrowed. "Every dish in the cabinet is trembling. The wind chimes are ringing outside with no breeze. And there's enough energy in this room to light up the town. You're doing something."

Kate looked at her reflection in the mirror. "I was only messing with my hair." She glanced at her mama but didn't meet her gaze. She'd also been thinking about seeing Geoffrey tonight.

"What's wrong with your hair?"

Kate pulled a section of her hair over her shoulder and draped it over her hand, letting the strands cascade down like a dark

waterfall. "Nothing. I was just trying a new style. Like the girls in town."

"What girls?" Ama asked.

Kate sighed. "The pretty ones, Mama."

"You're a pretty one."

Kate shook her head. "No, I'm not. Look at me. I'm—"

"You're what?" Her mama's voice sounded dangerous and edged with distaste. She crossed her arms over her chest and glowered.

At least half a dozen answers popped into Kate's head—dark, Indian, skinny, weird, awkward, uncool—but she answered, "Different."

"And you'd rather be, what? Exactly like someone else?"

Kate shrugged dismissively. "Maybe more like Sally Rensforth."

Ama laughed, but it coated everything in the room like ashes, leaving a taste on Kate's tongue that was as bitter as maror.

Her mama's mouth pinched. "You'd like to be the same as someone who has nightmares every night? Like someone who is still afraid of the dark?"

Kate whirled around and faced Ama. "You don't know that."

"Don't I? How about Martha Lee? You want to be like her?"

Kate hesitated. She knew she was treading on treacherous ground. "She's pretty. Lots of boys like her."

"She steals her father's liquor and hides it beneath her bed. She also steals from the drugstore on a regular basis. Patty Adams is in love with her first cousin. Sarah Connelly—"

"Mama—" Kate gasped.

"Don't mama me. Why would you want to be like any of them?"

Kate sank onto the edge of her bed. "People already think

we're weird enough without you sharing their secrets." She stared at her colorful, patchwork skirt that fell to her ankles. Not a single girl in town wore the same kind of clothes Kate did. Those girls all looked like they shopped on Main Street, while Kate looked like a girl who'd been dressed by gypsies.

"I'm only telling *you* their secrets, and I'm trying to prove that being like everyone else isn't always a good thing. Besides people in this town like to talk about other people's secrets, and that's how I know half of what I do." Ama sat beside her on the bed. She felt the anger whoosh out of her mama and disappear out of the room. Ama's fierceness was one of her scariest characteristics and also one of her most honorable. She pushed Kate's hair behind her shoulders.

Kate laced her fingers together in her lap and stared at her hands. "It was always so easy for Evan. He fit in with everyone."

Ama's spine stiffened. Kate knew her mama's grief was still raw and wild and had the ability to steal the sun, but Kate also knew her mama could hear Evan's name sometimes and still smile as though she carried beautiful memories of him around with her too.

"That was his talent," her mama said. "One of them. Yours are different. You're never going to be like the rest of them, like the other girls in town, Little Blackbird. You're going to be infinitely better."

Kate's shoulders sagged forward. Ama's words sounded exactly like what a mama should say to her awkward, gangly teenage daughter. "How could you possibly know that?"

Her mama smiled. "Trust me. And as for boys, you shouldn't be worrying about them right now. But if you were old enough for dating, boys would be stupid not to like you just the way you are.

You are a rare bird."

Kate was tempted to tell Ama about Geoffrey, to support her mama's belief that boys might one day find her interesting. But what would she say? *Hey, Mama, now that you mention it, I'm sneaking out tonight to meet a boy. I hope that's okay. I doubt he likes me, but he did say I was beautiful. I'll try to be back before midnight.*

Ama stood and walked toward the door. "Now, settle down in here before you set the house on fire. Your father and I are going to bed soon. Don't stay up too late."

Kate nodded, wondering if midnight was too late.

CHAPTER 5

WHEN GEOFFREY KNOCKED AT HER WINDOW, KATE WAS already dressed in a pair of faded jeans and a black tank top. She'd been waiting for him in the shadows of her room, unable to sleep, drinking cup after cup of lavender tea. She lifted the sash, inhaled a deep breath to try and calm her nerves, and crawled out into the darkness.

"Where are your shoes?" he asked.

"Don't need them," she said. "We're not going far."

He hobbled along slowly since the crutches sank into the soft earth of the garden, upsetting his balance. "What if there's an emergency?"

Kate glanced at the luminescent full moon. "For example, if you turn into a werewolf?"

Geoffrey laughed. "Why me? What if you're the werewolf?"

Kate stared at the moon's rippling reflection on the river as they approached the water. "Then you're definitely out of luck with that bum leg."

Geoffrey laughed again, and Kate shushed him. He looked over his shoulder at her house, which was shielded by mature pines. He stopped a few feet from the water. A half dozen

medium-size boulders alongside the riverbank near her house had been left ages ago as the shifting waters changed the size and course of the river with time. Geoffrey chose a flatter boulder and sat. He laid the crutches beside him. Kate hesitated. She couldn't sit beside him. That would be too close and inappropriate, and she wasn't sure she could sit still at all. Her insides squirmed like earthworms exposed after heavy rains. She unclenched her hands and chose a spot closer to the river, letting her feet dangle into the temperate water.

They sat in silence, listening to the water rush and ripple over smooth river stones. In the mildly humid night, crickets chirped, and an owl hooted from somewhere in the evergreens across the river. Kate closed her eyes and could almost pretend she was alone—if it wasn't for the way the air felt alive and charged or the way the fireflies darted around their bodies, drawn to them because of the energy. The warm wind sounded like reed pipes as it weaved through the trees. She tried to think calming thoughts, but her insides twisted and curled around themselves.

"Why do you live way out here?" Geoffrey asked.

Kate opened her eyes. "What do you mean?"

"Why don't you live in the city? It's not like you couldn't afford a nice house in town. Your dad makes—well, he makes a good living."

"Mama doesn't like living in town. She wants to live closer to nature."

"I guess I can understand that, but why the tiny house? Wait, that didn't come out right—"

Kate gaped at him. One second he was charming, and the next he was offensive. "It came out rudely," she said. "Is that

what you were aiming for? Not everyone can or wants to live in a mansion like Honeysuckle Hollow."

Kate refused to admit that she'd always wanted to see the inside of the Hamiltons' Queen Anne–style home and walk through their garden. Evan had been in the mansion several times and spoke of it as though it were a museum full of antiques, shiny floors, and sparkly crystal. It seemed like a place where royalty might gather and sip Earl Grey. The past spring Kate's daddy helped build a gazebo in the Hamiltons' backyard, which he said was immaculate and bursting with colorful flowers.

Geoffrey chuckled. "No, cool it. You make me nervous. Let me restate it."

Kate pointed at herself. "I make you nervous? How is that possible?"

"You're just so different from other girls. You're so . . . honest."

"And other girls lie?"

Geoffrey shook his head. "Nah, not exactly. They're busy trying to make sure everything they say and do is perfect and classy and proper. And you say whatever you want."

Kate gazed toward the river. "And that means I'm not perfect or classy or proper?" *Add more to the list of why it's no good to be me.*

"No, now, you're taking my words and twisting them all around. What I'm trying to say is that I like it. I like the way you talk to me. It doesn't seem fake."

"Believe me, if I could fake anything, I wouldn't choose this."

Geoffrey laughed again, and she turned to look at him, at

the way his eyes closed and his nose scrunched up. Her smile came unbidden.

"See, that's what I mean. You don't talk like other girls. I bet your biggest news isn't about your hair or your new dress or what Denise Maloney is wearing."

"Why would my biggest news be about Denise Maloney's clothes?" she asked.

"That's my point." He picked up a smooth pebble and tossed it into the water.

The moon's reflection burst apart into crystals of light, sending messages up to the sky. Slowly, the moon's light rippled across the water and put itself back together.

"To answer your question," Kate said, "my mama doesn't prize material possessions. She doesn't care about *things*. She loves nature and people and plants and animals. That's what matters to her. She's never wanted a big house full of breakable stuff to stare at or dust. We like our cottage out here. We have enough space for us. And my daddy says he wouldn't care even if they lived in a box as long as he could be with Mama."

Geoffrey fell silent for so long that Kate turned around to look at him. His gaze was cast far into the trees across the river. "My dad would probably be fine if my mom lived in a separate house."

"Why?"

"Have you met my mom?"

Kate shook her head. "Not directly."

"She's difficult. Demanding too." He created circles in the air with his long fingers. "She's wound way too tight, like a coil ready to spring out of here." He mimed a coil shooting off into the air.

"And your daddy?" Kate asked.

"A perfectionist all the way. I'm not sure he's ever taken a misstep in his life. That's probably why we—me and my brothers—are always seeing what we can get away with. When you know you'll never live up to anyone's perfect expectations, why not aim the other way and shoot for having fun and breaking the rules? Well, except Matthias. He's the good son."

"And you're not?"

"I dunno," he said with a slow smile. "I'll let you decide."

Her fingertips tingled, and the prickle spread up her arms, searing her skin as though she'd been in the sunlight too long. Deciding whether or not Geoffrey was a good son would require her to spend more time with him, to get to know him, to decide whether or not he was safe, whether or not she could trust herself around him.

He must have sensed her hesitation because when he spoke again, his voice sounded urgent, like one in need of a quick fix, one in need of reassurance. "Can I see you again?"

"I can't keep sneaking out like this. Sooner or later my mama is gonna find out."

"How? She's asleep."

Kate pulled her fingers through her hair. "You don't know her, so you'll have to trust me. She'll know." *Because if I keep rattling the dishes and trembling like an autumn leaf, she's going to see right through me.*

"My parents are going up to the lake for the weekend," Geoffrey said, leaning forward and propping his elbows on his knees. "Dad is meeting a medical school friend up there. Why don't you come over?"

The crickets stopped chirping, and the forest fell silent.

Kate turned her face toward the river because she couldn't look at him. She replayed his words in her mind, trying to pick each one apart to comprehend what exactly he was asking. "To your house?" What did that mean? No way he wanted her over for an afternoon of tea and conversations about the weather. Was he talking about something more mature, after sunset, moments that would be even more improper than their late-night meetings?

"How about Saturday afternoon?" he said.

Kate exhaled, and the river rippled away from her. "I doubt my parents would let me go over to your house without your parents being there."

He adjusted his cast on the boulder. "My brothers will be home."

She scoffed. "That's not helping."

"They could be chaperones."

Kate tossed a look of disbelief at him. "After you've just admitted that y'all are always breaking the rules?"

"Not Matthias," he said.

When she turned to finally look at him, he was grinning at her like Wonderland's Cheshire Cat. "A house full of young men and me is hardly appropriate. I don't know what kind of girl you think—"

"Don't," he interrupted. "Don't finish that sentence. I only want to see you. Let me think . . . Wait, how about you say you're going to Martha Lee's or Charlotte LaRue's? Martha's your age, and I've known Charlotte forever. They're friends of mine. Nice girls. They wouldn't care if you used them in secret."

"You want me to lie to my parents?" Kate asked.

It wasn't as though she'd never lied, but those had been

little lies, insignificant omissions, such as forgetting to put the lid on the flour canister and denying it or saying she liked her clothes just fine when all the other girls wore fashionable outfits and lipstick the color of poppies.

"You never break the rules? You're the good daughter then?" he asked. The moon turned his face silvery, and shadows hollowed his eyes and cheeks.

"I'm the only daughter."

"That doesn't answer my question."

No, it doesn't.

Geoffrey used a crutch to help him stand. Then he leaned down and grabbed the other one. Once they were situated below his armpits, he maneuvered off the boulder. "So what do you say? You want to say yes. I can tell."

Kate scrambled to her feet and brushed off the back of her jeans. "You can tell?" Could he see her trembling body? Did he know how much his offer affected the breath coming in and out of her lungs, how her heart beat madly?

He hobbled toward her, closing the distance so quickly she didn't have time to step away from him. She caught a whiff of his cologne, a tangy pungent scent that the guys were wearing these days so they all smelled the same. "I *want* you to say yes, so I'm trying to convince you. At least say you'll think about it."

"I'll think about it."

His expression revealed his feelings of triumph. "Here's the plan. I'll call you Saturday, and you act like I'm Martha calling to invite you over. Don't give me that look. Kids lie to their parents all the time. It's not a big deal, and it's not like you're breaking any of the big rules."

"You've classified the rules, have you? Some are bigger or

worse than others?"

Geoffrey huffed. "How is that different from the Ten Commandments? Aren't those the *big* ones, and all the others not mentioned are lesser? If we stick to the lesser ones, we're less *wicked*."

Kate tsked. "How long have you been working on that defense?"

His grin accentuated his handsome face. "It's a good one, isn't it? You say yes and ride your bike up the road. You can toss it in the woods, and I'll come pick you up. No sweat."

No sweat? The entire idea made Kate start sweating.

"You know the plan, and I hope to see you soon." He pointed himself toward the house and started picking his way across the uneven ground with more ease than she expected.

"Where did you park?" Kate asked, following along beside him.

"I borrowed Benjamin's car," he said. "Told him I was meeting a girl, so of course, he gets it. Benjamin is the master for sneaking out of the house, not that he has to sneak out anymore. At twenty-five he's too old for our parents to care. But I parked down the road a ways."

Kate stopped when she reached the edge of the garden and watched Geoffrey work his way up the dirt driveway, sticking to the shadows and then disappearing into the darkness once he reached the road. She crawled back in through her bedroom window, changed into her pajamas, and lay awake fretting about whether she was turning into an immoral, rule-breaking daughter. Then she wondered who had made all the rules, and what if the rule makers were wrong?

CHAPTER 6

ON SATURDAY MORNINGS AFTER BREAKFAST, KATE'S USUAL ROU-
tine involved gardening for hours before the intensity of the
summer heat made it unbearable. Her first task was to weed the
flowerbeds and the raised gardens. She dressed in a ratty pair of
shorts and a faded green button down, and she pulled her hair
into a loose ponytail. If her mama were home, she'd nag Kate into
wearing a sunhat, but it made her forehead itchy and sweaty, so
she rebelled this morning.

Kate still hadn't decided if she was going to try to sneak
over to Geoffrey's house. She weighed the pros against the cons,
but even after that she didn't have a clear answer. Was Geoffrey
worth lying for? She didn't know. How could she? She barely
knew him, and she barely understood the rebellious, almost
impulsive, temptation to go against the rules whenever he was
around. He *was* persuasive, and she could tell he was used to
getting his way. And how awful was it really for a teenage girl
to hang out with friends? Her peers did it all the time. Boys
and girls went to parties and dances together. They attended
pep rallies and football games in big groups. Just because *she'd*
never been invited to any of those things until now didn't make

her growing desire to be included some hideous, awful temptation . . . did it? Would her parents have a cow if she were honest about wanting to spend time with Geoffrey?

The purple and pink buds of *Echinacea purpurea* and dahlias burst into full bloom and leaned toward Kate as she pulled weeds from in between them. "Always so showy," she whispered with a smile. In response, a few dying blooms perked up and regained vivacity and color.

This sort of phenomenon had been happening her whole life—plants responding to her and acting unnaturally in her presence. Much more emphasis had been placed on Kate's cursed premonitions and how to halt them and their inevitable deterioration of her mind. An entire row in the garden grew only lavender, different varieties with various strengths for brewing teas, mixing salves, and creating tinctures. Dried lavender hung in the garden shed, was tucked into kitchen drawers, was sewn into sachets, and filled a canister in Kate's bedroom all throughout the year.

But ever since Kate could remember, living flora and fauna reacted to her moods and her words. She could also understand what they needed—more water, more light, more nutrients—and she cared for them just as someone might care for a family member. She hadn't known this reaction from plants was unusual until her mama explained that Kate had yet another extraordinary talent. At least this gift wasn't going to negatively affect her mind, but she'd questioned *why*. Had the gift-giver made a mistake and doubled up on Kate's? Her mama responded with an uncharacteristic laugh of delight. She told Kate that the giver of gifts never made mistakes, and one day the purpose of all talents would be made clear.

Her daddy looked over at Kate from across the yard. He stood tall and broad, resembling a Scottish Paul Bunyan with his thick black hair and beard. Although Sean had been the first American-born son, when he was sleepy or angry, his accent reverted back to the strong lilt of his parents', and Kate loved to hear it. It sounded like music, a rising and falling with a dream-like quality combined with his deep baritone.

Kate adored her daddy in a different way from how she loved her mama. Ama was strong-willed and sometimes thorny, with words that often felt like stinging nettles. But Sean was slower to respond, more thoughtful, and chose words that held strength without harm. Kate wondered how two so different could find commonality and then love. She knew fragments of the story about how her parents met. Most of the time all Sean would say was that Ama was the prettiest girl he had ever seen, and he knew she was the one he would marry. He saw her in town one day and was so distracted that he walked right into a light pole. Ama saw it happen and laughed before stopping to make sure he was okay.

Her mama had to be convinced to marry a Scottish-American because she grew up believing she should marry someone from her Cherokee tribe. Sean was persistent and gen-uine in his affections, and after a few months of courting her, Ama was won over by his charm, kindness, and intelligence.

Somehow being from two different worlds worked for them, and Kate couldn't imagine anyone else being more suited for each other. But the two different worlds—a mixed-race girl living in a mostly white-faced town—didn't work as well for Kate like it had for Evan. Kate didn't quite fit anywhere except at home in the garden. But now Geoffrey Hamilton had sprung

into her life, and the boundaries Kate always saw so clearly around herself were blurring.

Sean had spent the last hour digging up a tree stump. Kate lifted her trowel in a pathetic sort of wave. "How's the digging?"

He leaned against the shovel handle and wiped his sweaty brow. "Stubborn roots, but I'll get them. Who you talking to over there?" His lips lifted in a crooked grin.

"Myself!" He chuckled but Kate scowled at the flowers. She lowered her voice, saying, "Are you trying to give me away?" The blooms nodded their vibrant heads in the breeze. "You're supposed to be on my side, protecting our secrets."

Ama didn't outright ask Kate to lie to her daddy about her special gifts, but Kate understood that it was better to keep her talents a secret because most people preferred a simpler life. They wanted to believe in what they could see and touch, and anything that strayed toward paranormal or, God forbid, mystical was deeply disturbing. Her daddy loved her, but would he love her less if he knew she could do things others might label witchy?

Kate rocked back on her heels and thought of Geoffrey and of the deceptive plan he'd come up with for today if she decided to meet him. When he called, if she answered, he would know she wanted to see him. She would pretend he was Martha Lee asking for her to come over. The plan was almost laughable. Martha Lee, a rising sophomore like Kate, hadn't spoken more than a handful of words to Kate in her whole life, and her parents would somehow believe that the tides had shifted, the stars had aligned, and *now* Kate might actually have friends?

If the ruse worked, Kate would ride her bike far enough up the road not to be seen as she stashed it in the woods, and then

Geoffrey planned to pick her up in a car and take her home with him. It all sounded so devious.

She'd never been in the car with a boy other than Evan. She imagined what it would be like riding in a car with Geoffrey. Would the windows be rolled down to let in the summer wind? Would he play the radio so loud they wouldn't be able to talk to each other? Would he rest his hand in between the seats so that—*Stop it!*

Kate was startled by her own angry inner voice. If she kept thinking like that, she might as well mail her heart to Geoffrey in a box and say, "Do what you will." She slouched and patted her trowel against the ground. She had always wanted to see the inside of Honeysuckle Hollow, though, and there was the garden to consider too. Maybe one visit was worth telling a lie this time. Her stomach clenched. Kate looked up when she heard footsteps approaching.

"Ready for lunch?" her daddy asked.

Kate blocked the sun with her hand and looked up at him. She doubted she could eat anything if she tried, but she needed to act like everything was normal. Just a regular Saturday working in the yard with her daddy. "Sure."

Sean wiped his bear-size hands on his work pants, leaving behind smears of fresh dirt. "You're doing a great job with this bed. Those flowers are gorgeous. Look at all those blooms."

A dahlia dipped its bright-pink bloom toward her, touching her cheek with a gentle caress. The flowers were only responding to her energy, and she was probably charged with enough nervous energy to light up the whole town. "Mama's flowers always do well."

Sean gave her ponytail a gentle tug. "Give yourself some

credit. You work hard out here too. Now what should we eat?"

Kate stood, brushed the dirt from her knees, and stabbed her trowel into the soil. She followed him inside the cottage, pausing at the door to kick off her dirty shoes and place them beside her daddy's. "Is Mama coming home for lunch?"

Sean shook his head. "She's been delayed at Mrs. Ballister's. I think the poor old lady is worse than your mom anticipated. It might take her into the afternoon to finish up there."

Kate's pulse quickened. Her mama wouldn't be there when Geoffrey called. She wouldn't be able to see deceit making Kate's nose twitch or her ears itch. Kate pulled down the canister of dried lavender and a teacup. She filled the kettle with water and turned on the stove. Sean washed his hands in the sink and then grabbed two glasses from the cabinets. He filled one with tap water and drank half the glass.

Kate opened the refrigerator and looked over the contents. Although their fridge was never empty, they didn't have a large supply of food stored in it. At Ama's command, they ate a lot of fresh fruits and vegetables, whatever was in season. "We could have something easy, like turkey sandwiches, or I could warm up last night's chicken and vegetables."

Sean sat at the round kitchen table, looking like he always did—a man too large for the average size chair and small table. "Is there any more of that peanut butter pie in there? We could have that for lunch."

Kate's eyebrows rose, and she glanced toward the table where her daddy sat.

"Don't look at me like that. That's the same look your mom gives."

Kate smiled. "I won't tell."

Her daddy's lips quivered at the corners before a smile stretched across his face. "We'll have to swear on it."

"Daddy, you know I'm not allowed to swear. And Mama will know we've had pie. She'll notice the missing pieces because she notices *everything*."

"We'll blame it on the squirrels."

Kate gave him an incredulous look. "Squirrels?"

Sean winked at her. "She won't believe that for a second, but it'll make her laugh, and she has a beautiful laugh, doesn't she? You cut the pie. I'll grab the plates and forks. But first we need music." Sean crossed to the far side of the living room and turned on the portable radio. The channel was already tuned to the rock and roll station broadcasting from Atlanta. "Only You" by The Platters drifted through the house.

Kate grabbed the pie from the refrigerator and closed the door with her hip. Then the kettle whistled at the same time the phone rang, and Kate nearly dropped the pie. She grabbed the kettle, turned off the burner, and slipped the pie onto the table. Then she snatched at the phone and gripped it in her hand, turning her knuckles white.

"Muir residence."

"Hi," Geoffrey said. "It's me, Miss Kate."

This was it. Be a liar or be a good daughter. She swallowed and looked at her daddy. He swayed to the music in his lumbering way and pulled lunch plates from the cabinet. Sean glanced at her, waiting to learn who was on the phone.

She closed her eyes. "Hey, Martha. How are you?"

When Geoffrey spoke, his excitement crackled through the phone line. "You're coming over? Can I pick you up in half an hour?"

JENNIFER MOORMAN

"Can you please hold while I ask?" Kate pressed the receiver to her chest until she realized that her heart pounded so loud that Geoffrey could probably hear it over the line. She moved the phone behind her back and toyed with the long, spiral cord. "Daddy, do you care if I go over to Martha Lee's house this afternoon?"

His brow furrowed, and when he didn't answer immediately, Kate's heart kicked into panic mode.

She realized his hesitation wasn't because he objected but because of confusion. *No one* had ever called for Kate. "Oh, well, um, who's Martha? A girl? I mean, a girl from town? From school?"

If he wanted specifics, Kate could inform him that Martha was one of the most popular girls in her class, and the chances of her inviting Kate to her house were as probable as Kate being chosen as homecoming queen. Kate wasn't sure what bothered her more: lying to her daddy or the look of complete surprise on his face because a girl from school might actually invite Kate anywhere.

"Yes, sir. She's a girl in my grade. She lives in town. I could ride my bike there. That way you wouldn't have to drive me. We'll probably just hang and do girl stuff," she babbled.

His confusion magnified, creasing long trenches into his brow. "What's girl stuff?"

Kate shrugged. She had no idea. "Brush our hair and talk about boys?"

"Sounds dreadful," he said, but he was smiling. "Of course you can go, but you'll need to be home before dark. You sure you want to ride your bike? I don't mind taking you into town."

"No, no, that's okay, but thanks." She pressed the phone to

her ear. "Hi, Martha? Daddy says it's okay. I'll ride my bike. I should be there in an hour."

"Which means I'll see you at our meeting spot in half an hour," Geoffrey said.

Kate hung up and pressed her lips together so that her hitching breaths wouldn't reveal her excitement, which was rapidly outpacing the pang of guilt she felt.

CHAPTER 7

AFTER SHOVING A PIECE OF PEANUT BUTTER PIE INTO HER mouth at an alarming rate and drinking two cups of lavender tea, Kate changed into jeans she rolled up at the bottom, a white button-up shirt, and her saddle shoes—last year's Christmas present from her daddy after she begged for at least one piece of modern fashion. Ama had argued that Kate's clothing was *just fine*, which it was, if nobody cared about Kate fitting in. As much as she acted like she didn't care that the town didn't accept her, a part of her desperately wanted to belong.

Kate hopped on her royal-blue Schwinn ballooner bike with its cushy seat, whitewall tires, and classic wheels. It was one of her most prized possessions, and today it was taking her somewhere she'd never been before—to meet a boy who might actually be interested in her. *In her.* The stifling wind buffeted Kate as she zoomed up the road toward the spot where she'd meet Geoffrey. The wind felt like it was pushing her back toward her house an inch for every four she moved forward. It could have been a sign that she should turn back home, but Kate wasn't paying attention to signs. She crouched over the handlebars and pedaled harder and faster until strands of her dark hair clung to the beads of sweat on

her face and neck.

By the time she arrived at the designated spot to conceal her bicycle, her clothes were damp with perspiration, and she sucked in gulps of air. When she climbed off her bike, her legs trembled, making her feel as though they had been replaced with Red Vines. She would have rested by the roadside, collapsed even, but paranoia that her mama would drive over the next hill had Kate pushing her bike deep into the wooded area.

She laid her bike on its side and dragged a fallen pine branch over and covered it. Then she whispered a prayer that no one would find her beloved bike and take it for their own. She didn't need the added complication of explaining how her bike was stolen, which would lead to the whole lie unraveling faster than she could create a new one. Kate crept to the edge of the forest and listened for the approaching engine of a car. She waited a scant few minutes before a red car drove over the hill and slowed.

The driver pulled the Ford Thunderbird onto the roadside, and he leaned over and rolled down the passenger-side window.

"Kate," Geoffrey called in a rough whisper.

Kate burst out of the trees and ran to the car. She opened the door and hopped inside before she could change her mind. Her legs stuck to the leather seats, drawing attention to how sweaty she was. She caught sight of herself in the side-view mirror and gawked at her disheveled hair. Her embarrassment heated her from the inside as though she'd swallowed a coal and now it smoldered in her stomach.

"Well, good afternoon, Miss Kate," Geoffrey said.

She self-consciously pulled her fingers through her tangled hair. "It's windy."

"That it is. Nearly pushed me off the road a few times."

He studied her, and Kate noticed how tightly his skinny fingers gripped the wheel. She shifted on the seat, her legs sticking to the leather as though she were made of taffy. He turned on the air-conditioning.

"Want to cool down for a minute before we go?" he asked.

Kate nodded her head, realizing how enclosed they were inside the car, how peculiar it felt to be alone with a boy other than her brother. New beads of sweat dotted her forehead, and she reached up to swipe them away.

The air-conditioning circulated the scents of men's soap and leather. Sunlight reflected off the dashboard, creating starbursts in Kate's vision. She glanced over at Geoffrey as he wrapped his arms around the wheel and leaned forward on an exhale. His crutches were propped in the backseat, and she wondered how well he could drive while wearing a bulky cast on his right leg. He turned his face to look at her.

"I didn't think you'd actually agree to this," he admitted. "What changed your mind?"

That was a great question for which Kate didn't have a ready answer. Why had she agreed? Was she so desperate to keep Geoffrey interested? That wasn't exactly it. "Curiosity," she finally said.

"About?"

Kate shrugged and turned a vent toward her face. Her black hair lifted and blew behind her shoulders. "Everything." About seeing Honeysuckle Hollow, about experiencing riding in a car with a boy, about getting to know who Geoffrey Hamilton really was.

"You won't be disappointed," he said, shifting the car into drive and turning it onto the road.

"I'll let you know."

Geoffrey laughed, and Kate slouched in the seat to hide herself until they turned off her road and headed into town. She doubted they'd pass her mama in town or on Dogwood Lane, which was Geoffrey's street, and no one driving past would assume Kate Muir was in the car with Geoffrey Hamilton. Kate felt certain she was invisible to most of Mystic Water's townsfolk. When they pulled into the driveway of Honeysuckle Hollow, Kate leaned forward in the seat, already captivated by the front façade of the mansion.

Rudbeckia hirta and *Heliotropium amplexicaule* bloomed alongside azaleas in the front garden that bordered an expansive porch. "The *Rudbeckia* and the heliotropes are beautiful."

Geoffrey pulled into the garage and turned off the engine. "The what?"

"The flowers. The black-eyed Susans and the purple flowers."

He unhooked his seatbelt. "Oh yeah, Mom's gardener picks out the best plants for the yard."

"She doesn't garden?" Kate asked.

Geoffrey looked at her with a smirk and opened his car door. "And ruin her manicure?" He slid his legs out of the car, careful with the cast. "Shall we?"

Kate opened her car door and inhaled a slow, deep breath. She smoothed her hand down her hair and tried to push the wrinkles from her shirt. She glanced at her saddle shoes and noticed dirty smudges. She licked her thumb and quickly wiped away the grime. At least some part of her was like the other girls in town, even though shoes didn't magically make her become one of them.

Geoffrey leaned up the front seat and grabbed his crutches from the back. Kate followed him through the interior garage door that opened into a short, narrow hallway wallpapered in a

cream paper covered in blooming pastel-pink peonies. The hallway branched to the left and to the right. He turned left, and they entered the airy, light-filled kitchen, which was large enough to enclose her family's entire kitchen and living room combined. The room smelled like lemon and wood polish. A half-eaten creamy-white frosted cake sat beneath a glass dome. Sunlight gleamed off the polished round kitchen table tucked into the breakfast nook and off the high gloss wood floors. Through the kitchen windows Kate glimpsed the backyard, and she stepped closer to a pair of French doors.

Where Kate's family garden was wild and diverse, the Hamiltons' garden was orderly and manicured. Shaped boxwoods created separate spaces, working as natural fencing, and others were shaped into ovals that looked like green Easter eggs sitting in terra-cotta pots. A winding, geometric tile path disappeared behind a row of boxwoods, and a narrow, man-made stream divided the yard into two sections. An oak tree provided shade for a large portion of the yard, and cardinals flew in and out of it. Honeysuckle vines covered the rear fence. Kate had often felt as though she watched the world from outside of a snow globe, fingers pressed against the glass, wishing she could be inside just once, yet accepting she'd always be an outsider. For the first time in her life, she'd finally slipped into the world she'd been separated from. If Evan could see her now, what would he say? His voice moved through her mind like a backyard breeze. *Took you long enough, Little Blackbird.*

The kitchen opened into a living room filled with antique, lavish furniture and an ornately carved wooden mantel framing a pass-through fireplace. An oil painting of the Hamiltons hung above the hearth. The sons looked like boys, and Geoffrey looked

to be around five. The next son was Matthias, then Richard, then the oldest, Benjamin. Built-in bookcases lined one entire wall, and an assortment of items decorated the shelves—books, photographs of the family on vacations, vases, a globe made of polished marble mounted on a brass axis.

Music played from one of the downstairs rooms, and Kate recognized the song as "Rock Around the Clock." Geoffrey propped his crutches against the countertop and opened the refrigerator. "Want something to drink?"

"Sure," Kate said, standing halfway in the kitchen and halfway in the living room. She shoved her hands into her pockets.

Honeysuckle Hollow looked like a house no real person lived in. It reminded Kate of mansions in novels, peopled by fictional characters who drank tea all day and took strolls through elaborate gardens while ordinary people did all the work. She was afraid to touch anything, and she glanced down at her saddle shoes. She lifted each one to check the bottoms for dirt she might have tracked in from the woods. Would she leave behind traces of her unworthiness?

Geoffrey used a bottle opener on his key ring and popped off the tops on two sodas. He handed her one of the glass bottles. "Welcome to Honeysuckle Hollow. Want a tour?" He clinked his glass bottle against hers.

The bottle quivered in her hand, ringing out a melancholy tone. "Who wouldn't?"

Geoffrey chuckled before drinking half his soda. He put the bottle on the counter, adjusted the crutches beneath his arms, and pushed out his elbow for her to take hold.

"Is this dangerous? Me holding on to you while you try to move on crutches?"

"What's life without a little danger?"

Kate hesitated before touching him. Sneaking around with Geoffrey was one thing, but being close enough to touch him might be crossing the line society had already drawn between them. He lifted his elbow higher as if that would remind her to take it, so she wrapped her fingers around his bicep. How was he able to make something dangerous seem commonplace and acceptable? The most dangerous adventure Kate had taken before she met Geoffrey was carrying her daddy's axe to the shed.

She felt the tautness of his muscles beneath her fingers, and she adjusted her grip. What would her mama say if she knew Kate was touching a boy? Kate almost laughed—touching a boy seemed further down the list of what she should be worried about, sneaking out being at the top and lying about spending an afternoon with Martha was a close second.

Geoffrey walked Kate through a sitting parlor and the formal dining room across the hall from it. Both rooms were full of opulent upholstery, velvet curtains, Persian rugs, and heavy, dark furniture—some of the most beautiful craftsmanship Kate had ever seen. A crystal chandelier hung in the two-story foyer, and Kate stared at the hundreds of rainbows flashing on the walls and across the parquet floor as the sunlight poured through the high windows.

The house looked as though no one actually lived in it. Every item was carefully placed and arranged. There was no dust or scratches on the hardwood. No childhood handprints smeared on the walls, no stray books or drinking glasses left sitting around. No plants grew in corners or bloomed on shelves. The plush draperies battled to keep the sunlight from filling too much of the rooms, which grew shadows and swirled cold patches of air. The

lack of life closed in around Kate, suffocating her. She inhaled deeply. When she exhaled, the chandelier crystals tinkled together like fragile, never-played wind chimes.

"Four of the bedrooms are upstairs. Ben converted the downstairs office into his bedroom when we were older, but Dad changed it back when Ben went to college. Now that Ben's working with Dad at the insurance company, he owns an apartment closer to town. But he's here *a lot*, mostly because Mom still feeds him whenever he wants. Richard finished college last year, but he still lives here, and Matthias will graduate next spring, although he's been talking about medical school, so that'll mean another four years. I doubt he'll ever come back here to live at home. That's not his style."

As soon as Geoffrey started talking about college, Kate realized that he would be going off to college in the fall just like Evan had two years before. Geoffrey would be leaving Mystic Water in a little more than a month. The French doors in the kitchen opened, and a burst of wind rushed down the hallway and whirled around them.

"You're going off to college in the fall, right? Will they convert your room when you're gone? Make it a guest room?" Kate asked.

Geoffrey shook his head. "I'll still come home during university breaks and the holidays, and it's not as though they get a lot of out-of-town guests. Not except for family."

"Geoffrey!" a male voice called.

"Come on," he said, giving her hand a squeeze before leading her back through the house. "Let me introduce you to my brothers."

Three tall young men stood in the kitchen. Matthias was the most familiar to Kate because he had been good friends with her brother. Although she would have known all the young men to be

Hamiltons, she would not have known Richard, the second oldest, from Benjamin, the oldest. They could have passed for twins except that one's hair was darker and longer. Kate guessed Richard had the longer hair because the other brother had an angry red line marring the side of his cheek, a tell-tale sign of healing after a car wreck.

Benjamin and Richard held brown glass bottles of Budweiser, and Matthias drank a Coca-Cola. The oldest two leaned against the countertop and laughed at a joke Kate hadn't heard. With all of them, except Geoffrey, being older than twenty, she felt like a kid in a room full of adults.

"Tiger Lily has arrived," Benjamin said, looking at Kate. A mighty wind pushed one of the French doors all the way open, and the doorknob slammed into his elbow. He cursed.

Kate's jaw clenched.

"Shut up, Ben," Matthias said before his gaze met Kate's, offering an apologetic expression.

"This is Kate Muir," Geoffrey said. "Kate, this is Benjamin, Richard, and Matthias."

Richard lifted his bottle and said hello. His longer hair looked rebellious for a Hamilton. It gave him the air of a musician or an artist, but maybe he was neither. Maybe this was one of the ways he chose to break the strict rules laid down by their father.

"Hi," she said, not wanting to meet anyone's gaze.

Benjamin tilted his head. "Are you Evan Muir's little sister?"

Kate's eyes drifted toward Matthias, who gave her a small smile. She nodded because she didn't trust her voice could escape her too-tight throat.

"He was a helluva football player," Benjamin said. "Want a beer?"

Kate nearly choked on her response. Did older boys really ask underage girls to drink with them? "No, thanks. I have a Coke."

"I'll take one," Geoffrey said. "Sure you don't want one?" he asked Kate.

She gave him a disbelieving look and shook her head. Wasn't it bad enough she'd lied so she could sneak out with him? She couldn't come home reeking of beer. Regret skulked into the room and wrapped itself around her. What was she doing here, in a room full of strangers who thought it was okay to give a sixteen-year-old alcohol? Maybe she was being too rigid, but she hadn't lost all of her morals. Geoffrey opened the fridge to grab a beer.

"What's the name of the family two doors down?" Benjamin asked. He tilted back his bottle and finished the rest of his beer. "Grab me another one, will ya?" he asked, looking at Geoffrey.

"Down which way?" Matthias asked.

Benjamin pointed east. While balancing on one foot, Geoffrey used his opener to pop off the tops on two beers. He passed one bottle to Benjamin.

"The Lees," Matthias said.

"Yeah, the Lees. I saw their daughter, Martha, I think, and her friend in the yard a little while ago. She's grown up," he said with a smirk that caused Kate to shudder. "I invited them over."

Panic zinged up from Kate's toes all the way to her chest, where it lodged itself. She looked at Geoffrey, but he still wasn't paying attention to her. The brown bottle in his hand held him captive while he drank. She didn't want anyone to know she was at Geoffrey's house. Martha would tell everyone she saw, and then it would get back to Kate's parents, and then Kate would be grounded until she was seventy-six.

"Their daughter is sixteen, Ben," Matthias said.

Ben raised his bottle. "So?"

"So, isn't that a little too young for you?"

Benjamin made a show of counting on his fingers. "Nine years. If you'd seen how excited she was for the invitation, you wouldn't question it." Benjamin took a long drink of beer.

"I'm always going to question your motives," Matthias said.

Benjamin walked past Matthias and clinked their bottles together. "Maybe I invited her over for you. Or for Tiger Lily to have a couple of playmates." He winked at Kate as he passed her and walked out into the garden. Richard laughed and followed Benjamin outside.

A vein pulsed at Kate's temple. Warning blasts were going off in her head. She turned to Geoffrey. "Take me home."

Geoffrey nearly spewed beer from his mouth. "What? Why?"

She placed her half empty soda bottle on the kitchen counter and walked toward the garage door. "Now, please."

"Wait, Kate," Geoffrey called. He hobbled to catch up with her in the hallway. "Why?"

"I can't have girls like Martha knowing I was over here when your parents were away. Do you have any idea what that would make me look like?"

Geoffrey pulled a face. "Martha won't care."

"Yes, she will," Kate argued. "She'd care so much that she'd probably blab to the entire town as soon as she gets home today."

"Stay," Geoffrey said. "You just got here."

Kate's heart pounded so hard she felt nauseous. "Why? So your drunk brother can come up with other insulting names to call me?"

"He's not trying to insult you. That's his way. He teases."

If Kate had lost all of her manners—and was considerably

braver—she would have told Benjamin to get bent. Instead she
said, "Please, take me home, Geoffrey. This wasn't a good idea."

Matthias stepped into the hallway. "You can't drive her home,"
he said.

Kate's eyes widened before she straightened her shoulders. "I'll
walk then."

Matthias wrinkled his brow. "What? No, I'll drive you.
Geoffrey, you've been drinking." He pointed at the bottle in
Geoffrey's hand. "I'll drive Kate home. We don't need another car
wreck."

Geoffrey groaned. "I've had one beer."

"I said no," Matthias responded.

Geoffrey pushed his fingers through his dark hair causing it to
stick up. "This did not turn out right."

For a moment, Kate's expression softened. Geoffrey had
wanted things to go differently too, but none of that mattered now.
Not with Benjamin's insults, not with the alcohol, not with Martha
Lee exposing Kate's lies.

"Good-bye," she said. Without giving Geoffrey time to
respond, she opened the door and stepped into the garage.

Matthias took the keys from Geoffrey and joined her. She
climbed into the car, buckled her seatbelt, and prayed to melt into
the seat so she didn't have to live through another second of this
terrible idea. For the first few minutes, they were both silent during
the drive to her bicycle. As soon as they drove over the town bridge
and toward the outskirts of town, Matthias spoke up.

"I'm sorry about my brother."

"Which one?" Kate stared at the trees as they blurred past the
window in streaks of deep green.

Matthias tapped his fingers against the steering wheel. "Mostly for Ben."

"Because he's a rude drunk?"

Matthias laughed. "Among other things, but yes. And for Geoffrey."

"What for?" she asked, looking at him.

"He's young," Matthias said. "He doesn't always know how to handle a situation. But he is right about Ben. Ben can be a jerk, but he teases a lot too. He wasn't trying to insult you. In his own way, he was calling you a princess. You know, the princess from *Peter Pan*?"

"I know who Tiger Lily is. I can read," she snapped. "I'm only half-Cherokee. It's not as though I'm some other species. I'm still a girl, and I was born in this town. I'm not that different from anyone else. I have feelings, ya know?"

Matthias glanced over at her. "Who are you trying to convince? Me or yourself? I know all of that."

Did he? The Hamiltons were used to fitting in, to being the admired family. They were used to being the most popular boys in school and getting everything they wanted. Did someone like Matthias really know what it was like to be set apart because of something he couldn't control?

"Pull over there," Kate said, pointing out the window to a spot up ahead.

Matthias balked at the idea. "I'm not dropping you off on the side of the road."

"No, my bicycle. It's in the woods." Kate's ears warmed, and her cheeks flushed. She stared straight ahead. "Here is fine. I'll ride my bike from here."

Matthias pulled onto the shoulder of the road. "Why is your bike in the woods?"

Kate exhaled. "Geoffrey picked me up here. He . . . he couldn't very well pick me up at my house."

"Because you're too young to date?"

"Date?" she blurted with a sarcastic laugh. "We're not dating." Sneaking out of the house twice was not considered dating. In fact, she didn't even know what they were doing other than being inappropriate. "I told my daddy I was going to a girlfriend's house."

"Why?"

For so many reasons. Kate sighed. "Heavens to Betsy, Matthias, why do you think? Your parents are away. I've never even been to a boy's house before, and I certainly wouldn't be allowed to go if his parents weren't home."

"And yet you did," Matthias said. The corner of his lips lifted into a half smile.

"A mistake." She opened the car door but didn't meet his gaze. "Thanks for the ride."

"Kate!"

She paused with her hand on the door, finally looking into his pale-blue eyes. Matthias's kind eyes made her want to believe that there was still good in the world.

"I'm sorry," he said.

Kate shrugged. She hated the pity she saw in his expression. "I'm used to it." She slammed the door harder than she intended, and she didn't look back as she ran into the safety of the woods. Once she found her bike, she slumped against a tree, covered her face with her hands, and cried. Tiny fern fronds pushed themselves up through the soil around Kate's body. They grew a few inches and unfurled their rolled heads, pressing in against her body as

though offering comfort. Kate sobbed harder, and only the birds came down to console her.

CHAPTER 8

KATE RODE HER BIKE DOWN THE DRIVEWAY, STOWED IT IN THE shed, and dragged herself inside the house. Her daddy was preoccupied with architectural plans and looked up from the kitchen table papered in blueprints only long enough to ask if she had fun—to which she responded, "It was a new experience." If he noticed what she knew would be swollen, bloodshot eyes from crying, he didn't acknowledge it.

Kate went straight to the bathroom, undressed, and stood beneath the scalding hot water in the shower until she was sure she'd washed away the dirt and sweat from her body. She wished she could wash away the lingering sadness and disappointment too. As she toweled off, she tried to rub away the ache in her chest, but her insides felt painful like a poison ivy rash.

She tried rereading *Peter Pan*, one of her favorite stories, but her thoughts wandered all over the place, and her emotions were running rampant. She swung from feeling embarrassed by her lack of social skills on display at the Hamiltons to feeling rejected by Geoffrey and his brothers to a surge of guilt brought on by lying to her daddy and sneaking around with Geoffrey. He wasn't

worth all of these feelings and confusion. He'd tried to give her a beer, for Pete's sake. Kate groaned her irritation and went outside to ask nature to calm her.

When Ama came home at dinnertime, Kate was still sitting down by the river, tossing pebbles into the water and sketching pictures of Honeysuckle Hollow's chandelier into the dirt with her finger. Someone walked through the grass toward her, and Kate knew it was her mama, barefoot and determined.

"Martha Lee's?" her mama asked.

Kate didn't look up or turn her gaze toward her mama, because Ama could *see* the things people didn't say out loud. "For a little while."

"I didn't know you were friends."

Kate shrugged. "Just getting to know each other."

"Did you find the alcohol beneath her bed?"

"Mama!" Kate protested. "Nice girls don't snoop under people's beds."

Ama sat down beside her. Her skirt flowed around her legs like a blanket as red as a cardinal's wing. "I was only asking a simple question. Your dad said you didn't stay long."

Kate exhaled. *Stayed too long*, she thought. "I didn't feel well."

Ama harrumphed. "Could that be because you had peanut butter pie for lunch?"

Kate looked at her. "Squirrels?"

Ama laughed, and her daddy was right. Her mama's laugh sounded melodious and magical. She didn't hear it often, but when she did, Kate could see why her daddy had fallen for the mysterious, complicated Ama. "As if I would believe that nonsense."

"He knew you wouldn't."

"He admitted that it was all his idea, so I should give you a reprieve. Did you have a good time at Martha's?"

Kate shrugged and tossed a torn blade of grass into the water. "Depends on your definition of a good time. It was different. They're different."

Ama picked up a pebble and tested its weight in her palm. "How so?"

"They're rich."

Her mama laughed again. Sunbeams changed directions and shined on her face, illuminating her skin. "You mean they live in a big, fancy house. *Rich* has other meanings. They have wealth, yes, and it's easy to see when it's on such obvious display, but people are not always rich in the ways that matter."

Kate had heard all of this before. Money didn't buy happiness or love or fulfilment, but it did buy beautiful dresses and makeup and sometimes even friends. She and her mama sat in silence for a while, and Kate watched the sun drop below the pines across the river, casting a red-orange glow behind the trees, looking like a distant forest fire.

Kate hadn't expected her mama to understand. Ama's definition of rich was having good health, having overflowing happiness, having one's family close, and being surrounded by nature. All of that was well and good, but Ama didn't care that Kate didn't fit in with the popular kids. She had zero sympathy for Kate's feeling of rejection.

Kate wanted her mama to just once see it from her perspective. "It's like they live in a completely different way than we do. Everything they have looks antique and expensive. It's like a dollhouse. Everything is perfect. Even *they* look perfect, like they walked right off the set of *Ozzie and Harriet.*"

JENNIFER MOORMAN

"Boring," her mama said with a smile.

Kate's jaw clenched. "Mama, you don't understand."

"I never do," Ama said seriously.

Kate frowned. "You never cared that Evan wanted to hang with them."

Ama's hands stilled and her gaze traveled across the river. "Oh, I knew why that was happening."

"Why?"

Ama folded her hands together in her lap. "Evan was never mesmerized by their riches or their way of life. They were drawn to *him*. They needed *him*. He had something they often lack."

Kate's eyebrows knit together. "And what is that?"

"The light." Her mama's sigh bent the reeds lining the river, and they dipped toward the water.

Kate thought of the sunlight trying to press its way inside Honeysuckle Hollow, only to be held at bay, only to be let inside when allowed. She wondered if Geoffrey's family had constructed ways to keep the light out of their hearts too.

No one in Mystic Water had been able to construct a way to keep out Evan. He walked around as though he had happiness tucked away in his pockets, and he gave it away for free to anyone who needed it. Her mama was right. Mystic Water needed people like Evan. But she hadn't inherited Evan's ability to bring happiness and joy to others. The only thing she inherited was a cursed gift, and Mystic Water, without outwardly saying it, had turned its back on what they didn't want—another busted-up person.

Ama stood. "Come inside. It's time for dinner."

Kate reluctantly stood but immediately felt as though all the blood rushed to her head, and she swayed on her feet. Ama kept walking, unaware that Kate stumbled forward unsteadily. Kate's

86

vision undulated, and the world looked like she was looking at it through a glass jar full of aloe vera jelly. She reached out her hand toward her mama and tried to speak. Blackness swooped in from the periphery, and Kate felt herself falling.

Sunlight glinted off black-and-white checkerboard tiles. Red vinyl seats lined up along a powder-blue countertop. Bells jingled. A cold sweetness coated her tongue. Cigarette smoke choked the sugary air. A pair of glasses tumbled to the sidewalk. A brown blob melted in the heat. Nasal laughter irritated Kate's ears. Someone whimpered.

Kate woke up to a hard slap against her cheek. Her mama gripped Kate's bony shoulders and shook as though trying to shake dirt from a throw rug.

"Mama," Kate moaned, and the shaking stopped.

"You're going to be the death of me," Ama said angrily. "Did you forget your tea again?"

"Huh? No . . . what?" Slowly the backyard came into focus, and the dull buzz in her ears retreated, returning life to sharp detail all around her. Kate sat up and rubbed her forehead. A steady ache throbbed inside her skull. "I had a vision," she said, understanding what had happened.

"That's obvious," Ama said, helping Kate to her feet. "Did you forget your tea?"

"No," Kate said quickly. "No, I promise. I drank at least four cups today." She hadn't wanted anything bad to happen at Geoffrey's. Although she hadn't been able to stop the day from turning from hopeful to unfortunate. At least the lousy time at Geoffrey's hadn't been because she passed out and had a stupid vision. Pieces of the vision drifted through her mind like flower petals caught on the wind. Kate tried to reach out and grab them.

"It's getting worse then," Ama said, turning her back on Kate and pacing away from her.

Her words snapped Kate back to attention. "Worse? Why would you think that?"

Ama whipped around and marched back toward Kate. Her voice was quiet and measured. "Because you're drinking tea and yet you still had a vision. There are other possibilities. The tea isn't strong enough, the lavender wasn't mature enough, you need more than you used to. We'll try one thing at a time." She grabbed Kate's arm, causing Kate to look directly into her mama's oil-black eyes. "Don't worry. We'll figure this out. I won't let this win."

Let this win? Ama made it sound like Kate was in a battle with her own body. What if her body won? Wasn't that what Ama assumed would happen anyway? They were just delaying the inevitable moment when Kate's mind snapped into a million fragmented pieces that could never reassemble.

"It's time for dinner," Ama said, ending the discussion as though it had been settled. But Kate didn't feel settled *at all*.

During dinner, Kate pushed her carrots and broccoli around on a blue plate with a chipped edge that revealed the darker material beneath the lacquer. Her daddy's plate was white, and her mama cut her chicken on a china plate patterned with red toile de Jouy. Kate would bet her favorite plant guidebook that the Hamiltons never ate on cracked, mismatched dinnerware. The Lees probably had matching dishes for every occasion. Kate imagined their conversation. *We're having meatloaf? Oh, let's dine on the floral motif. Tonight is roast chicken? We must use the gold-rimmed Japanese pattern that just arrived.*

That night Kate fell asleep thinking of Peter Pan and how she

would always be Tiger Lily and never Wendy, the girl everyone remembered, the girl everyone wanted to be.

The following morning Kate awoke and blinked in the soft sunlight streaking across her bedroom floor. A square of shadow disrupted the straight beams of light. Something was stuck to a windowpane. Kate threw off her covers and rushed to her window. She unlocked the latch and pushed up the sash. Humid summer air poured into the room, slinking down the wall and covering everything with a sticky mist.

Kate reached outside and snatched a taped piece of paper from the glass. She unfolded the creased stationary and held her breath.

Dear Miss Kate,

I should apologize for yesterday. I wanted to spend a day with you in the garden, getting to know you better. Nothing turned out as I planned, and I didn't even get to take you home. I hope you will forgive the disappointing day. Would you be willing to meet with me again? If you are, a group of us are going to the park this afternoon at two, and you are welcome to join us.

Sincerely sorry,
Geoffrey

Kate read the letter three times before she refolded it, sat on the edge of her bed, and slid the note beneath her pillow. She passed glances toward the hidden note. *A group of us*, she thought. *Who's us? Did it mean his family? His friends? Girls from the neighborhood?*

She couldn't possibly go. After yesterday's disaster, did she

even want to go? Was it worth putting herself out there again? She could act like this never happened. She wouldn't have to suffer through the anxiety of declining his offer because she wouldn't have to see him or call him or write a return response. She could go on with her day and pretend he'd never stood at her darkened window, never thought of her, and never left behind an epistle of apology.

She sighed and slipped her hand beneath her pillow. The paper felt real enough against her fingers. Maybe the apology was real as well. Geoffrey had put a lot of effort into coming all the way out to her house just to say he was sorry, *and* he was inviting her to a group outing. Another occurrence that had *never* happened to her. What was normal for most kids, and especially for Evan when he'd been in school, was going places with friends, slumber parties, drive-in movies, and school dances. The list seemed endless, and each activity had escaped Kate's grasp. Until now.

She allowed herself a small smile because, regardless of who might comprise this group, Geoffrey wasn't ashamed to have her join them. It wouldn't matter if everyone looked at her and believed she had stumbled into the wrong party, because Geoffrey would know she belonged there.

It's a yes, then?

Kate dressed, brushed her teeth, and found her parents at the breakfast table drinking Maxwell House coffee and eating scrambled eggs and grits. An empty plate sat on the table waiting for her.

"Hey," she said, trying not to sound as breathless as she felt, "can I go meet some friends at the park today?"

"Well, good morning to you too, Little Blackbird," her daddy said.

She slid one arm around his shoulders and gave him a squeeze. He smelled like pine trees and cut cedar. "Good morning."

Her mama's coffee cup clinked against its ceramic saucer. "Who are 'some friends'?"

Kate assumed Geoffrey wouldn't be inviting her to spend time with his family, so the obvious "us" he mentioned would be other kids. She scrambled to come up with names. Geoffrey had mentioned two girls, so it felt safe to assume they could be among the group. "Martha Lee, Charlotte LaRue, and some other people from their neighborhood. Probably Geoffrey Hamilton . . . a few of his friends."

Sean's fork rested against his plate as he stopped eating. "Boys?"

"Yes, sir." Kate tried to make eye contact, but his hazel eyes looked at her as though he couldn't quite figure out who had replaced his daughter with this imposter. She wondered what he saw now—a daughter who might actually grow into a woman who would finally be accepted in Mystic Water?

His forehead creased, and his hand visibly clenched. "But boys will be there."

"Daddy, it's in the park. Groups go there all the time to have picnics and hang."

"But you don't," he said.

Anger snapped like a broken twig inside her. "I'm well aware that I'm an awkward nobody and no one ever invites me any-where, but other kids do this all the time," Kate said. Her throat tightened. It was one kind of heartbreak to know that kids her own age thought she was uncool, but it was a deeper kind of wound if her parents agreed.

"Your dad doesn't mean that," Ama said.

He shook his head. "Absolutely not. I only meant that I don't know how I feel about you being around boys."

Kate's lips parted, and she glanced at her mama. Would Ama agree that she shouldn't be allowed to go, or would her mama support Kate being able to experience a different part of the world around her? "But I'm around boys all the time at school. We'll be in public, Daddy. Completely out in the open. During daylight."

Her parents looked at each other. Sean's shoulders lifted in question, and Ama nodded. When her daddy picked up his fork and continued eating, Kate unclenched her fingers.

Ama lifted her coffee cup again and looked pointedly at Kate. "Only if your dad drops you off. No riding your bike into town. At least he can see if he approves of the people in the park."

Kate sighed. Sometimes she thought her mama judged the town as harshly as the town judged her family—both sides believing they weren't judgmental at all. "Mama, you know these kids. They're not roughnecks."

"Are you sure about that?" she asked.

"Mama," Kate said with a small groan.

Ama stood from the table and filled a plate with eggs and grits. She slid the plate in front of Kate along with a cup of steaming lavender tea. "Maybe your goodness will rub off on them."

"Oh, yeah, I bet they all want to be just like me," Kate said, stabbing her scrambled eggs with a fork.

"You'd be surprised."

Kate ate her breakfast and drank the tea like an obedient daughter, and even if her parents were skeptical about this unusual get-together, Kate felt excitement building in her like

a blocked river pushing through a beaver's dam. It started as a trickle and increased in intensity with each passing minute. Yesterday's disaster had the potential to be completely replaced with a new opportunity and another chance to spend the day with a handsome boy and his friends. For the first time in a long time, Kate imagined everything that could go right instead of fretting about impending disappointment.

CHAPTER 9

BY THE TIME KATE AND HER DADDY NEARED THE PARK, HER muscles quivered, and she bounced her knees up and down. She wished she'd brought a cup of tea to drink while they drove, just to ensure *nothing* would happen. Sunlight beamed off the hood of the car, making it difficult to see anything in front of them. Sean turned onto one of the streets that lined the perimeter of the park, and Kate scanned the grassy area for kids her age. She saw a couple of groups of young people sitting on quilts with picnic baskets weighing down the corners.

Two young men threw a football back and forth, and Kate recognized them. The ball sailed from Matthias's hands, and his aim was straight. Geoffrey barely shifted his body at all, catching the pass with his long, thin fingers. An ankle brace replaced Geoffrey's white cast, and there were no crutches in sight. Geoffrey caught sight of them as their car approached, and his green eyes flecked with gold found hers. She pressed herself back against the seat and stared at him, feeling the energy as it twirled its way up her spine and dispersed throughout her body like a starburst, shaking her like a tuning fork. Geoffrey lifted his hand in a wave before walking toward them.

Sean slowed the car, pulling alongside the curb. Kate felt her heart rising toward her throat, and she swallowed, trying to open up the passageway for air. "You can drop me off here," she said in a breathless voice.

Sean shifted the car into park. She fumbled trying to move out of her seat, and her sweaty fingers slipped off the door handle. She grabbed the plate of lavender cookies her mama made for the get-together, and the plate tilted in her hand like a seesaw. Sean caught them and righted the plate in her hands. His gaze drifted up and out through the windshield.

"Is that Geoffrey Hamilton?" her daddy asked.

"Yes, sir," Kate said. She flung open the door when Geoffrey was halfway to the car. It didn't look as though Geoffrey had any intentions of stopping and waiting for her to approach him. He was headed straight for them, displaying no fear of having to interact with her daddy. Sean wouldn't have assumed Kate had any sort of relationship with Geoffrey—even a speaking relationship—and Kate worried Geoffrey would appear too friendly with her.

"Thanks, Daddy. I'll see you later."

"What time should I pick you up?" he asked.

Kate paused. She had no idea how long these sort of outings lasted, seeing as how she'd never been to one. Before she could come up with an answer, Geoffrey stood by the car. He grabbed her car door and leaned down to look inside at Sean. Sweat glistened on Geoffrey's forehead and neck. His red-striped button-down shirt had been rolled up to his elbows.

"Good afternoon, Mr. Muir," Geoffrey said. "It's good to see you."

"Good to see you too, Geoffrey. What time, Kate?"

Kate glanced at Geoffrey. "How long do you think we'll—I mean, everyone will hang?"

Geoffrey shoved the football beneath one arm and shrugged. "A few hours." He looked at Sean. "Matthias and I can bring Kate home if you like. I don't mind."

Kate watched indecision narrow her daddy's eyes and thin his lips. He twisted his bear-size hands on the steering wheel. He was probably trying to decide whether or not he wanted his only daughter to be left alone in the car with two young men.

"You remember Matthias, don't you, Mr. Muir?" Geoffrey said with an easy smile. "He's a few years older than me and played ball with Evan. He's finishing his last year of college and plans to attend medical school at the university. He just made the Dean's List again, and he's apprenticing under my dad this summer at his practice."

"Yes, of course," Sean said. "A good kid." His jaw relaxed, and he nodded his head at Geoffrey then scratched his beard. "Thank you for offering. Kate, you need to be home before dinner."

She could barely believe her daddy agreed to let Matthias and Geoffrey drive her home. "Yes, sir. Thanks, Daddy."

Geoffrey waved to Sean. "We'll have her home on time, Mr. Muir." Then he shut the car door.

Kate waved as her daddy drove away, and she saw his eyes watching her in the rear-view mirror. She was actually standing in public with Geoffrey Hamilton, and her heart responded with quick, fluttery beats. The afternoon smelled of freshly cut grass and a nearby barbecue grill. She could also smell Geoffrey's cologne mixed with sweat and laundry detergent. When her gaze drifted to a gathering of people sitting on quilts, everyone was watching them. Her spine stiffened.

"I didn't think you'd come," he said.

"And miss all the stares?" she asked. She grabbed a fistful of her black skirt in one hand and squeezed the plate of cookies in her other.

Was it too late to shout for her daddy to stop? Could she toss the cookies into the air and run home?

Geoffrey moved in between the line of sight of his group. "What stares?"

She angled her head toward the others, and Geoffrey followed her gaze.

"Ah, well, they're curious. They've been expecting you. I told them you were coming."

Kate raised her eyebrows. "But you just said that you didn't think I was coming."

"I was staying positive," he said with a slow smile. "And I'm glad you did."

She looked up at his face, unable to stop herself. Her insides softened like dandelion seeds, feather-light and full of air pockets. Kate felt the attraction to Geoffrey return. It didn't matter that yesterday she felt stupid for going to his house and that part of her hoped she'd never seen him again. She imagined a rope, looped with a slip knot, cinched around her waist, tugging her in his direction.

Kate took a deliberate step away from Geoffrey. "I noticed you weren't proclaiming your own good qualities to my daddy," she said, braving another look at him.

Geoffrey grinned. "What good qualities?"

She shied away from his intense stare and laughed nervously, shaking her head. "I'm having second thoughts about spending time with you today."

Before Geoffrey could comment, Matthias walked up to them. He took the football out from under Geoffrey's arm and tossed it into the air. She watched it rise and fall. "Hey, Kate. Good to see you again."

Kate wanted to forget that less than twenty-four hours ago Matthias dropped her off on the side of the road after a terrible first visit to Honeysuckle Hollow. She wondered what her schoolmates were thinking. Based on the intensity of their stares, they were probably both baffled and intrigued. Kate wondered if they would ignore her today just as they normally did in school. Or did the usual rules of only speaking to cool kids not apply during the summertime?

Kate focused on Matthias instead. Yesterday's pity for her wasn't present in his sky-blue eyes. A hint of peppermint drifted on the breeze.

"Hey, Matthias. Nice throw." She pulled back her arm and mimicked his passing stance. The plate of cookies teetered in her hand, and Matthias steadied the plate.

He lifted his open palms in front of his body and shrugged. "If medical school doesn't work out for me, I'm thinking of trying out for the Browns."

Geoffrey snatched the football from the air when Matthias tossed it up again. "Keep dreaming, Matt. You're too scrawny."

"Which makes you a definite no for football then," Matthias joked.

"Hey, I'm wiry. Quick and agile," Geoffrey said, flexing his bicep.

"Don't forget skinny and reminiscent of an ibis," Matthias teased, and he laughed when Geoffrey punched him in the arm.

The sunlight warmed Kate's dark hair like cast iron on a

hot burner. She reached up and combed her fingers through it, thinking she should have pulled it back from her face or at least tried to style it. The other girls had rolled or pinned up their hair, but Kate's was long and straight and lying flat against her back.

"Your cast," she said, looking at Geoffrey. "It's gone."

"Nothing gets past you," he said, bumping into her with his elbow. He walked with a slight limp toward the picnic blankets, and Matthias fell into step beside them. "Got it taken off just this morning actually. Matthias did most of the work. It's a little uncomfortable, but, God, I was sick of that cast. My leg itched so badly. I had to beg Dad to let me remove it early. He advised against it, but I'm going to take my chances."

As they neared the picnic blankets, Kate couldn't concentrate on Geoffrey's conversation. Her skin burned beneath the stares of those waiting and watching, and although the group smiled, a few of the girls' faces reminded Kate of porcelain dolls whose expressions were painted and forced.

"Hey, guys, y'all know Kate, I'm sure," Geoffrey said. "But just to be proper like my mom taught me, this is Kate Muir. Kate, this is Sally Rensforth, Martha Lee, Charlotte LaRue, Betsy Cavenaugh, Ted Fletcher, Mikey Gill, John Kane, and you know Matt."

A chorus of heys greeted her. Kate tried to smile, but her lips felt stiff and unresponsive. She managed to say hello just as a strong breeze rushed across their faces and carried her voice with it. She imagined it tangled in the oak trees and then gusting off into the scorching, blue sky.

The girls sat on one quilt and the boys on the other for propriety's sake. Martha eyed Charlotte, who didn't pick up on Martha's questioning gaze, so she scooted over, trying to make

room so Kate could join them. As soon as she was settled in her new spot, Martha smoothed out the skirt of her polka dot dress, fanning it around her lower body in a perfect semicircle. She looked like she was posing for a magazine photo shoot.

Martha Lee's round face was pretty in an all-American way. Her blond hair, dark-blue eyes, and pink, glossy cheeks resembled the standard of beauty Kate had seen on paper dolls in department stores. Martha Lee wasn't stunning like Grace Kelly or glamorous like Elizabeth Taylor. She had a simpler elegance like Doris Day. With her pearl earrings and bright-pink lips, Martha was popular and coveted, and it was obvious why the older boys wanted to pin her.

Kate tried to control her breathing in an attempt to stop her insides from feeling as though she'd just sprinted over the suspension bridge spanning across Murphy's Gorge. She sat between Martha and Betsy and placed the plate of lavender cookies in front of her. Kate was so nervous that she almost burst out laughing, thinking of how she'd supposedly been at Martha's house the day before. She contained her mania by folding her hands together in her lap and clutching them together like someone holding pixie dust during a windstorm.

Kate couldn't help but notice that all the girls were dressed in a similar fashion. Full, brightly colored skirts ballooned around them, covering their legs, revealing only their identical ballet flats. Martha's and Betsy's dresses were sleeveless and dipped at the neck in a rounded curve, while Charlotte's and Sally's dresses had sleeves that stopped at their elbows, cuffed in white trim that matched their white, scalloped collars. Their dresses drew in tightly about their waists, which was meant to accentuate their feminine curves, something Kate did not have.

When the girls stood, they probably resembled an assortment of fine baby dolls, their skirts swinging from their waists,
looking like church bells. Kate had worn her cleanest, simplest
outfit, but her sapphire-blue top and calf-length black skirt did
nothing more than make her feel like a thistle among the roses.
Even if she'd owned an identical dress that matched the girls, she
would more likely resemble a broomstick in a dress rather than
a blossoming young woman.

Martha's full, candy-pink lips smiled at Kate. The distinct
gap between Martha's two front teeth looked much wider up
close, and Martha's black mascara was thick and clumped about
her lashes, looking as though she'd applied it with a paintbrush.
Kate had seen Martha's pink-and-white polka-dot dress in a shop
window on Main Street a few weeks ago, and she'd wanted so
badly to ask her daddy if he'd buy it for her. But Ama made most
of Kate's clothes, and they were sensible, or so her mama told her
again and again. Kate doubted Martha's parents ever told her she
couldn't have a dress because it wasn't practical. Why did clothing have to make sense? Why couldn't it simply help someone
look better, prettier, more like the rest of the world?

"Have you eaten yet?" Martha asked in a voice that seemed
to flow from her nose, pinched and slightly whiny. "We packed
hors d'oeuvres and drinks."

"I'm starving," Betsy said.

Martha pursed her lips. "You're always hungry, Betsy. You
might want to go easy."

Betsy was a rising sophomore too, and she and Kate shared
most of the same classes. She was quiet and studious, and Kate
suspected she was part of this group because her dad owned the
local bank. Money offered easy entry into popularity. Betsy's gaze

fell into her lap, and she smoothed her thick fingers down the fabric of her skirt. Betsy was shaped like an upside-down mushroom, wider and thicker than the other girls, with arms and legs that were smooth, pale, and doughy. Her full face reminded Kate of a cherub, rosy-cheeked and kind. Her small, upturned nose was nearly lost in the plumpness of her cheeks, but her round light-brown eyes—bright and twinkling—were the highlight of her face.

Charlotte cleared her throat and sent Betsy a small smile. She opened the basket nearest her. "We've brought fruit and crackers and cheese and what else?"

"I made pimento cheese sandwiches." Martha smiled at the boys. "It's my grandma's recipe, the one that wins first prize every year at the fair."

"Mama baked sugar cookies this morning, so I packed a few dozen of those," Sally said. "And Betsy's mama made cucumber sandwiches, didn't she?"

Betsy nodded and tossed a shy glance toward Kate, making eye contact for a second before staring down at her hands again.

"Enough girl talk. Can we eat?" Ted asked from the other quilt. "Geoffrey made us wait long enough for the—for Kate."

Ted averted his gaze when Kate looked at him. Kate didn't know much about Ted other than that he was a year ahead of her in school, he liked to hear himself talk, and he played football about as well as she did. He played ball because that was what all of his friends did, but Ted's fingers might as well have been slathered in lard when he was on the field. He was built like a brick wall—solid, square, and red-faced—and although he should have been a heavy-hitting linebacker, he was better suited for the debate team. He had a face like someone who'd fallen on a

shovel before his nose could grow, so his side profile was flat and accentuated his broad, high forehead.

Ted leaned his head back and blew cigarette smoke toward the stretching sky. John and Mikey sat to his left. They had just graduated high school in June, like Geoffrey. They'd been friends of Geoffrey his whole life, and Kate had seen them together for as long as she could remember. She wondered what it would be like to have lifelong childhood friends.

John resembled a thousand other young men his age, common and average looking with short-cropped sandy-brown hair. Kate knew he excelled at chemistry and calculus, but he still managed to be a part of the popular crowd. She assumed if someone snuck into the in-crowd as a kid, it was difficult to be weeded out when everyone discovered he was a genius and loved turning hardwood into charcoal in a backyard barrel. John pulled a cigarette from his shirt pocket and reached for Ted's lighter that lay between them on the quilt. He wedged the cigarette between his lips and cupped his hands around the lighter as he brought it to his mouth. When he lowered his hands, Kate watched the tip spark like a miniature fire.

Mikey was one of the most attractive boys in town. His sandy-brown hair swept across his forehead, a little too long to be deemed completely acceptable, a little too hip for Mystic Water, but Mikey didn't seem to care. His dark-brown eyes studied everything, and his smile was slow and genuine. Kate knew he was kind. Mikey was the sort of boy who always opened doors for women, who stopped and helped people who dropped their homework in the school hallway. If she had to pick teams, Mikey would be one of her first choices.

Prompted by Ted's whining, the girls opened the picnic baskets. They passed around red plastic plates and blue gingham

cloth napkins, reminding Kate of people who worked on assembly lines. Soda bottles and an opener were passed around next, and those were followed by plastic silverware.

Kate watched how the girls arranged their plates and how they unfolded the napkins and draped them across their laps. She copied their movements precisely. Finally, platters were arranged in the center of the quilts, and everyone shifted around, no longer bound to the rules that dictated how they must sit. With the food in the center, they sat on the borders of the blankets, anchoring the fabric to the prickly grass.

Geoffrey sat down beside Kate, and she smiled as she passed him a plate of sandwiches. "Well, thank you, Miss Kate," he said as he positioned his leg and brace out of the way.

She inhaled, smelling the scent of his soap. "Don't thank me yet. You haven't tasted them."

Geoffrey eyed the pimento cheese oozing from the squishy, crustless white bread. "Why don't you try one first?"

"No, thank you," Kate whispered but kept her grin in place, aware that others were watching her. "I don't eat goopy orange cheese sandwiches."

The wind gusted hot, sticky air across the grass and tried to snatch napkins from laps. Kate's spine stiffened. The skin on the back of her neck felt as though a dozen spiders skittered across it. When she looked away from Geoffrey, Martha was smiling at her.

"So, Kate," she said in a voice that sounded rehearsed and bogus, "I guess you heard all about Geoffrey's accident." Kate nodded. "And he's doing so well now, aren't you, Geoffrey? When I heard what happened, I was so worried you'd be in a cast all summer."

Geoffrey popped a square of white Cheddar into his mouth

and shook his head. "Wouldn't have wanted that. No way to spend my last summer before college."

Martha leaned toward Kate as though she had a secret to share. She spoke in a soft voice for dramatic effect, but she clearly intended for the group to hear. "Did he tell you about his helper?"

Kate spun the chilled soda bottle around in her hands, cooling her palms. "I don't know what you mean."

Martha's superior expression annoyed Kate. "The one who helped him after the wreck, after Benjamin went for their parents."

Kate stopped moving; she stopped breathing. Her eyes searched Geoffrey's face, but it was Matthias who caught her gaze. He moved his head side to side, barely an inch in each direction. Kate understood. "Didn't the doctor take care of you?" she asked, looking pointedly at Geoffrey. She offered a slight smile at Martha. "I'm sure Dr. Hamilton and Matthias have been great helpers to have around too."

Martha's wide smile showcased a smudge of pink lipstick on her front tooth as the sunlight glinted off her glossy lips. "I guess he didn't tell you about the other person."

Kate stifled a groan. *You mean me, Martha?*

Geoffrey cleared his throat. "These cookies are swell, Sally. Tell your mom to sell these at the candy shop. I'd buy them."

Martha looked put out that no one wanted to hear more of her secret story about Geoffrey, which obviously wasn't a secret to anyone in attendance.

Sally's cheeks flushed, and she tugged one of her blond ringlets. It bounced back into place, and she giggled. "She'll be glad to hear that."

"Hey, Kate, what kind of cookies did you bring?" Geoffrey asked. He pointed to the unwrapped plate resting on the quilt

near her knees.

"Oh," she said. She pressed the glass bottle into the grass behind her until it propped up by itself. Then she unwrapped the plate. "Lavender cookies."

Geoffrey took the plate from her hands and placed a cookie onto his knee. Then he passed the cookies to John.

"Are they actually made with lavender?" Charlotte asked. Shoulder-length chestnut-brown hair framed her heart-shaped face. Dark eyebrows arched over her deep brown eyes, giving Charlotte a sweet appearance.

Kate nodded. "Yes, fresh lavender, but you can use dried too."

Ted reached for a cookie and wrinkled his nose. "Isn't lavender a flower?"

Was he that obtuse? "Yes. It's also an herb, a very useful one."

Ted passed the plate. He sniffed the cookie and then stared at it as though waiting for it to perform a trick in his palm or poison him through his fingertips. Kate resisted the urge to tell him to put it back if he wasn't going to eat it. Making disgusted faces at someone else's food was rude.

Charlotte lifted a cookie from the plate. "They smell lovely. I've never thought about adding an herb to cookies. The only seasonings my mom uses are salt and pepper."

Kate smiled at Charlotte. "Thank you. I'll give the compliments to my mama. I don't bake nearly as well as she does."

Geoffrey bit the cookie in half and chewed. "They're good."

"Don't sound so surprised," Kate said, but she was grinning at him, and he winked at her.

"I'm out there in a lot of ways but not so much with food." He shoved the rest of the cookie in his mouth. "Just eat it, Ted. Quit being such a wet blanket."

"Why would anyone want to cook with flowers?" Ted asked before taking a bite.

"Lots of flowers have healing and healthy properties. People have been using flowers in their cooking and medicines for thousands of years," Kate explained, knowing she sounded like a defensive and pretentious know-it-all.

"Who? Witchy people?" Ted asked and guffawed, but no one laughed with him.

Everyone gaped at him, and Kate knew why. He was voicing out loud what everyone in town already whispered. Mrs. Muir and her daughter were witchy people. Crazy Indian folk. Sure, the architect father and the poor dead son were okay, but those Muir women . . .

Kate's eyes narrowed, and she clenched her jaw. "I don't understand the question. Are you implying that people who use herbs are witches? You must think your mama is a witch for using herbs then. She buys peppermint oil from my mama and dabs it on her windowsills to keep out evil spirits and negative energy. But it's only keeping out the spiders since obviously you're still coming in and out of the house."

Geoffrey choked on his pimento cheese sandwich. Matthias snorted and then laughed so loudly that the glass bottles hummed. Martha sprayed soda from her nose and squealed.

Ted stared at Kate—mouth agape like a bass on a riverbank— and then he looked at the cookie in his hand. He nodded at her. "Point taken." He lifted the cookie in a salute and shoved half of it into his mouth. After chewing with his mouth open, crumbs falling onto his lap, he said, "These are pretty good."

Matthias's laughter spread like a warm breeze across the quilts. Soon everyone was laughing and snickering, and even Martha giggled as she dabbed the soda from her dress. Kate

looked around at their happy faces and thought, *I did this?* Was this what it felt like to be a part of a group, to be welcomed and accepted? Geoffrey's arm pressed into hers, and she looked at him. Summer warmth unfolded in her chest like a fern frond, rolling out slowly, stretching, testing the limits before spreading completely.

"I'm glad you're here," he whispered.

"Me too." And she meant it.

CHAPTER 10

THE AFTERNOON HEAT NEVER RELENTED, RISING INTO THE HIGH nineties. The gathered group dried out on the quilts like plucked rosemary stalks in the sun, and before long, every extra beverage had been drunk, and they needed more. Kate wiped sweat from her forehead as the sun mercifully dipped behind the clouds.

"I promised your dad I'd get you home before supper," Geoffrey said after the conversation lulled. "It would be best if I didn't break that."

"Agreed," Kate said, but she wasn't ready to leave.

She wasn't ready to give up these moments of finally feeling as though she belonged. She hadn't skirted the outsides of this group; she'd been pulled inside. Going home meant returning to her little house in the woods with her childhood room that was still as simple as the day she'd been born. Sketched crayon drawings from elementary school still cluttered one of her desk drawers as though they were all afraid to let go of the past. The well-worn quilt on her bed had been handmade by her grandma, and her closet was stuffed with rainbow-colored clothes sewn by her mama. Rather than elegant prints or posters of heartthrobs, Ama had hung an ancient Cherokee spear on Kate's wall, saying

it would protect her. Kate doubted any of the other girls' rooms looked like hers, as though it belonged to a strange child.

In a way, Kate had trapped herself in her childhood, in a time when Evan was alive and being happy felt easier. Maybe it was time to move forward in her life, throw out the crayon drawings, and step into a teenager's life. Today was the first day when she believed that could be possible.

Kate looked around at the group. During the afternoon, they had gone for walks, tossed around the football, and taken refuge in the shade, and now they were rearranged on the quilts. Matthias sat next to Charlotte, who had graduated in the spring with Geoffrey, and Charlotte stared at Matthias, mesmerized by the conversation. Kate recognized the expression on Charlotte's face—an expression Kate feared she had given to Geoffrey. Kate lifted her hands and pressed them to her chest. *Hold on to your heart*, she thought for Charlotte. *Unless . . . unless it's already gone.* And Charlotte looked really gone.

"Hey, Matthias," Geoffrey called across the blanket. Matthias paused his conversation. "You ready? We need to get Kate home."

Matthias nodded, but Kate saw Charlotte's disappointment before she shoved it behind a smile. The Hamilton boys' leaving caused everyone to decide it was time to pack up and go home too. Even though Kate didn't want the day to end, it had been the most fun she'd had in years. In her happiness she considered skipping across the park to Matthias's car. And she would have, but the wind blew stifling, muggy air that caused Kate to pause and stare up at the sky. Thin, wispy clouds swirled like mini tornadoes. Waves of heat lifted from the asphalt and slunk across the park, burning the grass as it raced toward her.

"You coming?" Geoffrey asked.

Matthias glanced at her over his shoulder but kept walking. How could they not feel the approaching menace? The sky darkened, and Kate quickened her pace. *I can outrun it*, she thought. The humid air in her lungs turned frosty, and she felt the slivers of ice breaking apart, splintering through her.

"But I drank my tea," she mumbled. Her vision shadowed, and her steps faltered. Her mama's cookie plate slipped from her hand. Matthias turned and looked at her before her knees buckled and she undulated like underwater sea kelp. Then she felt the needle-sharp blades of grass stab into her cheek. Darkness folded over her like a shroud.

Fingernails clawed at her chest and shoved at her throat. Hands gripped her waist so tightly that she thrashed and yelled, choking on her own voice. She kicked against the window again and again and again, but no one heard her. Desperate pleas of mercy rushed out of her tight throat. She angled her body away from the heavy weight pressing down on her and kicked the window.

Kate gasped and flung herself into a sitting position. The confined space was replaced by the blazing sun and colors so bright she couldn't keep her eyes open. She clutched dry grass in her hands, balancing herself upright.

"Whoa, whoa, whoa," a male said. He sounded like a record played on the wrong speed, deep and elongated.

Sounds around her picked up speed and intensity. A blue jay threatened an intruder. A car drove past on the nearby street. A dog woofed in delight.

"What's wrong with her?" another male asked. "Is she having a sort of fit?"

"Nothing's wrong with her. She passed out. People do this

all the time in the summer when they haven't had enough water and get dehydrated."

"You think that's it? Remember that boy who had that fit at school when we were kids? The one who nearly bit off his tongue? You think she has that?"

"That was epilepsy. This is nothing like that."

Kate doubled over and stared at her knees tenting her black skirt. On each inhale, she smelled the stink of men's cologne, soured by sweat and cigarettes. She blinked in the glaring light. Her heart raced, and tears filled her eyes before splattering on her skirt. A hand touched her back tentatively as though she were a wild animal that might attack.

"Just breathe," the voice said.

She obeyed, pulling in one ragged breath after another until she stopped trembling.

"That's it. Keep breathing. Everything is okay." The hand moved up and down her back, imprinting a lazy figure-eight pattern into her skin. The voice soothed her, and she believed his words.

"Is she going to be okay?"

Geoffrey. The voices finally connected with faces in her brain. *And Matthias.*

A premonition. She was still in the park with them. Of all the lousy times to become the freak. What if her mama was right and she *was* getting worse? How much longer would she have her sanity? Would she start losing it faster than water spilling through her fingers? Kate inhaled deeply, wiped her eyes, and lifted her head. Geoffrey crouched at her feet, looking at her with a concerned expression. Matthias knelt on his knees beside her. It was his hand on her back. His blue eyes studied her.

"Hey," Geoffrey said, "you okay?"

Kate nodded. "I'm sorry . . . I must have gotten too hot. I do that sometimes. Overheat." Her hollow voice sounded like a liar's. She couldn't meet his gaze.

Matthias stopped rubbing her back and stood. "Let's get you home."

Geoffrey held out his hands to her, and Kate flinched, remembering hands that gripped too tightly, that made her blood run cold. She closed her eyes and inhaled slowly. The vision wasn't about him. It was probably not even anyone she knew. She reached her hands out to him, and he pulled her up. His hands held hers for a moment longer than necessary, and she wanted to enjoy the awareness of his skin against hers, but she felt as though the knob controlling every one of her senses had been turned past the highest notch. The premonition lingered like dregs in the last of the tea.

"Should we get her some water?" Geoffrey asked Matthias. Then looking at Kate, he said, "Are you okay to walk?"

Kate tried to smile, but an ideal afternoon had been ruined by her family's curse. "I'm fine, really. It happens sometimes. It's no big deal."

"God, it sure looked like a big deal. You were out cold. You crumpled like a rag doll. I've never seen anything like it. But you're sure you're okay? You think you just got too hot out here? 'Cause it's been brutal today," Geoffrey said.

Brutal. Kate thought of fingers that bruised, shouts that were buried in someone's shoulder. She shivered.

"Let's get you home," Geoffrey said, agreeing with Matthias. "At least let's get into the car where it's cooler."

Kate nodded and Geoffrey kept glancing over at her as they

walked. At the car, Geoffrey popped open the trunk to load it with their belongings. Matthias unlocked the passenger-side door for Kate, but he didn't open it wide enough for her to slip inside. Instead, he stood in the way.

"You were ice cold," Matthias said quietly. He reached out and pressed his fingertips against her forearm. "Still are."

Kate stared up at him. His eyes reminded her of blue hydrangea blooms, ringed in indigo. Her pulse tapped against her temple.

"I've seen heat exhaustion and overheating. That's not what you experienced."

"Okay." What else could she say? She couldn't admit she'd had a premonition. They'd likely leave her standing alone in the park while they laughed themselves all the way home. Crazy Kate, that's what they'd call her.

Geoffrey arranged their stuff in the trunk and spoke, but Kate couldn't understand what he was saying. Matthias's knowing gaze trapped her like an ant in pine sap. She swallowed.

"Do you want to tell me what it was?" he asked.

Kate shook her head. "It doesn't matter what it was," she whispered. "I'm okay now."

His fingers tightened on the passenger-side door before he relented. He passed her the cookie plate and stepped away. Kate climbed inside and rested the plate in her lap. Geoffrey closed the trunk and opened the backseat door. Matthias slid behind the wheel, started the car, and didn't say a word for the entire ride.

When they arrived at her house, Geoffrey tried to walk her to the front door, but she refused to let him.

"Why?" he asked as he leaned against the passenger-side door.

"Because," she said.

"Because why?" he asked, his voice taking on a whiny tone.

"Because it'll look like . . . like it's important." *Like we're important.*

A smile stretched across Geoffrey's face. "Oh, you mean it'll look you're jacketed?"

Kate's gaze met his. She held her breath.

"We could be, you know," he said, leaning toward her.

Hope rose up in Kate like a daffodil bursting through the ground at the first sign of spring. "Even after today?"

Geoffrey stopped smiling. "Why not? Because you passed out? What do you think I am, a complete jerk? I don't care about that. I care about you. Can I see you tonight? Someone needs to check on you."

She wanted to slide her hand into his and say yes, but she couldn't keep sneaking out. "I'm fine, and I'll be sleeping." He still wanted to see her after she collapsed in the park. Why wasn't he acknowledging that she was probably as weird as everyone said?

"I'll knock," he said.

Kate's mouth tugged up at the corners. How could she say no to him? Did anyone? "I'll think of answering," she said.

She caught Matthias's gaze through the windshield, but his expression confused her. He looked unhappy and frustrated. So Kate turned and hurried to the front porch before she admitted that there was no way she would be able to fall asleep knowing Geoffrey would be coming to her window.

Kate lifted her bedroom window and glanced over her shoulder at her closed door before slipping one leg out and then the other. After easing the window shut, she shoved her hand into her pocket and pulled out a small sachet of dried lavender. Then she ran through the darkness down to the river's edge. She knelt along the bank, tossed the dried herbs into her mouth, and then cupped river water in her hands and drank.

No more premonitions tonight. Please.

She heard a far-off sound of a car door closing mixed with the night music. Crickets chirruped, and tree frogs made quacking noises followed by high-pitched peeps, a strange and steady chorus. A few minutes later someone stepped on a dry twig and snapped it. Before Geoffrey could walk to her window, Kate whistled the tune of a whippoorwill.

His dark silhouette paused in the backyard, and he glanced toward the river. His tall frame cast a shadow as thin as a cattail against the side of the house. Kate raised her hand and waved at him. His gait was uneven but quiet as he strode across the yard.

He sat down beside her on the bank, not bothering to keep his brace away from the water. "Nice bird call."

Kate grinned. "They don't call me Little Blackbird for nothing. I can mimic lots of birds—" She stopped talking, realizing too late that she was sharing personal information with him. Had they reached that stage? Kate had nothing to compare this ritual to. How long did two people dance around each other, both on their best behavior, before they dropped the pretenses and became who they truly were? When did the genuine bonding happen, if ever? Kate still wasn't sure if bonding with Geoffrey was an innocuous idea.

"They call you Little Blackbird?" Geoffrey's voice betrayed his smile.

"Yeah."

"That's cute . . . Little Blackbird," he said and chuckled.

She frowned at him even though he couldn't see her expression in the darkness. "My family, *not you*."

"I'm not allowed?"

"No."

His laugh rushed across the river, and a family of bobwhites rustled from the reeds like a weaving bird train before disappearing again. "You came outside early," he said. "What if I hadn't come?"

"Was that an option?" she asked. After his repeat nighttime visits, she hadn't worried that he wouldn't show up tonight. Was that a possibility? Was he planning on winning her heart and then disappearing with it? *Could* he win her heart? She moved a hand up to her collarbone, feeling her fluttery pulse beneath her fingers.

"Of course not." He leaned back on his hands and stretched his legs. "How're you feeling?"

"Fine," she said. "Just like normal." Because even premonitions were normal for her.

"Matthias says it's good to carry water around with you during the summertime so you can stay hydrated." Geoffrey leaned over his knees and untied his tennis shoes. He pulled them off and set them away from the water. Then he removed his brace and socks.

Kate looked at Geoffrey's silhouette. "Is that all he said?"

He shifted closer to her. "About what? Hydration?"

She stared at their feet. Hers were bare and rested at the river's edge. Tiny waves lapped against her heels when the river swelled over rocks and pushed the water to the edges of its boundary. Geoffrey's legs stretched much farther than hers, reaching into

the water, wetting his long, narrow feet.

"About today. About me," Kate said.

Geoffrey turned his shadowed face toward her. "Was there anything more to say?"

"No. No, I just thought because he's a doctor—or a doctor in training—that he might have some insight."

"Nah, he just reminded me to always drink water. Instead of beer," he said with a sarcastic chuckle.

His words caused the memory of her short time at Honeysuckle Hollow to resurface. Kate hadn't been taught that alcohol was innately wrong, although she'd heard more than a few kids at school—the ones who attended church often—whisper about the evils of drinking. Kate didn't care so much about the drinking as she did about breaking rules. There were laws in place about underage drinking, and her parents taught her to follow the rules. Geoffrey wasn't twenty-one, so his drinking broke the law. "Is that something you do often?"

"What? Drink beer?" Geoffrey shrugged. "Depends on your definition of often."

"Every day?"

"Definitely not," Geoffrey said. "Mom doesn't like it, and she would never let us sit around and drink in the house."

"So you only do that when she's away." Kate pulled a blade of grass from its roots and slid her fingernail up the spine, splitting the blade in half.

Geoffrey looked at her. "It's a good time to do it." The owl hooted across the water, and Geoffrey turned his face to the darkened forest. "It's a good time to do a lot of things when she's away."

"Like what?"

"Live."

Kate almost asked what it was like to live in his world, but she knew he wouldn't understand. He probably didn't even realize how different their lives were, or if he did, he didn't see the great chasm spanning between them like she did. Instead, she asked, "What about college? What are you going to study?"

"Dad wants me to study law like Ben and Richard or medicine like Matt," he said.

The wind pushed clouds across the night sky so that they covered the sliver of moon, cutting off the feeble light. Kate and Geoffrey slipped into a darkness so complete that Kate had trouble seeing her own body. She heard Geoffrey shift in the shadows and then felt his arm press against hers. The warmth of him so close to her made her body tingly.

"Which one do you want to study? Law or medicine?" she asked.

"Did I say want?"

His irritation rippled over her skin like goosebumps. She rubbed her hands up and down her arms. "Why would you study a subject you didn't want to?"

He scoffed. "Because it's what Dad thinks is right."

"And . . . you don't have any say?"

"Oh, I have a say, but it makes sense to study law or medicine. Those two professions will definitely make money."

"Money isn't everything," Kate said instinctively, hearing her mama's voice in her head. The clouds shifted again, and thin rays of moonlight trickled down onto them, outlining their dark forms.

"Isn't it?" Geoffrey asked. "It gets you what you need."

She sat up straighter, feeling defensive, not understanding her own response. "Not everything."

Geoffrey turned to face her, which made her profoundly

aware of how close they were sitting. His body felt too near hers, with his arm against hers, warming her skin, and their hands side by side.

"Yeah? What can't it get you?" Geoffrey asked.

She leaned away from him, letting particles of air move in between their bodies. "Happiness. Love."

Geoffrey shook his head. "You don't think money attracts those things? It can't buy love, but women are attracted to money—"

"Not all women want money," Kate argued, pulling her knees toward her chest, creating a barrier between them.

"Don't they? Don't all women want security? To be taken care of? A house? Nice clothes? The ability to go out and do what they want?" He rotated his body so he faced her, and his knees pressed against her thigh. "You don't want nice things?"

Kate's desires tugged inside her, closing her throat. She did want nice clothes like the other girls. She wanted red lipstick and ballet flats in multiple colors. She wanted to fit in so badly. She didn't have the charm Evan had, but wealth could give her what she needed to belong with them.

What wouldn't Kate give up to be like them, to be a part of their world? She stretched out her legs and stared at Geoffrey's shadowed face.

"I want nice things," she whispered. Shame burned through her belly, consuming her. "But at what price?"

"What if you didn't have to give up anything? What if you could have it all?" Geoffrey asked, his voice as quiet as hers.

"No one can have it all."

He moved one hand to her thigh, and Kate looked down at his thin fingers spanning across her jeans. She paused on an inhale, and she lost feeling in her fingertips as blood rushed to

her heart. When she lifted her gaze, he was so close. So close she could hear him breathing.

"What if we could?" he asked as he leaned toward her.

"Impossible," she said, unable to move as she watched him come nearer the way a rabbit watches a wolf approach from across the meadow. He was going to kiss her.

"Is it?" Geoffrey pressed his lips against hers. Warm and gentle. A chaotic crickets' chorus erupted from the reeds near the eddy. A mockingbird bulleted out a song. Then Kate panicked. She jerked away from Geoffrey, nearly tumbling over backward. "What? What is it?" he asked, pressing his hand against her thigh to keep her from moving farther away. "Did you hear someone?"

"I—I don't—I don't know what I'm doing. I've never kissed anyone," she blurted. She slapped her hand over her mouth.

Geoffrey laughed, and Kate felt the emotions swell so brutally in her chest that she feared she would crack open. She blinked rapidly because her vision blurred with tears. Her mind screamed, *Get out of here! Get out now before you make a complete fool of yourself!* She tried to stand, but Geoffrey had a firm hold on her thigh and grabbed her wrist.

"Cool it," he said. "It's okay—"

"But you laughed at me," she said, squirming, looking anywhere but at him.

"Not at you. I was surprised. You're a Dolly, you know that?"

She stopped resisting him. He thought she was adorable? She stared at the river. The moon's reflection created a thin, wavy line that divided the course in half. "I'm adorable because no one has wanted to kiss me?"

"Just because you haven't kissed a guy doesn't mean no one has wanted to kiss you."

Kate made a noise in her throat. "The likelihood that

someone has wanted to kiss me is zero. I'm probably the only sixteen-year-old who's never been kissed."

"I doubt that."

The feeble light painted Geoffrey's face in black and gray. "But out of your friends? Am I the only one?"

"My friends are different. And different doesn't always mean better either. It doesn't take much for a guy your age to have kissed a girl. Guys are willing to kiss the first girl who agrees, regardless of whether or not we really like her. And I like that no one has ever kissed you before. That makes me the first."

Geoffrey slipped his hand from her wrist and grabbed her hand. Kate shivered. His fingers closed around hers. The owl hooted. Was the bird approving or disapproving? She looked across the river toward the tree hollow where she knew the owl liked to perch.

"Kate," Geoffrey whispered, "stop thinking so hard and look at me." Before she could turn her face all the way toward him, he was there, as close as a breath, kissing her. Kate's thoughts jumbled together. *Am I doing this right? What am I doing? Will Mama wake up and find us? Should I—*

Geoffrey rubbed his hand up and down her bare arm, awakening sensations in her skin, causing her lower lip to tingle. She leaned into him, drawn toward him like a sunflower to the light. Her fingers ached with a desire she'd never felt. She needed to touch him, to see if he was real.

Kate reached up her hand and placed it on his shoulder and then slid it to the summer-warm bare skin on his neck. She felt his pulse quicken beneath her fingers. Her fingertips found his jawline and then his face, where stubble had grown prickly like fresh thorns on a rose bush.

Geoffrey slid his arm around her waist and pulled her toward

him. Kate's breath escaped in a sigh that caused Geoffrey's hold to tighten. He was too close, invading her space, her thoughts, stealing her breath. A tremble started low in her belly and then shuddered out to every nerve ending. She put her hands on Geoffrey's chest and pressed.

When the space between them widened, they both inhaled deeply as though they'd been denied air.

Geoffrey exhaled. "I don't believe it."

Kate pressed her lips together and closed her eyes. "Don't believe what?"

"That you've never done that before." He rubbed the back of his neck and chuckled. "I wasn't even standing up and my legs feel useless."

Nervous energy caused Kate to laugh. She covered her mouth, smiling against her fingers. Then she sat up straight and looked at him. "I'll get better," she said plainly.

Geoffrey's laugh bounced across the water, skipping like a polished pebble before it shook the trees on the opposite bank. The owl hooted again. Geoffrey pulled her against him into a quick hug before setting her upright again. "If you get better, my heart might stop."

I'll give you mine.

"We can keep practicing, though, if you want," he said, moving closer, and Kate grinned in the darkness, feeling like she'd been granted a wish to live this one night in someone else's life.

CHAPTER 11

A FEW DAYS LATER KATE WAS IN HER BEDROOM RE-ALPHABETIZ-
ing the books on her shelf. She'd paused with the reshuffle long
enough to open her worn copy of *Peter Pan* and read her favorite
passage.

"You need to get out of this house," Ama said, barging into
Kate's room without knocking. "Get out into the garden. Move
the wood pile around. Plant those asters. Anything. Just get out
of the house."

Kate startled. "Ma'am?"

Ama created swirling patterns in front of her with her hands.
"The air is pink and purple and shot with electricity. Everywhere,
Little Blackbird. I don't know what's going on with you, but I can
barely breathe in this house with you. You're sucking up all the
oxygen."

Kate knew exactly what was going on with her. *Peter Pan*
brushed against her hip when she lowered her hand. "I'm sorry."

"Don't be sorry, just get outside. Get that restless energy out
of your system. Shoo," her mama said, swooping into Kate's room
and pushing her out the doorway. "And don't come back inside

until it's gone."

What if it would never be gone? Kate hadn't heard from Geoffrey in a few days. She knew he had family plans to visit an aunt and uncle in Macon, Georgia, so she hadn't expected him to show up at her window until he was home again. But that hadn't stopped her from daydreaming about him. Hadn't stopped her from reenacting their kisses on repeat in her mind.

She walked into the backyard. Did she even want this euphoric feeling to be gone? She never wanted to forget how it felt to be kissed. How Geoffrey kissed her until her lips were too pink, and he'd imprinted himself there. She touched her fingertips to her lips, and even though it was days later, she felt the ghost of him still lingering.

A patch of sunflowers exploded into bloom, shooting golden petals from their heads like fireworks. The petals twirled through the air before landing at Kate's feet, leaving the sunflower heads naked and trembling. Kate inhaled sharply. She scooped up the petals and ran from the yard, intent on hiding the evidence.

Kate ran all the way through the pine forest until she reached the divide where her family's land ended and the state park's began. A shallow ravine was all that separated the Muir property from the protected state land. The only architectural structures her daddy ever planned to build on their property were their cottage, the shed, and a future greenhouse. The rest of the land was untouched and would stay that way. They didn't need more than the natural divide because people never wandered far from the hiking trails, and as long as she'd been alive, no one had ever shown up in their backyard. The need for fencing seemed unnecessary.

Kate wandered through the pines, dropping sunflower petals

like Hansel had dropped breadcrumbs. She reached the edge of the valley inside the park and leaned against a tree trunk, looking down at the sun-soaked green land below. She had hiked down to the valley's basin numerous times with Evan, but today she only wanted to sit on the edge and see if the wound-tight energy would leak out of her, see if the wind would take more and more of it from her body on each exhale.

She thought about the time she and Evan had been hiking in the basin the summer before he left for college. They'd been laughing because Evan had tripped and fallen into stagnant water and smelled like a dung pile. Then she had collapsed, still as death, because of a premonition. Kate closed her eyes and remembered.

Evan leaned over her, his face blotting out the August sun. He slipped one arm beneath her back and lifted her into a sitting position.

"Quick! Don't think. What did you see?"

They'd been playing this game since her tenth birthday. Evan had ways of making the detestable easier to swallow. He made her ability seem less like a curse and more like a gift.

"A tombstone in the sunlight. New and shiny. An angry cat stuck in a tree in Mr. Parker's yard. Some guy with dark hair eating birthday cake."

Evan laughed. "Wow, those are tough to piece together. Let's see . . . The cat went for a walk in the cemetery and then decided it was time to go home. Home is Mr. Parker's house, of course. He has a fat cat named Gertrude. But it's Mr. Parker's birthday, and he wanted to eat his cake in peace. So he refused to let Gertrude in, and now she's mad as fire and hissing at him from the tree."

Kate chuckled and rubbed her eyes with fisted hands. When

she lowered her hands, she stared at Evan. Her throat squeezed and tears swirled in her eyes.

"Hey," he said, sitting down beside her, "what are those for? You didn't like my story?"

Kate shook her head. "No. I mean, yes, I did, but it's not that. It's . . . you're leaving."

"For college, not forever."

Kate frowned. "It'll feel like forever. I won't have anyone when you leave."

He smiled at her. "You have this whole town."

Kate huffed. "This whole town thinks I'm your weird baby sister."

Evan laughed. "First of all, it's obvious you're not a baby anymore. You do have that habit of blubbering and whining like one—" He winced when Kate hit his arm. "Okay, okay, I wasn't serious, but you're wrong. No one has ever told me they thought you were weird."

Kate stood and brushed herself off. She wiped at her eyes. "No one is going to tell you that. Everyone likes you."

Evan stood and puffed out his chest. "What can I say? I'm irresistible."

Kate rolled her eyes. "And humble."

Evan laughed and slipped his arm around her shoulders. "You'll always have me, and you should give the town a chance. You might see that they aren't so bad."

"But what about . . . about, well, you know."

"Your gift?"

"Curse."

"Gift," Evan said and squeezed her shoulder. "They'll probably think it's the coolest superpower they've ever heard of."

Kate scoffed. "You always look on the bright side."

"Is there another side?"

"You are so irritating when you're optimistic," she teased. "And you smell like a cow patty."

"I aim to please."

Kate looked at him, and they both laughed. The sun warmed their cheeks, and she prayed for the summer to stretch on forever.

A twig snapped behind Kate and snatched her from her memory. She glanced over her shoulder. A young man skidded down the slope, flailing his arms and knocking into low branches. He barely stopped himself from landing flat on his back, not more than thirty feet away from her. Kate jumped to her feet.

"Geoffrey?" Her hand flew to her chest. "Are you okay?" She rushed over to him, too surprised to see him to register the way her whole body thrilled at the sight of him. "Why are you out hiking in your brace?"

A wild trumpet vine wound around the trunk of a pine tree and stretched at least ten feet above their heads. As soon as Kate neared it, buds appeared on the vine and burst open, popping like bang snaps, exposing red-orange blooms.

"Whoa," Geoffrey said as a trumpet flower cracked open beside his head.

Crocus leaves knifed up through the soil around Geoffrey's feet like emerald blades before pushing buds up through their center and unfolding purple, white, yellow, and fuchsia flowers.

Kate's eyes widened. *No, no, no! Go back to sleep! What are you doing?*

Geoffrey stared at the flowers with an expression of absolute astonishment. "What is going on? This is weird, right?"

131

"Uh, no. It's normal, but people don't usually see this when it happens," Kate lied. She inhaled deeply and exhaled, trying to release the frenetic energy that zipped through her, making her feel as though her heart had donned a pair of roller skates and raced around inside.

Geoffrey stood slowly, brushed off his clothing, and stepped away from the flowers. As he moved, the trumpet vine reached out a tendril for him, and Kate slapped it away. "Stop," she whispered through gritted teeth.

Geoffrey stopped walking. "What?"

Kate glared at the vine, and it pulled itself tighter against the tree. "What are you doing here?" she asked. "I thought you were in Macon."

Geoffrey smiled at her. "Got home last night. Couldn't get home fast enough. My aunt and uncle live outside the city in Nowheresville."

A thought occurred to her. "How did you know I was here?"

"I knew it was you," he said. He opened his hand and bright-yellow sunflower petals fell from his fingers. "I had the strangest feeling when I was driving up to the park. Mom has her ladies' luncheon up at the pavilion, and she left her secretarial something or other at the house. I dropped it off for her, and on the way back down, I pulled into Whitman's Overlook. I don't know why, but I kept feeling as though I needed to. And what do I see when I look down? A trail of gold winding through the trees. I had to follow it, and the whole time I kept thinking about you."

Geoffrey stepped closer to her and reached out for her hand. She met his hand halfway, yearning to feel his skin against hers, hoping it would calm her. His fingers and palm were sticky with

sweat but warm and alive. He'd been thinking about her? She stared down at their interlocking fingers and smiled.

"Did you cast a spell on me?" he asked.

When she looked up at him, she could tell he was teasing, not insinuating she was a witch like Ted had. "I don't know those sorts of spells. Only the ones to turn you into a toad."

"I know a few people you could cast that one on."

"I bet you do," she said.

He squeezed her hand. "I wanted to see you soon," he said. "And here you are. What are you doing out this way?"

Kate motioned over her shoulder with her thumb. "I like to come here sometimes and think. I have a favorite spot that over-looks the valley."

"Show me?"

Kate turned and led Geoffrey a few feet to where she'd been sitting. "It's quiet here. Most people don't hike through this section, because there are no man-made trails. But it's a nice hike down to the river. Evan and I used to come here all the time. Once you're down by the river, you're not likely to run into any-one. It's like you're alone in the world."

"Which means if you were attacked by a bear, no one would know it," he chuckled.

She shook her head. "You won't likely see a lot of bears around here. They're higher up in the mountains. There's not enough food for them here."

"Unless they want to eat hikers."

"Stray hikers with leg braces."

He pulled her closer to him as though it weren't an inap-propriate thing to do, and she didn't push away. Instead, with her face pressed against his chest, she stared at the checkerboard

pattern on his shirt. Sapphire and ivory. Pale-cerulean shadows were created when the two colors mixed. Instead of calming her, Geoffrey's nearness intensified her emotions, spiraling out from her stomach, filling every space.

"I missed you," he said.

She peered up at him. Hope felt like fireflies in her chest. Sparking, pulsing, glowing. "You did?"

He slid his hand up her arm. "Of course. Who wouldn't? I'm glad you left a trail for me."

"I didn't leave it for you," she said honestly. In her rush to escape her thoughts of him, she had left a trail as bright as a comet's tail, leading him straight to her.

"Of course you did," he said. He lowered his head toward hers. "I want to kiss you again. I can't stop thinking about it. Maybe that's why you left the trail for me to follow. Maybe you wanted to be kissed again."

"Maybe."

"Can I?"

Would anyone ever say no to that? Kate nodded.

As soon as she closed her eyes, he was already there, his lips against hers. The pent-up energy inside her ricocheted. His arm slipped around her waist, and she pressed one hand onto his chest. His heartbeat struck against her palm. Her breaths shortened, leaving her dizzy and faint. She clutched onto Geoffrey so he could anchor her to the earth, because otherwise the next gust of wind would lift her into the air like a kite.

He pulled away from the kiss long enough to say, "We should do this every day for the rest of summer. What do you say?"

Feeling bold, she answered him with a kiss and thought, *Please.* Her mama wanted her to get rid of the energy, but who

would ever want to escape this?

For the past week, Kate and Geoffrey had been meeting every day in the park's forest like a couple of thieves stealing away to count their loot. They picked different locations each time, and every day, Kate concocted some reason why she needed to be outside for hours at a time. The lies were piling up like garbage, and Kate wondered when she'd suffocate beneath the mess.

Today's spot was the sacred area that had once belonged to her mama's Cherokee tribe. Visitors to the area could see fifteen original and reconstructed buildings, as well as the burial ground. The area was designated as hallowed ground by the Cherokee, but it was also a national landmark. Kate doubted the rangers would want kids monkeying around in the trees, which was where Geoffrey presently sat. Would her mama feel as though they were being disrespectful? They weren't vandalizing the site, but when Kate had visited the area with her mama, they had always been quiet, not even speaking to each other.

"Get down from there," Kate demanded. "And be quiet. They can probably hear you in the next county. I'd rather people not know we're up here."

Geoffrey grinned down at her from his perch on the fat oak branch. His legs dangled, his ankle finally free of the brace, and he leaned over, propping his elbows on his thighs. "Come up here, and I'll shut up."

Kate fisted her hands on her hips. "I'm not climbing that tree. If the park rangers show up, we'll be trapped like raccoons."

Geoffrey groaned. "God, will you stop worrying about the

rangers and live a little?" He motioned dramatically to her.

"I live just fine," Kate argued. "What if—what if my mama finds out?"

"Cool it, will you? Your mama hasn't found out yet. I doubt today is the day. Now, are you coming up here, or are you going to be a scaredy-cat?"

Kate exhaled and scanned the area. There was no one in sight, and she didn't hear anything but cardinals and finches in the trees. The summer was disappearing, and when it was gone, it would take Geoffrey with it, leaving Kate with nothing but the fall and its slow death toward winter. How could she deny him the time he continued to ask for, especially when she began to live for the moments she spent with him?

She looked up at him. "I'm always bending the rules with you."

"Bending, not breaking."

"If we get caught, I'm blaming you. I'll tell them you forced me into the tree."

"Deal."

Kate climbed the oak in a matter of seconds, and she swung onto the branch beside Geoffrey.

"I wanted you to see this view," he said, scooting closer to her. Bark tore from the limb and dropped to the forest floor.

Kate's brow furrowed. "But we can see the same view from the top of the ridge."

"You're right. I really wanted you to come up here so I could kiss you."

She gaped at him.

"What? Have you ever been kissed in a tree?" he asked, grinning at her, tempting her.

Kate shook her head. She'd never been kissed anywhere until him.

"Then, I have no choice but to kiss you so you can cross it off your list."

Kate choked on a short laugh. "I don't have a list."

"We could start one." Geoffrey moved his hand through the air as though he were writing a note. "Number one, kiss Kate in a tree. Check."

Kate laughed, and Geoffrey kissed her. Their kisses were improving, not that any kiss had ever been bad, but they'd come into a rhythm with each other. Kate felt herself learning more about what seemed to excite him and what she liked too. But they didn't do much else when they were together, other than necking. She wouldn't have complained about it, but the relationship—if she could call it that—felt heavily weighted on the physical. They didn't talk much about themselves, and Geoffrey wasn't interested in sharing personal information. Most of what she knew were things she'd known for years or learned from other people. Since she hadn't been in a relationship before, she figured this might be how they all were. Maybe teenagers necked for weeks before they ventured into other areas of getting to know each other.

Kate leaned back, and Geoffrey looked slightly disappointed. She cleared her throat. "Should we do something different tomorrow?"

Geoffrey's brow furrowed. "What do you mean?"

"Go into town, eat ice cream, walk through the downtown park," she said, suddenly feeling foolish for bringing it up. What if he thought those activities were boring? Would he lose interest?

Geoffrey looked questioningly at her. "Can you do that?

Would your parents let you be alone with me?"

"Oh," she said immediately. "Probably not, but we could get your friends together, couldn't we?"

He hesitated. "You want everyone to know? About us?"

Her heart thumped a few anxious beats. Did she want anyone to know? What would they think? Did she care what they thought? Yes, she did. How devastating would it be if they told Geoffrey he was making a mistake being with her? Then she'd lose the last few weeks she had left with him. She grabbed his hand. "Forget I said anything. I'm okay with just doing this."

"You sure?" he said, and she was slightly bothered by the look of relief on his face.

But Kate nodded. *For now.*

CHAPTER 12

A FEW DAYS LATER GEOFFREY HAD PLANS AND COULDN'T MEET Kate in the park. After spending so many consecutive days together, knowing she wouldn't be seeing him left her feeling discouraged and bored. Kate wandered into the kitchen to make tea. She found a ballpoint pen on the kitchen table, and she marked fourteen even lines on the inside of her palm. Fourteen days was all she had left with Geoffrey before he left for college.

"Your brother was never so moody."

Kate startled at the sound of Ama's voice. Lavender tea sloshed from her teacup and dripped down her fingers. Using a hand towel, she wiped the spill from the floor.

"One day you're bouncing around like you've eaten nothing but sugar all day, and the next you're gloomier than a rain cloud." Ama grabbed a cup from the cabinet and put the kettle back onto the stove. She lit the burner to heat the water. She sat at the kitchen table and pointed at the chair nearest her. "Want to talk about it?"

Kate looked at her mama. She knew Ama wasn't *really* asking her if she wanted to sit; she was *telling* her to. That's how most

conversations were with Ama. While her words came out as a question or a suggestion, she fully expected her requests to be met.

Today Ama looked tired, a bit worn around the edges like she'd been working too hard for too long. Her eyelids dropped, and the tiny creases stretching from the corners of her eyes were deeper grooves than they'd been. Her wide, full lips traveled downward at the edges like someone who'd walked into an unfavorable situation. But even in her exhaustion she was beautiful.

Ama's beauty was considerably different from the traditional looking women revered these days. Her features were sharp and squarer than the soft cherub-faced women in town with their pale cheeks and button noses. Ama's otherness caused men to stop and stare, which had as much to do with her beauty as it did the air of confidence and strength that surrounded her. Ama would never be described as frail or dainty, and she did not possess the Southern woman's gentility—nor did she strive to attain it. Even with Kate she was often blunt without the tenderness that Kate sometimes craved.

Kate sat at the table. "What do you want to talk about?" She purposefully avoided her mama's gaze.

"What's gotten into you lately?" Ama asked.

Kate shrugged. "Other than the tea? I'm just bored today, that's all." A flush colored her cheeks.

"That's all, is it?" Ama asked. The kettle whistled, and she crossed the room to fill her cup. "Why didn't you sneak off into the park today?"

Kate's hands trembled on the cup, so she placed it on the table and folded her hands together in her lap. She spoke only

when she was certain she could control her voice. "Sneaking off? I've told you or Daddy where I'm going."

"So you have," Ama said, sitting at the table again. She bounced a tea strainer in her cup, tinting the liquid a pale golden hue. "You wanted to stay home today and sulk around here instead?"

"I'm not sulking," Kate argued.

Ama sipped her tea and watched Kate over the top of her cup. "Have you seen the snapdragons this morning?" She pointed toward the back door.

Kate opened the door and glanced into the yard. The entire grouping of snapdragons drooped over like they suffered through a drought. Their customary bright blooms now displayed shriveled petals and weak stems.

"You know as well as I do that they symbolize lies, deception, and indiscretion," Ama said. "Anything you want to tell me?"

Kate felt a quiver jolt through her body. She pasted on the sincerest smile she could and shook her head. "I'll water them." Then she rushed out of the house before Ama pulled the truth out of her.

While Kate was watering the snapdragons and begging them to return to life, Sean came home. He walked around the side of the cottage and greeted her. "Hey, Little Blackbird, I was hoping you'd be here. You know what I've been craving?"

"A way to keep Mama from asking me questions?" Kate mumbled.

"What's that?"

"Nothing," Kate said and smiled genuinely at her daddy. "What have you been craving?"

"Cookies from Bea's Bakery. I have a meeting in town this

afternoon. Would you like to ride with me and grab our favorites from the bakery?"

"Yes!" she answered immediately. Anything to get away from Ama for a while. Kate had no desire to tell her mama about Geoffrey, but she feared that if left too long in Ama's presence, she might reveal the truth. Kate hoped to one day be honest about her relationship with Geoffrey, but she wanted to wait for the perfect moment, and today wasn't it.

Kate pushed open the door of Mystic Water's downtown bakery and inhaled the scents of baking sugar cookies and vanilla cake. The display cases at Bea's Bakery overflowed with chocolate donuts, red-velvet cupcakes, crullers, jelly-filled Danishes, and chocolate chip cookies. A caramel chocolate cake sat beneath a glass dome.

The owner, Beatrice O'Brien, walked out from the back room. "Good afternoon, Kate." She wiped her hands on her pink apron. "I was hoping I'd see you this week. Tell your mama thank you for her lavender cookie recipe. It fills the kitchen with the most peaceful smell, and they sure are good. I can barely keep Joe from eating them all as soon as they're out of the oven."

Kate nodded. "Yes, ma'am. She'll be glad to hear it. My daddy loves them too." Kate walked to the first display case, and her eyes widened.

An expression of surprise lifted Beatrice's eyebrows. "I see you've spotted a new creation. Those are the double chocolate chunk brownies. They're for chocolate lovers and for those who are falling in love and need to calm their nerves. Want to try a piece?"

Kate's mouth dropped open. Were her feelings for Geoffrey obvious? She wasn't falling in love . . . was she? "I, uh, well, I—"

Beatrice laughed. "I thought I spotted a dewy-eyed expression on your face." She opened the display and grabbed out a brownie using a flimsy paper square. "Young love is always so exciting and so distracting. See if a few bites of this won't help."

Heat filled Kate's cheeks, a combination of embarrassment and gratefulness. She took the offered sweet and thanked Beatrice, then she bit into the brownie. The chocolate melted on her tongue. After a few moments, the knot in her chest loosened. "This is excellent, probably the most delicious brownie I've ever eaten."

Beatrice nodded her head. "I'm glad you like it. Now what else can I get you today? Is your daddy needing his usual?"

Kate nodded. "Yes, ma'am. A dozen chocolate chip cookies." She folded the paper square around the rest of her brownie. "And another one of these, please." If Beatrice saw that Kate had strong feelings for someone, then it was only a matter of time before her mama's question became more pointed and direct. Right now, Ama was trying to get Kate to confess to whatever had her emotions so unpredictable, but soon her mama wouldn't be as amenable. Kate would have to do a better job of controlling her feelings.

Beatrice packed a pink box full of cookies and added the extra brownie inside. Kate used the dollars her Daddy gave her, and she waved good-bye to Beatrice as she left. Dr. Alfred Hamilton, Geoffrey's father, and Matthias walked up the opposite sidewalk. Dr. Hamilton pulled open the door to the pharmacy. Before following his father inside, Matthias noticed Kate. His lips lifted in one corner like Geoffrey's did, and he nodded at her. She lifted

her hand in a small wave before turning away and heading down the sidewalk.

Seeing the Hamiltons made Kate miss Geoffrey more. The hours dragged by so slowly, and she felt she'd come apart inside before she saw him again. Kate glanced down at her open palm and counted the fourteen tiny pen marks again. Two weeks. And then what? Kate viewed the last day with Geoffrey like a person with acrophobia might view the edge of a cliff. Terrifying and paralyzing.

Kate carried the box of chocolate chip cookies around the corner to the small public garden enclosed by a low wrought-iron fence. She sat on a bench beneath an enormous magnolia that had been named the oldest tree in town. Her daddy would be in the meeting for at least half an hour, so she had time to tumble thoughts of Geoffrey through her mind.

Clouds stretched over the sun and created patches of shadow around the garden. Would Geoffrey write her from college? Would he drive home to see her on weekends? Her jaw clenched. That was foolish. She hadn't even met his parents. No one even knew the two of them were together—if they even were together.

A chill shivered over Kate's skin. Her fingers tingled, and her next inhale filled her lungs will ice. *No . . .* Kate tossed the cookie box beside her and slid from the bench. As soon as her knees hit the grass, the darkness dropped a sheet over her vision.

"Earth Angel" floated through the room. Waffle cones smelled like warm sugar and vanilla. Tennis shoes squeaked on black-and-white checkerboard tiles. Bells jingled. Unkind whispers drifted out the door as a cloud of cigarette smoke curled inside. A young girl stumbled over an outstretched leg. Eye glasses fell to the concrete, followed by a pitiful whimper. More snickers. Bile rose in Kate's

throat. Images burst apart and reformed.

Laughter, flirtatious and relaxed, filled the dark space. Smoke fogged the air between them. The burning end of a cigarette flared in the darkness. Heaviness shoved her back against the seat, forcing the breath from her lungs. She tried to jerk her arms, but they were pinned. Her shirt yanked open, and she panicked. Her heel hammered against the glass, and she shouted. Then she screamed, and then she cried . . .

Kate's eyes opened. Someone's hands were on her arms, and she flailed free, grasping at her shirt to make sure it was still on before scrambling backward like a crab. Her shoulders slammed into the magnolia tree, and she stared, gasping, at Matthias, who knelt in the grass.

"Kate," he said as he reached out his hand toward her, "it's me."

Her vision was doubled, like two worlds overlapping. She could see the roof of a car, a steering wheel popping in and out of view behind a man's shoulder. She trembled. Matthias touched her arm.

"Are you okay?" he asked. "You're ice cold."

She inhaled deeply. Her breath released in broken pieces. "I'm okay."

"What happened?" He moved to sit down next to her on the patchy grass.

"I . . . got too hot," she said. She closed her eyes, but as soon as she did, she saw the red flare of a burning cigarette dropping onto her chest. Her back stiffened, and her eyes opened. She touched her collarbone, feeling the ghost of a burn singeing her skin.

"Kate . . . I know that isn't true," Matthias said.

She swallowed. "It doesn't matter. Don't worry about it. I'm fine."

Matthias sighed. "Would it be so bad to tell me the truth?"

Kate made the mistake of looking at him. His pale eyes captured her, pulled her in, and she wanted so badly to tell him everything. A voice in her head cooed, *Trust him.* But she didn't trust her secret with anyone except her mama. "Yes."

He frowned. "Why?"

She shook her head. "Because . . ." She forced herself to look away. Kate opened her palm and stared at the pen lines marking how much time she had left with Geoffrey. What if telling Matthias the truth took away some of her days with his brother? What if he told Geoffrey how crazy she was and told him to stop seeing her? Would Geoffrey do that if he knew the truth? Her shoulders sagged. "You won't believe me, and if you do, you'll think I'm crazy."

"Have a little faith in me."

"I don't even know you," Kate said. She pushed herself off the grass and walked to the bench. She plopped down and grabbed the box of cookies.

"Evan knew me well, and he trusted me. He told me everything." Matthias stood and followed her. "You can trust me too." He sat down on the opposite end of the bench, putting plenty of space between them. "I wouldn't lie to you."

Kate smoothed her hands over the top of the pink box. She shrugged. "Not that it matters if you do think I'm crazy. You'd be just like everyone else in town."

Matthias's body tensed. "No one thinks you're crazy."

Kate scoffed. "Oh, they don't?" she asked sarcastically. "Maybe you're right. Calling me an Indian witch isn't the same as calling me crazy."

"Don't say that," Matthias said. His jaw was clenched,

creating a distinct square line down the edges of his handsome face. His hands balled into fists in his lap. Matthias seemed genuinely irritated that she'd speak badly about herself.

Her secret pulsed against her chest like a heartbeat. It wanted to be let out. She pressed her lips together and inhaled. Matthias shifted toward her on the bench. On the breeze, Kate caught a whiff of peppermint.

"Geoffrey doesn't think you're crazy," Matthias said.

"Not yet."

"Kate, come on."

Her secret chanted, *Tell him, tell him, tell him.* A blackbird swooped down from the magnolia and pecked at the shaded ground at their feet. It lifted its head and watched Kate, tilting its head before flying off.

On an exhale Kate said, "I see things."

"What do you mean?"

"The future, I guess." She shrugged. "I have premonitions. I mostly see broken pieces of the future. Imagine putting together a puzzle and then throwing it into the air. When it lands, there are pieces everywhere, scattered all over the place, nothing whole, nothing that seems to connect to anything else. I see those scattered pieces."

Matthias didn't respond, and after a few seconds, she looked at him. He watched her just as the blackbird had, with his head tilted, and she could tell he was thinking. But thinking what?

He nodded. "I see."

She hugged the cookie box to her chest. "You don't believe me."

"No, I do. I just wasn't expecting that. I don't have a proper response yet."

"You think I'm crazy." She slumped against the bench.

"No, and stop saying that," Matthias demanded. He propped his arm on the back of the bench and rested his knee on the seat so he could look directly at her. "What's it like?"

"Horrible," Kate blurted. Then she shook her head. "Not always. But sometimes they are."

"How do you know it's the future you're seeing?"

Kate stared at two bluebirds sitting on the low wall surrounding the garden. "Mama told me that my grandma had the same curse—"

"Curse?" Matthias's frown deepened.

"You can't possibly think it's a blessing, can you?" she asked.

"I think it's remarkable."

"That's because you don't have it. Mama told me it was the future I'd see. Sometimes weeks later, a small piece of my premonition might make sense. I see a ladder fall and hear a man shout. A week or two later, I'll learn that Mr. So-and-So fell off his ladder and broke his leg." Kate shrugged. "But it's not always that easy. Most of them are jumbled up. Plus, people can change their futures every minute by making one small change, and what I see might not always be the real future."

"Do you see people you know?"

Kate cut her eyes over to him but didn't look up at his face. "Sometimes I see faces but not as often as blurry images."

Matthias leaned back and scratched the dark shadowing of stubble on his cheek. "It must be challenging to see people you know. I'm guessing you don't say anything to them."

Kate tapped her fingers against the bakery box. "It's not really a conversation I can have with someone. Can you imagine me starting off with that? Hey, I saw a vision of you, and guess

what happens?" She gripped the cookie box as a deep hidden truth flung itself up her throat. "I saw Evan—" She clamped her mouth shut.

Matthias's eyes matched the pale blue of the sky. "What do you mean?"

The loss of Evan engulfed her like someone thrown into a brush fire, and she nearly choked on the sorrow. Why had she brought him up? Why had she revealed the one thing that filled her with unending shame?

"Kate?"

Matthias's hand on her arm dislodged the words in her throat. "I knew what was going to happen. I *wanted* to tell somebody, especially Evan. But Mama said it's against the rules to do anything about the future. I can't change it or even try to. It's not allowed for me to alter anyone's path. So I didn't tell Evan what I saw." Her throat closed. She'd let her brother die. She should have done *something*. Anything. But she'd been trapped by her own curse.

Matthias reached over and touched her hand. She looked down and saw she was crushing the corners of the cookie box, so she released her grip. The breath shuddered in her lungs.

"It's not your fault," he said.

Kate closed her eyes. "No? I knew it was going to happen, and I let it." She'd never told anyone about those premonitions. She'd been ashamed, afraid, and heartbroken. She could still see the busted car, the splintered windshield, his closed eyes. Every time Evan had come home from college, she'd told him she loved him, but she'd done nothing more.

"Kate." Matthias's voice was as gentle as rose petals. "It's not your fault. Evan wouldn't want you to carry around that guilt."

"But I *wanted* to tell him. I *wanted* to change the future because a future without Evan is awful. But . . . there are rules," she said, her voice trailing off. "And I have to assume the rules are meant to keep something worse from happening." She wiped at her damp cheeks. "But what could be worse than losing Evan?"

Matthias leaned down and picked up a crescent-shaped leaf. "Evan thought you hung the moon."

The pressure in her chest started lessening. Kate almost smiled. "He thought I was weird."

Matthias mirrored her expression, and for a moment, Kate was mesmerized by the Hamilton smile. "Was he right?"

Kate laughed unexpectedly. She sat up straighter on the bench and nodded. "Definitely."

The breeze passed through the magnolia and loosened a thick, fat leaf the size of Kate's thigh. It pirouetted through the air until it landed at her feet. She picked it up, measuring it against her small hand.

"Is that what happened to you at the park?" he asked.

Kate nodded.

"What did you see just now?"

Kate's grip tightened around the leaf, and her fingers pierced it. She opened her hand and released the leaf, and it floated to the grass. "I don't . . . I'm not sure." She slid one hand up to her neck. "Darkness. A small space, maybe a car. Someone smoking. Then . . ." She cleared her throat. "It's hard to explain what I see because a lot of it is how it makes me *feel*. Evan knew about my premonitions, but now only Mama knows. We haven't even told my daddy, and this is the first time I've ever talked to anyone outside the family about it." She studied Matthias's face. "What are you thinking?"

"I think I have a lot left to learn about the brain and what it's capable of."

A thought burst in her mind. Her desperation tumbled out in her words. "Please, don't tell anyone." Especially Geoffrey.

Matthias shook his head. "I won't. I promise."

"Kate, are you ready?" her daddy called from the entrance of the garden.

Kate looked at her daddy. "Be right there!" She jumped up from the bench and cradled the box of cookies. "Thanks."

"For what?" Matthias stood.

"For not thinking I'm crazy." She gave him a small, uncertain smile.

"Never."

Kate hurried across the garden toward the gate. She glanced once over her shoulder, and Matthias stood with his hands in his pockets watching her leave. The scent of peppermint drifted on the sticky, summer breeze.

Her daddy needed to stop in the hardware store, so Kate put the bakery box in the car and then joined him inside. Looking for nothing in particular, she wandered through the aisles. She'd drunk her lavender tea this morning, but still she'd had a premonition. Thankfully no one had been around except Matthias. As soon as she got home, she was going to drink at least a dozen cups of tea. She refused to accept that she was getting worse. Her great-grandmother had lived to be an old lady, so maybe Kate wouldn't lose her mind until she was at least seventy.

As Kate rounded the corner of an aisle, a box of nails fell

from the shelf and scattered across the floor. She knelt down and scooped the nails into a pile. Then she arranged them back into their box. Kate stood and went to place the box with the others, but she noticed everything on the entire shelf trembled. Tiny tremors rushed up and down the shelves in waves, rattling nuts and bolts, causing hammers to sway on their hooks. Kate backed away from the unit and bumped into someone. She whirled around.

"Geoffrey," she said on an exhale.

"I saw your dad and wondered if you'd be here." Geoffrey touched her arm. "He's near the front talking to Mr. Perkins." Without warning he pressed his body against hers and walked her backward until Kate felt the rigid shelf pressing into her back. Her emotions had swiftly swung from feeling anxious about the curse to feeling shocked to see Geoffrey. The entire shelving unit felt as though it quaked more and more violently. Geoffrey kissed her. So familiar now was the need she felt for him, along with the desperate ache when he was away from her. She locked their hands together, holding him near, needing to feel him closer and closer.

A tool down the aisle crashed onto the floor. Geoffrey pulled away at the sound, and the fog in Kate's brain shifted. She used the space between them to bring up her hands and push him away. "My daddy is in here," she whispered with wide eyes and a madly pumping heart. She pressed her hand against her chest.

Geoffrey leaned toward her again. "So?" he said against her lips.

Shoes clicked against the tiles with fast staccato beats. "Geoff—oh!"

Geoffrey stopped kissing Kate, and they both looked at

Martha Lee standing at the end of the aisle gaping at them, her pink lips open like a Venus flytrap.

Geoffrey shoved one hand through his hair. "Martha, hey," he said, "how're you?"

Martha's cheeks tinged deep rouge. She smoothed her hands down her floral-patterned dress. "This is certainly a surprise. I didn't mean to interrupt." When she looked at Kate, her brows joined together at the top of her nose as though squinting might help her see the situation clearer.

"You weren't," Geoffrey said. "I was just saying hello to Kate."

Kate's heart slammed against her ribcage so hard that she felt nauseous from the violent rush of blood through her body.

Martha pursed her lips. "Is that what that was?"

An entire row of monkey wrenches at the opposite end of the aisle fell from their hangers. The crash echoed throughout the store. Kate stared at the tools, trembling as though she'd been standing in the snow too long without a jacket. Was she causing this? If so, she needed to get herself under control before the whole store collapsed.

"What in the world is going on here?" Mr. Perkins, the owner of the store, asked. He hooked his thumbs behind his red suspenders and frowned at them.

"I'm sorry, Mr. Perkins," Geoffrey said as he stepped forward. "I'm not sure what happened, but the wrenches fell. Maybe their hangers weren't properly installed." He walked toward the fallen tools and began picking them up. "It's the strangest thing. I can help you tighten down the screws if you want."

Geoffrey smiled at Mr. Perkins, and the owner's face softened. "Maybe I do need to tighten the screws on those hangers." He leaned down and gathered wrenches in his beefy hands.

Sean walked up behind Mr. Perkins. He looked at Kate with raised eyebrows. "Are you kids okay?"

"Oh, yes, sir, Mr. Muir," Martha said with a mischievous smile that caused anxiety to spike in Kate's chest. "We're *great*, aren't we, Kate?"

Kate couldn't look at Martha. She could barely breathe. The cloying scent of Martha's floral perfume filled her lungs on every panicked inhale. Any minute Kate knew Martha could reveal exactly how she'd found her and Geoffrey kissing, hiding in the back of the hardware store like sinners.

Kate had to move her body, or else she might shatter in panic. She knelt beside Geoffrey and helped him gather the remaining wrenches. The metal tools trembled in her hands, clacking together like dice. Mr. Perkins and Geoffrey rehung them on the shelving unit. Kate heard Martha's shoes on the tiles, clicking toward them. Kate's back stiffened.

"Kate," Martha said, "I'd love it if you could come over today."

Kate stared open-mouthed at Martha. Was she serious? Kate promptly shut her mouth and cleared her throat. "Oh, well, I'm with my daddy today, and I have chores at home."

"That's okay, Kate, you can finish your chores later," Sean said. He smiled at Martha. "That's nice of you to ask. I'm finishing up in town, so I can drop her off at your house. Over on Dogwood, right?"

"Yes, sir," Martha said. "I drove Mama's car to town to get a new color of paint for the dining room. She's in a decorating mood." She waved her hands through the air, emphasizing the word *mood*. "Kate can go home with me from here. If that's okay, Kate?" Martha's pink lips widened, but her eyes remained

unchanged. While Martha's expression looked innocent and inviting, Kate felt an undercurrent of insincerity.

Kate glanced quickly at Geoffrey, but something outside the window had caught his attention. "I guess?"

Martha smiled so brightly that Kate blinked in the glare. Martha linked her arm through Kate's, startling her with the contact. "Wonderful," Martha said. "I'll drive Kate home later. Mr. Perkins, could I have a gallon of periwinkle in the best brand of paint you sell? Something good for dining rooms with lots of light. And crystal. Mama has a lot of crystal, you know. Geoffrey, good to see you again."

"Thank you, Martha," Sean said. "Kate, you need to be home by dinner."

"Yes, sir," Martha said before Kate could respond.

"Have fun," Sean said.

Martha pulled Kate away from the men, and Kate stumbled along beside her. She glanced over her shoulder at Geoffrey, and he gave her a small wave. If no one thought there was anything wrong with Martha taking Kate home for an afternoon, then why did Kate feel as though she'd eaten a handful of ants?

CHAPTER 13

Martha drove her mom's royal-blue Buick Roadmaster like the trunk was on fire and they were trying to outrun the blaze. She disregarded speed limits and rolled through a stop sign. Kate gripped her seatbelt in both hands and squeezed the black fabric as if that might somehow protect her from disaster. The radio blasted the rock-and-roll station airing out of Atlanta, and the car speakers strained to release the music at max volume without exploding from their mounts.

Martha took a left turn into the driveway so quickly that Kate's body smashed into the passenger door, and her head knocked against the glass. Martha laughed like she'd done it on purpose. Parking the car in the driveway, Martha grabbed her purse and got out. Kate opened her door and stepped onto the concrete, thankful to have her feet on solid ground. She considered telling Martha she'd walk home later just to avoid being in the car with her again.

The Lees' grand traditional colonial-style home was just as impressive as the Hamiltons' Honeysuckle Hollow. The architectural styles were different, but both were equally classic and distinctly Southern. Martha led Kate up the herringbone brick

pathway toward the front door, an entry Kate suspected she didn't use regularly but was intended to impress her guest. On the colonial there was no shortage of exterior detailing with its custom front entryway planters filled with blooming lantana and draping bright-green potato vines. Powdery gray-blue shutters complemented the crisp-white painted wood structure, and the black entry door fashioned a striking contrast. The flowerbox on the narrow second-floor balcony over the front entry burst with colorful geraniums and impatiens.

The front door opened into a two-story foyer with soaring ceilings. Kate caught a glance of the family room with a screened-in porch just beyond it. Large windows offered her a view of an expansive stone patio and landscaped backyard.

"Your paint is in the trunk. We'll be in my room," Martha yelled from the foyer. Her mother called a response from somewhere buried in the enormous house. "Follow me," she said to Kate in a sing-song voice that made Kate feel like she was being led toward a surprise attack. Martha marched up the switchback staircase, and Kate put her hand on the smooth railing, prayed she wouldn't have a vision, and followed.

Heels clacked across hardwood. Kate glanced over the railing at Martha's mama standing beneath the foyer's chandelier made of drop crystals and polished brass that reflected the afternoon sunlight. Her mama looked like a grown-up version of Martha, except with wider hips, more downturned lips, and eyes that were shadowed and heavier. She reminded Kate of a Madame Alexander Wendy doll that had been left outside for too many seasons, still beautiful but faded, not ready to accept that time had passed.

Mrs. Lee looked up at Kate, and the resemblance of her

experienced smile was a dead ringer for Martha's. "You girls have fun," she said, her words slurring softly, sounding like she was unconcerned about their level of fun. She wrung a kitchen towel in her hands and then walked off.

The sound of Kate's footsteps was lost on the carpeted runner spanning the length of the long, wide second-floor hallway. Doorways adorned with fluted molding and decorative corner pieces dotted both sides of the corridor, and ornate gilded-frame paintings hung in between doorway openings. Martha disappeared through a door halfway down the hall, and Kate lingered in the doorway before entering.

Martha's bedroom was an exhibition of pink and lace and muted light. Baby-girl pink and crisp white striped the wall behind a canopy bed draped with sheer white fabric tied with fuchsia ribbons to the bedposts. Ornamental white frames filled with mirrors of varying sizes decorated the striped wall. An antique white armoire with curving lines and a mirrored front towered against another wall and anchored a rug patterned with pale-pink roses and green vines.

A lacy duvet covered her bed, and overstuffed feather pillows resembled marshmallows leaning against the headboard. A dressing table with an oval mirror was littered with makeup. Pearl necklaces and gold chains with jeweled charms hung inside an open jewelry box, and a tufted pink stool was tucked beneath the table.

"Let's do something fun," Martha said, tossing her purse on the bed. "Charlotte and Betsy will be here soon, and I have a great idea."

"They're coming over?" Kate said, not sure if she should feel thankful for not being left alone with Martha or panicked for

having to appear normal in front of more people.

"I invited them before I went to town for Mama," Martha said. She walked over to a record player set up on a small table in the corner of her room. Martha listened to music in her room the same way she listened to music in the car—loud enough to vibrate Kate's chest. Elvis sang, and Martha shook her hips for a few seconds before she opened a door across the room and walked inside.

When she returned, she gripped a clothes hanger draped with an azure dress. She waved it beside her, and it rippled like a flag. "Makeovers!" Her pink lips turned down. "Quit standing around like a square and try this on."

Martha thrust the dress into Kate's hands. The cotton fabric felt as light and as soft as lamb's-ear. She held the dress out in front of her and studied the hourglass shape of it. Martha stepped out of her closet again holding a broad white belt with a round buckle.

"This will be perfect," Martha said. "Go on, try it on already." She shoved Kate toward an adjoining room that turned out to be a private bathroom.

"You have your own bathroom attached to your bedroom?" Kate gaped at the porcelain clawfoot tub with cast-iron taloned feet. A miniature chandelier hung from the high ceiling.

"Of course," Martha said as she closed Kate inside the bathroom. "Now, change." Her voice carried through the closed door.

This was what girls did together? Tried on each other's clothes? Kate hesitated for only a moment before a feeling of delight shivered through her as she thought of putting on the dress. Kate kicked off her shoes and changed out of her casual clothing. She shimmied the dress over her head. It was a half size

too large for her, but she caught her reflection in the mirror and gasped.

The dress was the exact color of the lapis lazuli necklace her daddy had given her mama last year. Kate smiled and twirled barefoot on the black-and-white bathroom tiles. She opened the door and stepped into the bedroom.

"Well, look at you," Martha said in surprise, studying Kate with a critical eye. She wrapped the white belt around Kate's waist and pulled it tight, slipping the prong through the farthest hole. She looped the extra length of strap through the buckle and stepped away from Kate. "You're tiny." Martha inhaled and pressed her hands against her own stomach. "Look at yourself." She pointed toward the armoire.

Kate stepped in front of the tall mirror. For the first time in her life, she looked like a baby doll. In a crowd of girls, she could slip right in, and no one would notice her. She'd be invisible, one of them, a replica.

"Go on, admit you like it," Martha said as she turned down the volume on the record player. "The dress looks good on you. That's your color."

"Thanks," Kate mumbled.

Martha grabbed the tufted stool beneath the dressing table. She picked up a silver hairbrush and smacked the stool's cushion. "Sit."

Kate obeyed because there didn't seem to be any other option. Martha smoothed Kate's hair into a low ponytail and held it at the base of her neck. Then she pulled the brush through the long strands. "Your hair is really soft and shiny. What do you wash it with?"

Kate thought of the natural soap and shampoo her mama

concocted in the kitchen. She didn't dare tell Martha for fear of sounding like Ama made witchy potions. "Whatever Mama gives me. What about you?"

"Same," Martha said. "She's obsessed with Lustre-Creme now. Somebody told her that Elizabeth Taylor uses it, and Mama was sold. It's okay, smells nice. Your hair is really long. Have you ever thought of cutting it?"

Kate's eyes widened in the mirror. She shook her head, and a few dark strands slipped through Martha's fingers and dropped to Kate's shoulders. Kate caught movement as someone stepped through the doorway into the bedroom.

"Charlotte!" Martha said in an exaggerated greeting. "You're looking particularly lovely today. Is that a new dress? Oh, hey, Betsy, did you two come together?"

"Mama dropped me off at Charlotte's on her way to the help with a fundraiser at the church," Betsy said. Her expression revealed her surprise. "Kate, I didn't know you'd be here. How are you? Golly, you look so pretty in that dress."

Martha fisted the brush at her cocked hip. "That's why I chose it for her. It's mine, but I haven't worn it in ages. I thought it would be a good fit for her."

Charlotte smiled. "It looks like it was made for you, Kate. That is definitely your color."

Martha's lips pursed, but she quickly recovered. "Kate and I were discussing cutting her hair. What do you think? She might look more fashionable with a trim."

Kate watched as both Charlotte's and Betsy's reflections moved into the mirror with her.

Charlotte stepped closer to the stool. "Do you want to cut your hair?"

Kate shifted on the seat and grabbed a section of her hair. She stared at the darkness spilling over her palm like a stream of melted chocolate. "I've—I've never really thought about it. Mama cuts it sometimes." Would a haircut be another step toward sincerely fitting in with everyone? "Do you think it's too long?" She stared at Charlotte's reflection.

Martha turned to Charlotte. "It's not *too* long. Unless you want a specific style, right? It's not going to hold curl. Betsy?"

Betsy moved in closer. She chewed her bottom lip and tugged at one of her own curls. "I think if you curled it in waves, you'd be the spitting image of Ava Gardner."

Charlotte's smiled widened. "You're right."

Kate scoffed, unable to meet her own dark-eyed gaze in the mirror. "The actress?"

"Do you know another one?" Charlotte teased.

"But she's . . . beautiful," Kate said, staring at her clasped hands. Charlotte eased Kate's hair from her shoulders and folded it in half, pressing it against the back of Kate's head and causing the hair to loop and stop at her shoulders. "And you're not? I think Betsy's right. With a few waves, you could pass for Ava."

Martha's lips curled like she smelled an acrid odor. "Hmm, maybe a version of her."

Betsy nodded. "A knockout version of her."

Kate shared a thankful smile with Betsy.

Martha hummed in her throat. "I guess I can see it. People say I look like Grace Kelly all the time."

Betsy's brow wrinkled. "What people?"

Martha ignored Betsy's question. "So what do you think, Kate?" Martha leaned her face close to Kate's so they were side by side in the mirror. "Cut it?"

"I cut my sister's hair all the time. Mama taught me how," Charlotte said. "I can do it if you want."

Kate exhaled and wondered what Geoffrey would think. A tiny smile tugged her lips up at the corners, and she nodded. Martha slapped a pair of scissors into Charlotte's open palm. "In the bathroom. I don't want hair all over my bedroom floor."

Half an hour later Charlotte opened the bathroom door and scurried out. "Don't come out yet, Kate." Talking to Betsy and Martha, Charlotte said, "Now, don't you two turn around until I tell you. Okay, Kate, come on out."

Kate rocked in place on restless legs. A fast pulse throbbed in her chest. She glanced at herself one last time in the bathroom mirror and inhaled a slow breath. Her hair had been cut at least five inches, and now it framed her face in waves and fell just past her shoulders. Dark berry stained her lips, and Charlotte had blended shimmering shades of tan and brown to her upper eyelids and brow bone. Thin black lines traced the edges of where her lashes met her eyelids, and black mascara elongated her thick lashes. A dusting of rich rouge highlighted her cheekbones.

When Kate walked out of the bathroom, Charlotte clapped her hands together and bounced on her toes. "Okay, y'all can turn around."

Betsy gasped, and Martha's pink lips parted as though she wanted to say something but couldn't. Kate squirmed beneath their stares.

Charlotte rushed over and draped a few curls over Kate's shoulders. "Doesn't she look stunning? You were right, Betsy. Ava

Gardner, step aside."

Betsy walked over. "Gee, Kate, you look, well, you look so exotic. Just like a movie star."

Kate fiddled with the belt around her waist. "I don't look like me."

Charlotte touched Kate's upper arm. "Of course you do. Don't be silly. This is still you. Just a different version."

"The fancy version," Betsy said with a wide smile that lifted her plump cheeks toward her eyes.

Martha cocked her hip to the side and pressed her lips together. Then she grinned without showing her teeth. "I wonder what Geoffrey will think."

Betsy and Charlotte both looked confused. "Why does that matter?" Charlotte asked.

Martha's eyebrows rose, and her smile widened, reminding Kate of an alligator. "Ask Kate."

Betsy's brow wrinkled deeper. "Ask Kate what? I don't understand."

Kate tried to swallow, but she felt as though she'd eaten a mouthful of dried lavender without water.

"Go on, Kate. Tell them."

Charlotte looked from Kate to Martha. "Tell us what? What is going on?"

"Kate and Geoffrey are together," Martha sighed dramatically.

Betsy made a choking noise in her throat, and Charlotte gaped at Kate.

"Geoffrey Hamilton?" Charlotte asked.

A shiver zinged up Kate's spine. "Yes, but we're not—I mean, it's not as though—we're not exactly *together*."

Martha laughed, but her throat sounded tight with cattiness.

"But you were kissing in the hardware store."

Betsy gasped again and clasped her hands together at her chest. "Oh my."

Charlotte blinked at Kate as though seeing her for the first time. Then she grinned and giggled. She grabbed Kate's arm and tugged her toward Martha's bed. They sat down on the edge of the mattress, and she reached for both of Kate's hands.

"Tell me *everything*," Charlotte said, her blue eyes sparkling with delight. "I can't believe you caught Geoffrey Hamilton's eye, and *not* because you're not beautiful because look at you, but because he's normally so . . ."

"Absorbed in himself?" Betsy added.

Charlotte snickered. "Yes, exactly that. Now, don't leave out any details."

"Well, they obviously enjoy kissing *in public*—" Martha blurted.

"Hush, Martha," Charlotte said, snapping her head toward Martha, "this is Kate's story."

Betsy plopped down on the bed on the other side of Kate, causing Kate to rise higher on the fluffy duvet. "Please, tell us everything," she said, echoing Charlotte's plea.

Martha huffed and dragged over the stool from the dressing table. She sat in front of Kate, smoothed her skirt over her legs, and folded her hands in her lap. "Yes, let's hear how you've won over Geoffrey's heart." Her voice sounded as rigid as her back looked.

Kate scoffed. "I haven't won over anyone's heart."

"Looking like this, you could win over the pope's heart," Betsy said.

Charlotte laughed. "Betsy, that's blasphemous, but you're

right." She turned her blue eyes back toward Kate. "Spill it."

Kate looked at Betsy's and Charlotte's eager faces before meeting Martha's curious gaze. She thought of Geoffrey, and her cheeks warmed. Charlotte squeezed her hands, and Kate refocused on her. They wanted to know more about *her*, and the warmth of that realization spread through Kate's entire body.

Her shoulders relaxed, and she smiled at her lap. "We've seen each other a few times."

"Like in the hardware store," Betsy said and giggled.

Kate blushed so hard that her palms began to sweat, so she let go of Charlotte's hands. "That doesn't usually happen. That was all Geoffrey. I wouldn't—you know, I wouldn't do that normally."

Charlotte sighed loudly. "But who can resist a Hamilton?"

Kate's head snapped up, and she and Charlotte shared a knowing look. "Exactly."

Martha made a motion for Kate to continue. "What else? We know about the store and the picnic. Where else do you see each other? Obviously, you two are closer than we were aware of."

An image of Honeysuckle Hollow rose in her mind, and even though the experience hadn't been pleasant, Kate was aware the bare facts would impress them. "I've been to his house."

Martha's nostrils flared. "He took you home?"

Kate nodded.

"To his room?"

Kate shook her head, and curls tumbled around her face. "Of course not. That would be inappropriate."

Martha snorted. "More inappropriate than necking in the hardware store?"

"Enough about the store," Charlotte argued. "We've all been overcome with the urge to kiss a handsome boy, haven't we?"

Charlotte narrowed her gaze at Martha. "Don't act like you didn't kiss Roddy Temple senseless behind the bleachers during that football game last fall."

Martha's body tensed. "Who told you that?"

Charlotte chuckled. "Everyone and their grandma could have seen you. Just so happens I did."

"My grandma did too," Betsy chimed in.

Martha tugged on her earring. "He was going back to college the next day, and he begged me for a kiss. I'd never kiss anyone in public like that." Her eyes met Kate's. "He *begged* me."

"Oh, cool it, Martha," Charlotte teased. "We don't care a lick about it." She looked at Kate. "We've all kissed a boy when we knew better."

"Not me," Betsy said glumly.

Charlotte reached over Kate and patted Betsy's leg. "Your time is coming, I promise. The right guy just hasn't come along yet."

Betsy sighed and clasped her hands together at her chest. "But when he does, I will neck with him anywhere." Then she giggled again. "Even in the hardware store."

That caused Kate and Charlotte to laugh.

"So . . . how was it?" Charlotte asked.

Kate blinked. "How was what?"

"The kiss," Betsy and Charlotte chorused.

Kate couldn't stop the warm tingle that started in her chest and spread all the way down to her toes. She smiled. "Oh, well, that . . . it was wonderful. All of them are." An embarrassed giggle bubbled up Kate's throat, and Charlotte and Betsy joined her.

Charlotte asked, "Where else have you been kissing Mr. Hamilton?"

Kate smiled into her lap as she thought of the imaginary list she and Geoffrey had been keeping of all the locations where he'd kissed her. "Way up in a tree."

They snickered more, and Betsy slipped one leg beneath her and sat on it, facing Kate. "That makes me think of kissing on the Ferris wheel at the carnival. Wouldn't that be romantic? You know the carnival will be here in a week. We should all go together."

Charlotte nodded. "That's a great idea."

"And we can invite some guys to join us," Betsy added. "Maybe the one for me will be there."

Martha lifted one shoulder. "Why not? We'll just have to keep Betsy away from the fried dough. Remember you ate so much last year that your dresses were too tight? Not a good chance of finding *the one* if your face is covered in powdered sugar."

Kate felt Betsy stiffen on the bed. Martha's smirk caused a knot to twist in Kate's stomach. She looked at Betsy. "I've never had fried dough. I'd love to try it with you. My Daddy says that when a man loves a woman, it doesn't matter if she's not the same size as everyone else or if she loves fried dough."

Betsy's face softened, and she smiled sweetly at Kate. "You'll love it."

Excitement rocketed through Kate, filling her with an unfamiliar emotion. She felt certain she was making friends. Not friends in books or in flowers or in her mama and daddy. Real ones. She would go to the carnival with girlfriends and see Geoffrey and maybe kiss him on the Ferris wheel. Kate's smile was reflected back to her on everyone's face except Martha's. The sun stole behind the clouds, darkening the bedroom before stretching shadows across Martha's scowl.

CHAPTER 14

LATE THAT AFTERNOON CHARLOTTE OFFERED TO TAKE KATE home, which gave Kate a reprieve from riding with Martha again. Charlotte drove one of their family cars, a two-tone Chevy Nomad painted seafoam green and pearl white. The dash was also seafoam green, and the front seat was made of vinyl and plush blue fabric. Betsy rode with them, allowing Kate to take the passenger seat.

The whole ride to Kate's house, Betsy leaned forward, resting her arms on the back of the front seat, and Kate turned an air vent toward Betsy's face so they could all appreciate the cool interior. Charlotte and Betsy talked about the upcoming carnival, what they'd wear, and what rides were the most thrilling. Kate listened with rapt attention. She wanted to absorb every detail, memorize every snicker, so she could revisit them over and over and never forget how it felt to be included.

Kate pushed open the front door of her house, still laughing at Charlotte's joke. Charlotte and Betsy waved at Kate through the windshield as they drove off. The living room and kitchen were empty, but a vegetable medley with roasted chicken sat warming on the stove.

"Mama?" Kate called. She heard voices in the backyard. She opened the backdoor and stood in the doorway. "Mama? Daddy?"

Her parents' arms were linked at the elbows, and Ama leaned into Sean and laughed. Kate wondered if her face lit up like her mama's when she looked at Geoffrey. She skipped into the yard, still on a high from the afternoon. She wanted to tell her mama how fun her day had been, how she had friends now, how they were all going to the carnival next week.

"Hey!"

Her parents turned in unison with the setting sun haloing their silhouettes in a blushing light.

Kate couldn't stop smiling. "I had the best time," she gushed.

Sean lifted his hand slowly and pointed at her head. "What have you done to your hair?"

"What have you done to your face?" Ama asked, stepping away from Sean, her skirt swishing about her bare feet.

Kate had nearly forgotten about her hair and makeup. She pulled her fingers through her shortened hair, feeling the roll of the waves. "You don't like it?"

"It's just—you look . . ." Sean stuttered, and then his words failed.

Kate felt her happiness draining away from her like a pulled plug in the bathtub. "Look what?"

His frown deepened. "You don't look like my baby girl. Where did you get that dress?"

"It's Martha's," Kate said. "And I don't want to look like a baby."

"You certainly don't now," Sean said with furrowed brow. "You look about twenty."

Kate's expression lifted. "Really?"

"That's not a good thing," he said.

His words sent a shock of cold through her body. Her toes tingled before the chill crept up her legs, into her stomach, and reached her chest.

Ama crossed the grass toward her. "Go inside and wash your face."

"Why?" The chill clawed up Kate's throat, choking her. "I like it. I think it looks pretty."

Ama squeezed her arm. Her jaw clenched and released. "Do as I say."

Kate looked at her daddy. His eyes were clouded and stormy gray, his jaw as rigid as a handsaw.

"But I don't want to," Kate said. "Doesn't it matter if I like it or not?"

"Next you'll be telling me you have a boyfriend," Ama said. The air around them felt dense and heavy, as though it fell from the trees and pressed against them.

"I might," Kate blurted.

Ama inhaled sharply. Kate saw the truth of her words register in Ama's wide eyes. The grass darkened beneath Sean's shoes as he walked toward them. "Do as your mom says. Go inside." His command shoved against Kate like an angry force. Her bottom lip trembled.

The bitter chill detonated inside her, and she stumbled toward the house even as her body stopped responding. Darkness pressed in at the edges of her vision, and her knees slammed into a stepping stone. Kate crumpled onto her side.

A young girl with oversize eyes magnified behind thick glasses stood in front of a display counter. "Blue Moon" echoed through the room. The girl carried a chocolate ice cream cone. Bells jingled.

A door opened, and sunlight streamed in. A male voice spoke, and the girl stumbled onto the sidewalk. A patch of blood stained the concrete. Images washed away and gathered into new ones.

Lips pressed against hers, angry and bruising. A hand fisted in her hair and pulled back her head. Her breathing hitched, and her scalp burned. She dropped flat on her back against the seat, nearly suffocating beneath his weight. He grabbed at the gaudy plastic necklace she wore and yanked. Small beads launched into the air like red plastic fireworks, raining down on her face, and his laughter exploded, echoing off the windows, as tears streaked the sides of her face.

"Please don't," she begged with her nose running and throat pinched tight in fear and desperation. "Please . . ."

"Kate, baby," someone cooed. "Wake up. Come back to me."

Kate's eyes opened, and she sucked humid air into her lungs. Night had fallen around her, and tiny blades of grass poked into her calves. She focused on a face leaning over hers.

"Mama?" Her voice croaked like a frog on the riverbank.

Ama exhaled and looked over her shoulder. "Don't call Dr. Hamilton. She's okay, Sean." Her mama's face leaned over hers. "Don't you dare scare me like that again." She lowered her voice. "You've never been out for so long before. Have you been drinking your tea?" Kate nodded. She'd been drinking lavender tea every day, more than once.

Sean knelt beside her. "You okay, Little Blackbird?"

Their previous anger had evaporated. Could she consider this one good thing about her curse? It eliminated their disappointment and replaced it with pity.

Sean looked at Ama. "You think it's her blood sugar?" Looking back at Kate, he asked, "Did you eat?"

Kate tried to remember. Martha had mentioned she'd already eaten before she met up with Kate, but Kate and her daddy hadn't eaten lunch before they went into the hardware store. At Martha's they'd drunk lemonade, but there had been too much giggling and talking to think about anything else. "No, sir."

"Let's get you inside. Your mom made your favorite—"

Ama cleared her throat, and Sean chuckled as he slid his hands beneath Kate's back and lifted her as though she were a baby doll. "Okay, so it's my favorite," he said, "but I know you like it too." He helped Kate to her feet.

She wobbled and rubbed the front of her neck, feeling the ghost of where a necklace had been. She remembered the feel of beads pelting her in the face as the man in the darkness of her mind laughed. The past few repeating premonitions felt like a melding of two separate events, and one distressed her more than the other. All of Kate's previous premonitions happened as though she were an observer, but this violent, disturbing vision in the car felt as though it were happening *to her*. But who would she be in a car with other than Geoffrey? The dominant, forceful man in her vision absolutely did not feel like Geoffrey. Kate shuddered.

She would avoid getting into a car with any man other than her daddy or Geoffrey for the next few weeks. Maybe she wasn't allowed to alter anyone else's future, but Ama never said anything about Kate altering her own. But what kind of sense did that make? Kate furrowed her brow as she let her daddy guide her into the house. She could alter her own future but not anyone else's? Once again Kate questioned the makers of the rules. What if they were wrong?

Inside the house, Ama told Kate to get cleaned up and then

she'd have tea and dinner ready. Kate stared at her reflection in the bathroom mirror. Mascara leaked down the sides of her face. Dark berry lipstick smeared below her lip. She looked like a bleeding watercolor left behind in a rainstorm. She scrubbed her face until it shone pink and raw, and she couldn't stop thinking about being trapped in a car with a boy whose intentions were vile. She met her reflection's gaze, pressed her trembling hands against the sink, and whispered, "What's going to happen if I change the future?"

CHAPTER 15

THE NEXT MORNING THE PHONE RANG, AND AMA ANSWERED IT while Sean and Kate finished breakfast. "Yes, she's here," Ama said. Kate stopped drinking her tea and looked at her mama. Someone was calling for her? She panicked for a moment, thinking it might be Geoffrey. Would that send her mama into a tailspin? Ama held out the phone toward Kate. "It's Charlotte LaRue." From the pinched expression on Ama's face, Kate assumed her mama hadn't forgiven what happened the last time Kate hung out with the girls—she'd come home with a haircut, wearing a new dress, and dolled up like a Hollywood actress.

Kate pushed back from the table and took the offered phone. Ama lingered close by, making herself look busy cleaning the kitchen, but it was obvious she wanted to eavesdrop.

"Hello?"

"Kate! It's Charlotte. How are you?"

Kate made eye contact with her daddy, but he looked away quickly and continued eating his toast. Ama ran a dishcloth over the clean countertop.

"Good morning," Kate said. "We're finishing breakfast. How are you?" She stretched as far out of the kitchen as the coiled

phone cord would allow.

"Martha, Betsy, and I are going into town this morning, and we'll probably go to Scooper's. You know they have a weekly special, and this week it's Betsy's favorite, so I promised her I'd go with her. Want to go? We could pick you up in an hour."

Kate's breath caught. Going to Martha's had been a shocking invitation, and then being included in a group attending the upcoming carnival felt like a dream. Now Charlotte wanted Kate to spend the morning window shopping and eating ice cream with them. In her wildest imaginings, Kate never believed she'd have friends the way Evan had, that Mystic Water would draw her into its embrace like a welcomed member.

"Hold please and let me ask," Kate said before covering the receiver with her palm. "Mama, can I please go to town with Charlotte, Martha, and Betsy? They want to walk around downtown and then stop by Scooper's. Charlotte can pick me up in an hour."

"Absolutely not," Ama said immediately. Kate's stomach dropped.

"Why not?" Sean asked.

Ama's glare caused Sean to sit up straighter in the chair. "Have you already forgotten what happened yesterday? Your daughter came home a stranger, and there could be boys involved."

Sean looked at Kate. "Charlotte, Martha, and Betsy?"

"Yes, sir," Kate answered. "Only the girls." Ama's gaze pierced through Kate's calm. Could her mama see her hopes that Geoffrey might be in town?

"I don't see the harm," Sean said. "I have work to do in town this morning, so I'll drop you off." Then he met Ama's steely gaze. "That way I can assure you of who's there." Ama stomped

off without responding, leaving a trail of angry sparks behind her.

Kate removed her hand from the receiver. "I'd love to meet you there," she said. "Daddy can drop me off in a hour."

An hour later, Sean pulled into a slanted downtown parking spot in front of the pharmacy. Charlotte and Betsy stood a few shop doors down in the shade created by maples planted along the sidewalk. The temperature hovered around ninety-five degrees, but a sticky breeze blew, lessening the intensity of the heat. Kate smoothed her hand over her ponytail. She hoped that pulling up her hair would keep her parents from staring like they still couldn't believe she'd let someone cut it. She opened the car door and smiled. "Thank you, Daddy."

He hesitated before responding, tapping his fingers on the steering wheel in rhythm with The Platters's song piping through the radio. "Have fun with the girls." Martha exited the pharmacy with Ted in tow, and Sean stiffened in the seat beside her. "You said no boys."

Kate frowned. If any boys joined them today, she didn't want it to be Ted. "We can't demand every boy avoid downtown. I'm sure she just ran into him in the store. He's a guy she knows from school." As she said the words, Ted lit a cigarette, crossed the street, and left Martha with Charlotte and Betsy. "There, you see. Only the girls."

Sean acquiesced. "I'll meet you back here at one."

Kate said good-bye and leaped out of the car. Betsy caught sight of her and lifted her hand in a wave. Betsy and Charlotte had worn shorts and sleeveless button-up shirts, just as Kate had. Relief moved through her because she looked like she belonged. Kate had been tempted to ask Charlotte was she was wearing that

morning, but with both her parents listening to the conversation, Kate didn't want more lectures about needing approval from others. They didn't understand what it felt like to be an outsider in school, an experience that was almost as awful as her curse. Martha was the standout in her peach skirt and white blouse with a strand of pearls and matching earrings.

"Hey, Kate," Charlotte said in greeting. "Your hair looks great pulled back like that."

Betsy adjusted her purse strap. "What did your parents say about the new style?"

Kate's shoulders tensed for a minute, remembering the previous night. "They were surprised," she said honestly.

"It's a noticeable change," Charlotte said. "But a great one. I'm sure they love it."

Martha patted a blond curl on the side of her head and gave it a gentle lift with her palm. "Are we going to spend all day talking about hair or shop?"

"Can't we do both?" Charlotte said lightly, and Betsy laughed.

Betsy slid her arm through Kate's and hooked them together. "Let's go to The Story Keeper first," she said. "Jack said he got in a new shipment of books. You're a reader, aren't you, Kate?"

"Yes," Kate said, feeling thrilled that Betsy knew and approved of something about her. "It's one of my favorite shops."

Martha groaned. "Who needs books in the summer? Don't you read enough during the school year? Let's go to Iris & Ivy."

Charlotte said, "The Story Keeper is on the way to Iris & Ivy, so let's stop by there first. Then we'll go to the boutique and finish off with Scooper's."

The Story Keeper's primary stock was books ranging from current bestsellers to antique collectibles. The shop also sold

other peculiar finds, such as treasure maps leading to fantasy worlds, needlepoint kits, fuzzy socks, wind chimes, and discarded keys used as bookmarks.

Every couple of months her daddy let her peruse the shop for a new book. Space was limited on her bedroom bookshelf, forcing Kate to be choosy with what she brought home. She sometimes faced the decision of giving away an older one to make room for the new.

Martha situated herself in the plush velvet armchair placed at the front of the shop, facing the wide-spanning bowed window. She fanned her skirt out around her legs and looked like a mannequin for sale in the front display among the books, oversize globe, and other oddities. Charlotte flipped through cookbooks, and Betsy followed Jack, the store owner, as he pointed out the new inventory.

Kate didn't have money for anything other than ice cream later, but she still wandered up and down the aisles, stopping by the romance section and wondering if Geoffrey would be joining them at the carnival. She glanced down at the fading pen marks on her palm. Thirteen days until he would pack up and leave for the university.

Martha's voice carried from the front of the shop. "Hey, Geoffrey, what a surprise! I don't think I've ever seen you in a bookstore before." Her nasal laugh rattled across the floorboards.

Kate popped out from behind the shelf and caught sight of Geoffrey, who was gazing around the shop as though looking for someone. When he spotted Kate, his smile widened.

"Just who I was hoping to see," he said, leaving Martha standing in the front area with an offended expression. He grabbed Kate's hand and pulled her up an aisle away from Martha.

Kate felt exhilarated and then immediately worried. She'd told her daddy there would be no boys and now Geoffrey had her cornered in the book shop. "What are you doing here?"

"Helping my dad at his office," Geoffrey said and then chuckled. "Cool it. I'm not helping with patients. I'm moving furniture around at his bidding. Ran into Ted outside, and he said y'all were in here. I only have a minute before I have to get back, but . . ." He leaned down and kissed her. Kate tensed at first and then leaned into him, savoring the warmth of his mouth against hers.

The kiss ended too quickly, and Kate didn't want him to go. What she really wanted was to find a dark corner in the shop and kiss Geoffrey until next year. Kiss him so long he couldn't go to university ever.

"We're going to the carnival in a few days," she blurted. "Are you going?"

Geoffrey grinned. "Yeah. If I don't see you before, I'll see you there for sure. Dad's keeping me busy for the next few days. I better cut out." He kissed her swiftly and strode off.

Kate leaned her head against the bookshelf and sighed, still feeling a light throbbing in her lips from where he'd pressed his mouth to hers. Martha appeared at the end of the aisle. "Oh, don't look so far gone. Don't you know anything about being coy? Men want what they can't have. They want the chase. You're too easy."

"I am?" Kate asked.

Martha rolled her eyes as though Kate was a helpless cause. "You have a lot to learn about men, Kate Muir."

An hour later after shopping in Iris & Ivy, a fashionable boutique full of women's clothes and stylish accessories, Martha had two full bags hanging on both arms. Kate had forced herself not

to gape at the money Martha pulled out of her wallet as though it were normal for a teenager to carry around fifty dollars in cash. Charlotte bought gloves and a summer scarf, and Betsy bought a pair of earrings that dangled when she moved her head. Martha dropped off the bags at her car, and then the girls walked to Scooper's.

Martha's words at the book shop about Kate not understanding men sprouted like seeds in Kate's mind, growing a garden of doubt. Did she have the ability to keep Geoffrey's interest? Or did only girls like Martha truly understand a man's needs and desires? Kate didn't understand the concept of playing hard to get. If she was interested in Geoffrey, the natural inclination was to admit it to him, and he wasn't shy about his attention. He'd come into The Story Keeper specifically to see her.

Betsy pushed open the door to Scooper's. Only a half dozen people waited in line. "Perfect timing," she said. "Most of the time the line would already be stretching outside. What flavor are you getting?" she asked Kate.

Sunlight reflected off the black-and-white checkerboard tiles. A few kids sat at the red vinyl seats lining the powder-blue countertop. A young girl dropped coins into the jukebox. "Earth Angel" serenaded them, and goosebumps skittered across Kate's skin. Inside Scooper's was cold not only to battle the outdoor summer heat but also to keep the ice cream frozen. Kate rubbed her hands up her bare arms.

"Did you hear me?" Betsy asked again, positioning herself at the end of the line.

Kate gazed at the colorful tubs of ice cream through the glass displays. "I like strawberry in the summertime."

"I'm getting the special, chocolate banana split," Betsy said.

"With extra cherries."

"Do you need extra anything, Betsy?" Martha asked, causing Betsy's excitement to dim.

Charlotte moved in between Martha and Betsy. "I'm getting triple chocolate in a waffle cone, and I'm asking for double fudge sauce. I say order the extra cherries."

Martha huffed. "I prefer butter pecan."

The line moved forward, and the song changed on the jukebox. When "Blue Moon" started playing, Kate shivered, and her palms felt sticky. She breathed in the sugary scent of warm vanilla. Another smell mingled with the sweetness, and when Kate recognized it, she stiffened. Lavender. Why did she smell lavender? She scanned the ice cream labels to see if Scooper's had added a lavender flavor, but they hadn't.

The door opened, jingling the silver bell hanging from the doorframe, and Ted sauntered in with a cloud of cigarette smoke following him. He spotted them and crossed to their group. Was he following them?

"Order me a praline pecan," he said to Martha. He grabbed her hand, opened it, and dropped money into her palm. "In a cup, no cone. I'll save a table for us."

Charlotte frowned. "Ted, we're having a ladies' day. Couldn't you get ice cream some other time or take it with you?"

Ted smirked. "Nope. Martha here doesn't mind, do you, Martha?" He winked at her, and Kate looked away from his leering expression. Martha didn't argue, but she also didn't make eye contact with Charlotte, who studied her curiously. Ted sat at a table near the front door and sagged against the seat back. His legs stretched out into the walkway.

The cash register dinged as a young girl paid for her ice

cream. When the girl turned to leave, Kate recognized Dani Moreland from school. Dani was a rising sophomore like Kate, and they had shared biology and literature together last year. Dani and Kate also shared another thing in common—they both loitered on the margins of their peers. Dani was a gentle, quiet girl but had the unfortunate need to wear the thickest Coke-bottle glasses Kate had ever seen. The extremely thick lens magnified Dani's eyes, giving her the appearance of a perpetually surprised beetle.

Dani's chocolate double scoop sat perched on top of a sugar cone. She pressed her mouth to the side of the melting ice cream and came away with chocolate smeared at the edges of her lips.

Martha snickered. "Isn't that the saddest thing? I feel awful for her." Martha's words sounded insincere, which she proved by laughing again at Dani. "Can you imagine looking like that? You'd think someone could help her. Those glasses are the worst."

The line moved forward, and Dani took another large bite of her ice cream. Kate's heartbeat quickened, and her gaze shifted to Ted, who stared at Dani like someone staring at a dung pile. The scent of lavender grew so strong in the air around Kate that it smelled like she stood in a field of it.

"She needs those glasses to see," Charlotte whispered. "If you asked her, she'd probably tell you she hates them."

"Why would I ask her anything?" Martha said incredulously.

Kate's stomach clenched. The line moved forward again, but her legs had become marble pillars. An overwhelming feeling of déjà vu caused her breath to hitch. Goosebumps covered her entire body.

Dani walked toward the front door, steadily licking the sides of her ice cream and not paying attention to what was going on

around her. She didn't notice the wicked gleam in Ted's eyes as he stood from the table and held open the door for her. Dani appeared so shocked by his chivalrous gesture that she didn't see how he purposefully stuck out his leg with the intent to trip her. In her mind, Kate immediately saw Dani falling, dropping her ice cream, and scraping her knees on the concrete sidewalk. With shocking clarity, Kate understood she was watching her premonition play out in real life. Her first impulse was to follow the rules and let Dani's life happen as it must. No interference.

But a fiercer, more passionate instinct took over. "Dani!" Kate shouted without realizing what was happening.

Dani visibly flinched and stopped walking. She stared at Kate in question. Ted's eyes narrowed.

"Be careful," Kate said, pointing at Ted's leg, which he didn't move fast enough for Dani to miss. Dani didn't respond, but she skirted around Ted, and scurried out onto the sidewalk without dropping her ice cream or falling.

Betsy was too focused on ordering her ice cream to observe what happened. Ted stomped toward them and glowered at Kate. "We could have had a good laugh."

"Don't you get tired of putting down others?" Charlotte asked.

"Nope," he said, and both he and Martha laughed.

Kate lost her appetite for ice cream, but she ordered one anyway so as not to draw attention to herself. Instead of sitting at the table with the girls and Ted, Kate used her daddy as an excuse to leave. Charlotte said she'd call in a few days about the carnival, and Kate left Scooper's in a mood somewhere between terrified and awestruck.

She had done the unthinkable. She'd altered the future.

What would happen to her now? Would she be struck by lightning from heaven like a disobedient biblical character? Would Dani's life somehow create a more tragic event for her today now that one had been avoided? As Kate walked, her ice cream melted and dripped pale-pink strawberry ice cream onto her hand.

When Sean found her, she was standing by the car, sweating in the sunlight, holding an empty ice cream cone with a puddle of pink at her feet. "Little Blackbird," he said cautiously. "Everything all right?"

She followed his gaze to her ice cream mess. "I don't know," she said. So far nothing horrific had happened since the altered future. No screams, no plagues, no angry Ama yelling at her. It seemed as though *nothing* had happened other than keeping Dani from hurting herself.

Sean opened the driver's side door. "If you don't know, who does?"

Kate tossed her empty cone into the trash and used the leftover napkins to wipe as much of the stickiness from her hands as she could. Something Evan said to her years ago resurfaced in her mind. When she got into the car, she looked over at her daddy. "Is Mama going to the Cherokee village soon?"

Sean started the engine. "Tomorrow, I think. Why?"

"I'd like to go with her," Kate said, stopping short of saying there was someone there she needed to talk to.

"You haven't been in years," Sean said, backing out of the parking space. "Any particular reason you're interested in going now?"

"That's it exactly," Kate said. "I haven't been in years, and it's time to change that." The time had finally come for Kate to find Aurora Catawnee and see what she knew about the curse.

CHAPTER 16

AMA RESISTED TAKING KATE TO THE CHEROKEE VILLAGE UNTIL Sean, in an unexpected display of dominance, told Ama she didn't have a choice. He argued that Kate should be allowed to visit the village if she wanted. The Cherokee were, after all, part of Kate's heritage, and Ama still had family members living there. Kate didn't understand why her mama felt so strongly about her not going, but she wondered if it had something to do with why she stopped taking her and Evan when they were kids.

Ama was silent for most of the car ride until they left the boundaries of the city limits. "I don't know why you're so insistent on going with me today." Her words carried a tone of displeasure.

"Why are you so insistent on me not going? You used to take Evan and me all the time."

Ama huffed. "Years ago, when you were children. You're not a child anymore."

And yet you still treat me like one, Kate thought. "I thought it might be nice to see the village. Visit with some people."

Ama's mocking laugh lowered the temperature in the car.

"Visit? You hardly know anyone in the village."

Kate frowned. "Maybe it's time I get to know them."

Ama said nothing more. When they arrived at the village, she parked in a makeshift dirt parking space beside a modest one-story home. "I have to attend to Walela this morning, then I planned to help with the bean harvesting. You can . . . walk around until I'm done with Walela. Don't walk too far."

Kate nodded, wanting to ask how far "too far" actually was, but she held her tongue, not wanting to further antagonize her mama's souring disposition. Ama hustled up the street, kicking up clouds of dust on the dry, cracked path. Kate hadn't been to the village in years, but not much had changed from the snapshots in her memory.

Rows of houses lined both sides of the main red-clay road that shot straight through the village. Other houses branched off on perpendicular side roads. Verdant fields surrounded them on all sides, a thriving boundary containing the people. A tributary of the Red River ran alongside a cornfield. The population of the village was probably around two hundred. Dozens of younger kids, much more than Kate remembered, ran around. In the rising summer heat, they played in thin cotton dresses and shorts without shirts, their laughter and youthful voices filling the air with a constant buzz of conversation.

The village was active, and people greeted one another on the main road as they passed. A group of men carrying hoes and other farming tools passed Kate as she walked up the road. They greeted her with a combination of surprised and wary expressions. A scent of baking corn carried on the stifling breeze, and Kate lifted the hair from her neck to allow the wind to cool down her sweaty skin.

She wondered how she would find Aurora Catawnee among the houses and the busyness. She didn't even know what Aurora looked like. Two bicycles leaned on each other along the road, and Kate paused long enough to notice they were at least ten years old based on their model and style. She remembered Evan had a similar bike when he was younger. He had tried to talk her into riding on the handlebars, which she declined repeatedly, and she smiled at the memory.

"What's the white girl doing here?" someone asked.

The voice pulled Kate from her thoughts, and she walked on, wondering again how she would find Aurora. She needed to find the older woman before her mama was done helping Walela. Should she stop and ask someone?

"Did you lose your way? This isn't where white folks come."

Kate stopped and looked behind her. Two Cherokee boys, probably fourteen or fifteen, stood beside the bicycles. Their brown skin glistened in the heat, and their black hair brushed against their bare shoulders. They stared at her with chest-nut-brown eyes.

"Are you talking to me?" Kate asked.

"See any other white girls around here?" the taller of the boys asked.

Kate glanced around the street and then brought her gaze back to them. The shock at being called *white* trapped a response in her throat.

"What are you doing here anyway?" the stockier boy asked.

Kate's voice finally emerged. "I'm not a white girl," she said, chuckling at the absurdity. "I've actually never been called *white* in my life."

The taller boy stepped forward, and his high forehead

creased when his eyebrows pinched together. "You look like a white girl to me."

"Well," the stockier boy said, "she does look a little brown."

Kate couldn't stop the laugh of indignation. She was too white for the Cherokee village and too dark for Mystic Water. "My mama is Ama Muir, and this is her tribe, which makes it mine."

Both boys looked stunned, but the taller boy recovered faster. "You must be a mix then."

The front door on the nearest house opened, and an elderly woman stepped out onto the low, covered porch. The potted lantana on her porch shivered as new blooms opened. Both boys snapped to attention and greeted her. The stout woman wore her silvery hair long and loose. Her bright-pink shirt accented her deep caramel skin. Life lines contoured her face, and her small, round eyes turned down at the corners and nearly disappeared with her disapproving expression.

"Jistu, Tokala," the woman said. "That is no way to treat family or a guest. Apologize and go."

To their credit, the boys looked sincerely ashamed and apologized quickly. Then they jumped on their bikes and rode off, leaving a trail of dust behind them. Kate turned back to the woman to see she was smiling.

"Come in," she said. "I wondered when you'd show up." The woman shuffled back through her front door, leaving it open for Kate to follow.

Kate hesitated and then stepped onto the slatted porch. The blooming lantana leaned toward her, and she bent over to caress the blooms in greeting. Kate moved to stand in the open doorway and peered into the house. "Excuse me? Were you expecting

someone?" Perhaps the woman was confused. Kate stared into the quiet light-filled living room. A ceiling fan clicked above a forest-green couch with faded patches where the fabric had worn thin. A handwoven rug spread out across the oak wood floors.

The woman moved into view in the living room. Her eyes were so dark it was impossible to see where the pupils ended and the irises began. "You are Kate Muir, yes?" Kate nodded. "And you were looking for me, yes?"

"Are you Aurora Catawnee?" Kate asked, fully stepping into the house and closing the door.

The woman nodded and walked away. Kate followed her into the attached kitchen, which was tidy and as small as Kate's bedroom. Wood cabinets hung above and were tucked below the sparkle-flecked ivory countertops. Salmon-colored walls showed signs of fading in the sunlight, and the linoleum floor, although clean, appeared worn down, brown, and muddy green. The copper hood vent above the stove and the copper drawer and cabinet pulls shined in the sun rays coming through the one curtained window in the room. A kettle whistled on the stove, and Aurora lifted it and poured boiling water into two stoneware mugs. Then she dropped a tea strainer into each one. Kate smelled lavender immediately.

"You're making lavender tea?" Kate asked, taking the offered mug from Aurora and following her into the living room.

Aurora sat on the couch and motioned for Kate to sit. "That's why you're here, yes?"

The mug trembled in Kate's hand, and she steadied herself as she settled onto the threadbare cushion.

"Before you ask, no, I don't have the vision, but why else would you be here? Ama's daughter, who I haven't seen in years,

shows up in the village after all this time. Ama has kept you away long enough, and finally you've made your own decision to find answers."

Kate cupped the mug tightly in both hands, feeling her pulse quicken at her throat. "And you have answers?"

Aurora smiled, lifting her full cheeks, deepening the lines framing her mouth. "I have some." She closed her eyes, inhaled the steam rising from the mug, and exhaled with a smile. She sipped the tea and raised her eyebrows. "Are you going to ask, or will we drink our tea in silence?"

Kate placed the mug on an end table, not trusting herself to stay balanced. She wrung her hands together in her lap. "I don't know where to start."

"Everyone starts at the beginning, but maybe you want to start in the middle, keep it interesting."

Kate relaxed at seeing Aurora's smirk. "Evan told me I should talk to you, but that was six years ago."

"Smart boy," Aurora said. "Why didn't you?"

Kate glanced down into her lap, feeling shame warm her cheeks.

"Ah, I see," she said. "You've been told I was the crazy lady." Aurora shrugged. "Is that any different from how you think of yourself?"

Kate's head snapped up, and she gaped at Aurora. It was as though the older woman had a front-row seat inside Kate's mind. How many times had Kate referred to herself as crazy? "Also cursed."

"Cursed?" Aurora said, appearing sincerely surprised.

"Did you know my great-grandmother?" Kate asked.

Aurora nodded. "She was a few years older than me, but we

grew up together."

Kate fidgeted on the cushion. "So you know about her curse."

Aurora sipped her tea. Crows cawed nearby, filling the silence with their cries. "I believe you mean her *sacred gift*."

Kate's laugh sounded hollow. "From what I hear, she didn't think of it as a gift, and neither does my mama."

Aurora placed her mug on the end table nearest her. When she turned back toward Kate, her eyes looked as black and hard as obsidian. "When only a piece of the truth is known, it's impossible to have clarity. Ama can't see outside of her own vision of the truth. She knows very little about her own grandmother."

Kate leaned forward, wide-eyed, almost hopeful that Aurora held some shred of information that might save Kate from a life of lunacy. "What do you know about her?"

Aurora's features softened like someone recalling a fond memory. "She was a wonderful girl. Clever, kind, quick-witted, and hard working. Very loving and funny too." Her lips pulled into a frown. "But after her visions started, she retreated into herself. She was ashamed of her abilities, said she shouldn't know such things about the people around her. So rather than embrace her gift and use it to help people, she fought against herself and tried to force her gift into what best suited her. She tried to pretend she didn't have it, and she became like a woman with a trapped cougar inside her. Violent, ill-tempered, unhappy."

Kate's body trembled on the couch, causing her teeth to chatter. She clamped her jaw tightly until she could control the shudder. "You think she could have embraced her gift and helped people? How?"

Aurora's confused expression caused her to pause without responding right away. The silence dragged on so long that Kate

reached for her mug of tea and gulped it down. "You see visions, yes?" Aurora asked. Kate nodded. "They are of the future, yes? Have you seen them *show up* in the present?

Kate nodded slowly, thinking about Evan and then about Dani most recently at Scooper's.

"Then you understand what I mean," Aurora said. "If you have a premonition of me falling off a ladder, would you not call me and tell me to avoid ladders or to be more careful? Time is irrelevant, yes, and more like water than like a straight line, so maybe you wouldn't know *when* I might come to harm on a ladder, but wouldn't it be worth it to warn me?"

Kate's heart pounded so quickly that she felt almost sick to her stomach. "But . . . but Mama said I can't alter the future or tell anyone about it."

Aurora's eyes widened as her nostrils flared. Her body went so rigid, she looked more like a statue than human.

Kate exhaled a shuddering breath. "Is that not true?"

"You remember what I said about having a piece of truth? Ama has the tiniest sliver, and somehow she believes she knows all. What else did she tell you?"

Kate felt a stab of guilt at betraying her mama, but she *needed* to know what Aurora knew about her visions. "She said it was a curse and that I would slowly lose my mind. The only thing that would slow the process and maybe give me some relief from the visions would be to drink lavender tea."

Aurora shook her head and a heaviness settled around her, causing her shoulders to slump. "The things we tell our children to protect them when it actually hurts them." She reached out and took Kate's hand. Aurora's leathery hand was warm and soft in Kate's, and she gave Kate's fingers a gentle squeeze before

pulling her hand back into her own lap.

"She said there were rules."

Aurora asked, "Who made these rules?"

Kate had wondered the same thing. "I don't know." Then in a flash of rebelliousness, she said, "Maybe some rules need to be broken."

Aurora caught Kate's gaze and smiled slowly. "Ama's intentions were to protect you, but her own fears have muddied the waters. That's why she stopped bringing you here. Did you know that?" Kate shook her head. "Most of our children are taught here in the village school, but Ama didn't want you and Evan to be separated from the children in town. She hoped by keeping you away and sending you to school there, you would be seen as 'one of them' rather than as someone different."

Kate made a scoffing noise. "I feel like Mama *doesn't* want me to fit in with them. She's constantly insisting I live a life that makes me different. My clothes, my activities, everything. Anyway, her plan to send us to school in town to ensure we wouldn't be seen as different didn't work well for me, but Evan fit in so easily."

"You know why?" Aurora asked. "Because he acted like he belonged there. They never questioned him. You, on the other hand, blare your difference like a siren." Aurora held open her hands. "But, Little Blackbird, you were not made to fit in with the ordinary folk. Once you stop fighting who you are, then you can embrace all of you, even your sacred gift."

Kate leaned back against the soft couch, her mind racing with thoughts and more questions. "You think there's a chance I won't lose my mind to the curse?"

Aurora frowned. "You keep calling it a curse and you will.

Watch your words. Change them. Make them help you, not harm you."

Kate cleared her throat and felt optimism sparkle inside her. "You think there's a chance I won't lose my mind to my sacred gift?"

Aurora's deep belly laugh filled the small living room. "What do you think?"

Kate answered honestly, "I haven't felt this hopeful in years."

Aurora's genuine smile swelled Kate's heart. "There's your answer."

CHAPTER 17

FOLLOWING KATE'S REVELATORY TALK WITH AURORA, KATE spent the first few days afterward in a mental fog. She felt like someone had taken the completed puzzle of her life and tossed it into the air, causing pieces to scatter everywhere. It was as though someone had unlocked a door, a door she'd never seen before, and given her permission to walk through. She battled what she'd been taught against new possibilities. What if the rule makers weren't the only people who were wrong? What if her mama had been too?

Kate wasn't sure how to handle finding out her parents were wrong about life or that they had taught her untruths. Aurora *had* told Kate that Ama thought she was doing the right thing according to her own beliefs. But what happened when Kate's beliefs didn't fit with her mama's?

When the questions became too complicated or the flowers in the garden acted too strangely because of her emotions, Kate shifted her thoughts to more pleasant ones, like Geoffrey. She hadn't seen him in days, not since their encounter at The Story Keeper, but Charlotte had called last night to catch Kate up on the latest news and to invite her to the carnival.

According to Charlotte, Geoffrey and a few of his friends had been preparing for their move to the university. They'd been to campus for orientation and to buy their course books. They'd also been moving personal belongings into the dorms. The university required all freshmen to live on campus, and the reality of Geoffrey moving away became more solid than ever. Charlotte also mentioned that Matthias had applied to medical school, which was no surprise, but the Hamiltons had been celebrating that too.

Although the temptation to mope attempted to smother her happiness, Kate focused on the upcoming carnival. Charlotte invited Kate to join them at Martha's house so they could all ride together, and Kate desperately wanted to. She watched and waited for the perfect moment to ask her parents, which was no easy feat since her mama had been more tense and displeased ever since she and Kate visited the Cherokee village together. One night after dinner, Sean had gotten Ama to laugh, and Kate knew it could be her only opportunity. She sprung the request on them, and caught in an instant of joy, they both agreed.

But a few days later when it came time for the carnival, Kate had to beg her parents to drop her off at Martha's house. Ama complained that they'd always gone to the carnival as a family, but Sean convinced her mama to let Kate go with her friends. *Friends*, Kate thought. Even now in her mind the word sounded sacred, and she buried it in her chest just to feel its warmth. Then Ama argued that Kate didn't need to wear the blue dress that Martha had given her because it wasn't "sensible attire" for a carnival. Kate remembered Aurora said Ama wanted her children to fit in with the other kids in town, so Kate explained that *her friends* would be dressed similarly, and she only wanted to

belong. Ama relented.

Sean parked in the Lees' driveway, and Ama turned around in the front seat to look at Kate. "Did you drink your tea?"

Kate nodded. "Yes, ma'am."

"Don't waste your money on carnival games. They're all rigged. Don't get on any rides with boys, and stay away from the Ferris wheel. Don't eat too much sugar or fried food, or you'll pay for it later. Don't go into the—"

"Mama," Kate said, "maybe the list of what I *can* do will be shorter."

Sean snorted a laugh in the front seat, and Ama glared at him. He propped his arm on the seat and looked over his shoulder at Kate. "What your mom means is have fun."

"That's not what I mean," Ama argued.

"Can I go?" Kate asked. As soon as Sean agreed, Kate jumped out of the car, saying, "I'll meet up with you later." Then she ran up the path leading to the Lees' front porch.

Before Kate could ring the doorbell, Betsy threw open the front door wearing a red sleeveless dress cinched at the waist with a chunky black belt. She grabbed Kate's arm and pulled her upstairs where Nat King Cole blared from Martha's bedroom. They spent the next half hour changing outfits, applying makeup, fixing their hair, and giggling. Knowing she would be seeing Geoffrey soon, Kate thought she might explode with happiness.

Martha, Betsy, Charlotte, and Kate piled into Charlotte's Chevy Nomad. The radio blasted so loudly that the windows rattled in their frames, and the girls sang along with Buddy Holly at the top of their lungs. Kate smiled so widely that her cheeks ached.

Kate looked down at her new pair of black ballet flats, a gift from her Daddy. She'd nearly cried when she opened the shoebox

and saw them shining beneath white tissue paper. She clicked her heels together and thought about Geoffrey and how he might react to this new version of her. With her hair done and makeup applied, would he see her as someone to be proud of? Would he describe her as his knockout girlfriend?

Charlotte pulled into the field that hugged one side of the carnival, which acted as a temporary parking lot for the crowd. The girls climbed out and straightened their clothes and checked their makeup in the side-view mirror. Martha twirled and watched her blurry striped reflection spin in the car's paint.

Charlotte spritzed on perfume and tossed the bottle into the front seat. "Let's go," she said with a wave.

Long before they paid the admission fee, received handfuls of pink tickets, and entered through the arched gateway into the carnival, Kate smelled popcorn, melting sugar, and hot frying oil. Colorful lights twinkled and pulsed all around her. The Ferris wheel looked like a circular rainbow of color twirling round and round against the starry night sky. A multitude of sounds peppered the air—shouts, laughter, the pipe-organ music of the carousel, carnival workers calling people to their rides and booths, ringing bells. When she entered the carnival, Kate spun around in a complete circle as she'd always done as a child, trying to take everything in all at once.

Charlotte touched her arm and motioned with her head. "Come on, Kate. Sally is already here, and so are the guys."

Geoffrey, Matthias, and Mikey sat at a game booth firing water pistols into the mouths of clowns while the clown hats rose higher and higher in a race to the top. The guys taunted one another, and when Kate heard Geoffrey's laughter, her heart squeezed. Just the sound of his voice caused her pulse to race.

They hadn't spent any time together in days, and she was eager to be near him.

Sally sat on the stool next to Matthias, but she wasn't playing the game with them. Instead, she sat pulling spun sugar from a ball of cotton candy that looked like a fluffy pink balloon on a cardboard stick. Ted and John smoked cigarettes off to the side of the booth while watching to see who'd win the game.

Ted looked away from the clowns and noticed the girls. He dropped his dying cigarette onto the dirt and snuffed it with the toe of his shoe. "Check out these beauties." He ogled them in a way that made Kate feel like she had ants on her skin.

Martha leaned over Geoffrey's shoulder. "Who's winning?"

He glanced up at her and then cursed as his clown hat lost momentum. "I was until you distracted me."

Martha laughed and shoved his shoulder. Matthias's clown hat set off a whirl of alarms and blinking bulbs as it reached the top first.

Mikey replaced his water gun into its holster. "Matt, did it ever occur to you to let someone else win?"

Matthias grinned. "Never."

The booth operator handed Matthias a stuffed koala bear with marble-size black eyes and a red bow tie. Matthias quickly passed the prize to the nearest girl, Charlotte. Her shock faded into a sweet smile. Kate recognized the longing in Charlotte's eyes, but Matthias caught sight of Kate, and she fidgeted beneath his intense stare.

Kate peered down to make sure her dress was presentable and her shoes weren't disgusting from walking through the field. When she glanced up, Matthias still watched her with knit eyebrows.

Geoffrey's eyes roved over the group. He scowled at Martha. "I thought y'all were bringing Kate."

"They did," Matthias said, elbowing Geoffrey in the ribs and nodding toward Kate.

She attempted a genuine smile and lifted her hand in a small wave.

Geoffrey's thick eyebrows rose on his high forehead. "Oh my God," he said, crossing the center of the group and standing in front of her. He grabbed both of her hands and then spun her around. "Would you look at you? You look so different."

Kate stopped spinning. "Different good?" Her breath held. Someone squealed from a carnival ride.

"God, yes," he said.

Betsy nudged Geoffrey with her elbow. "Doesn't she look like Ava Gardner?"

Geoffrey nodded his head. Disbelief dilated his pupils, rimming them with a thin line of gold. "You could be her twin. Her better-looking twin." He touched Kate's hair. "I like this."

Kate smiled at the ground, shivering as his hands slipped through strands of her curls.

Martha stomped over. Her red lipstick had smudged onto her top teeth. "Come on. Are we going to stand here all night, or are we going to ride something?"

Ted hooked one arm through Martha's. "Only if you're my riding partner." He pulled a silver monogrammed flask from his shirt pocket. "Pick me up?"

Martha grinned up at him, batted her eyelashes, and uncorked the flask. She swigged it and then returned the flask to Ted. "Let's go." She tossed her blond hair over her shoulder. "Are y'all coming or not?" she said, walking off with Ted and not

waiting for a response. They pushed a path through the crowd.

"Shall we?" Geoffrey asked. He slid his arm around her shoulders and tugged her toward him. Kate leaned into the warmth of his body, wondering if the night could be any more wonderful than it already was.

They found Martha and Ted standing in line for the House of Mirrors, and the rest of the group filed in behind them. Sally shared her cotton candy with Mikey and John, focusing her attention on each boy in turn as though she hadn't yet decided which one she wanted to attract. Geoffrey grinned at Kate like he was as excited to see her as she was to see him after the string of days apart.

"What?" Kate asked, smoothing her hand down her hair.

"You," he said, leaning his face toward hers. The scent of his cologne mingled with the smell of dry hay that lined the pathways. "You look amazing. I really want to kiss you."

Kate knew Geoffrey would kiss her right then, right there, if she let him, but it wasn't proper, and there were too many people around. "Not here."

He tilted his head toward the fun house. "Inside?" He leaned closer, and his whisper tickled her ear. "Should I add it to the list?"

John pushed a silver flask into Geoffrey's shoulder, breaking his close contact with Kate. She caught sight of a monogram that engraved the metal before Geoffrey's thin fingers grasped it. He swilled the liquid around in the flask and then took a sip. He offered it Kate.

She shook her head, glancing around at the others. Would Charlotte or Betsy drink tonight? Would she be the only girl not participating? The pungent scent of alcohol floated around them

before the next breeze snatched it away.

"Want something to drink? A Coke?" Geoffrey asked. "Looks like we'll be in this line for a while."

"A Coke would be nice, thank you."

Geoffrey leaned down and kissed the top of her head before hurrying off toward the nearest concession stand. Corn kernels burst out of large vats and filled glass machines with buttery fluffy popcorn. Hotdogs rotated beneath heat lamps. The sizzle of frying dough beckoned people from every direction. A red balloon, released by a young girl, drifted into the night sky, and Kate followed its ascent until the darkness absorbed it. Betsy's red hair ribbon untied itself, and Charlotte paused in her conversation with Matthias to help retie the bow.

Matthias shifted his body to face Kate. His blue eyes studied her. "New look?"

Kate shrugged. "I guess."

He pushed his hands into his pockets. "It'll take a bit of getting used to."

A scream erupted from the House of Mirrors, and a group of high school kids stumbled out the exit, laughing and hitting one another.

She returned her attention to Matthias. His expression unnerved her. She couldn't tell if he was disappointed or uncertain. Kate clasped her hands together to stop herself from combing her fingers through her hair. "Why? It's still me."

"Is it?"

She narrowed her eyes as annoyance sprang to life within her. How dare he act as though she were a different person just because she wanted to look like the other girls. What was the big deal if she wanted to belong? It didn't matter in that moment that

Matthias was asking the same question she had asked herself. "Of course it's still me. A better version." Heat spread through her belly, and she adjusted her belt.

Matthias shook his head. "A better version implies that the old version needed to be replaced, and I would disagree strongly with that idea."

Kate's irritation faded into wisps of surprise, circling in her chest. She stared at him. Before she could respond, Geoffrey pushed his way in between them in line. He handed her a cup filled to the brim with dark liquid. "One Coke with extra ice." He held another cup out toward John. "Top me off, will you?" John poured liquid from his flask into Geoffrey's cup.

Kate wanted to ask how much he'd had to drink, how much all the guys had been drinking, but she saw Charlotte remove a small wine bottle from her bag, and Kate didn't want to sound like the immature kid. She sipped her Coke, and so far, no one was acting in the ridiculous ways her mama had warned her happened when people got drunk. Kate wondered if Evan had ever drank with them. Would he have thought this behavior was normal?

Based on her mama's descriptions, Kate thought alcohol turned people into strange creatures who yelled and cried and threw fine china at one another, but she'd never actually seen anyone drunk before. She drank most of the Coke by the time they moved to the front of the line, so she tossed it into the trash can.

The snaggletooth man standing guard at the ride entrance asked Kate for three tickets, and she handed them over with a hesitant smile. "Is it scary?" she asked him.

He grunted. "Not when you've seen what I've seen."

Kate's mouth formed a small *o*, and Geoffrey slipped his hand into hers as they entered the House of Mirrors. Warbling music blared inside the first shadowed room, sounding as though the record player had become seasick. The floor pitched at an awkward angle, and the ceiling lowered, forcing them to bend over to walk. Soon, they were crammed into a narrow hallway that spilled out into an octagonal room with black walls and twinkling lights on the ceiling. The doorway closed behind them as they entered. The sounds changed as they entered different spaces, and this music reminded Kate of an icy wind blowing through wind chimes.

The room appeared to have no doors, which meant no way out. Kate's heartbeat gained momentum, and soon she felt the rapid pulse in her fingertips. Ted and John began moving their hands along the walls.

"There has to be a hidden door," Martha yelled over the music. She moved toward the nearest wall and slid her hands over the smooth surface.

While everyone was busy touching the walls, Geoffrey pulled Kate across the room and away from the others. In the twinkling lights, he looked down and winked at her. He motioned with his head toward the back wall and leaned toward her.

"I remember this room." He placed his hands on the wall and pushed. It cracked open, and Kate's eyes widened. "Come on."

"What about the others?" Kate asked, trying to look over her shoulder, but Geoffrey pulled her through the opening, and the wall closed behind them.

Geoffrey and Kate stood on a small landing. Through an archway she saw walls of mirrors framing concentric, circular floor panels that spun in slow, lazy circles meant to confuse the

patrons. Each floor panel moved in opposite directions, so they created a circular maze of mirrors and passageways. The room was completely devoid of sound, and the silence unnerved Kate.

"Don't worry about the others. They'll figure it out. They have Matthias, and he always finds a way," Geoffrey said. He pulled Kate's body against his. "I've been wanting to kiss you all night. You look like a movie star."

Geoffrey's mouth was warm, and he tasted slightly sour from the alcohol. She lifted up on her tiptoes and pressed herself closer to him. He slid one hand up the back of her neck and into her hair. She fisted his shirt in her hands. When she opened her eyes, she saw hundreds of Kates and Geoffreys kissing each other in the spinning mirrors. They were surrounded by themselves, lost in the moment.

Geoffrey pulled away and pushed his fingers through his hair. "God, I missed that. I can't imagine not being able to kiss you whenever I want."

She smiled into his chest. "You can." Forever.

He kissed down the side of her neck, and Kate shivered. "Whenever I want?"

She closed her eyes and sighed. "Yes."

The wall behind them swung open and knocked into Kate and Geoffrey. Matthias stepped through, followed by the rest of the group.

Martha fisted her hands on her hips. "There you are. You could have told us you found the door."

Geoffrey shrugged nonchalantly. "We just got in here."

Martha lifted an eyebrow. "Looks like you got in here long enough to have lipstick smeared on your face."

Geoffrey wiped the back of his hand across his mouth. Kate

stared at the berry stain on his hand, and she touched her finger-tips to her lips. Matthias stepped onto the first revolving platform and disappeared behind a wall of mirrors. Kate's eyes widened, but she followed him with Geoffrey close behind.

The spinning floor disoriented her immediately. She stumbled and watched herself stagger from twenty different angles. She saw Matthias in the reflection, but she couldn't see him in person. Soon, everyone's reflections spun around her as they stepped onto the platform. Their voices filled the void of silence and echoed.

Through openings in the mirrored walls, one by one, the group disappeared, and Kate spun alone on the platform, watch-ing multiplied versions of herself staring right back at her. But her reflection resembled a stranger—a more mature, prettier girl who only faintly resembled the sixteen-year-old Kate who ran around barefoot in the grass wearing patchwork skirts.

In the distance, Matthias appeared. Hundreds of him moved closer and closer to her. It was impossible for her to tell from which direction he approached her. She swayed on the platform. Then he stepped through one of the doorways, and his hand reached out and closed over her forearm, stabilizing her.

"Lost?"

Kate knew she should thank him, but his earlier comment still irritated her. "Sent to rescue me?"

Matthias chuckled. "I wasn't aware you needed saving."

She watched their reflections turn round and round, watched Matthias's smile charm her in a hundred different angles. The annoyance disappeared, and she saw her reflections smile. "Even if I did, I wouldn't admit it."

Matthias laughed again and, still holding her arm, led her toward a doorway. "Geoffrey can't stay in this section too long. It

makes him motion sick. He sent me to find you."

Kate and Matthias wove their way through the moving mirrored walls until they stepped through one final opening into a
room full of fun-house mirrors. There was a mirror that reflected
a tall paper-thin Charlotte and a mirror that made Sally's head
swell to the size of a beach ball. There was a mirror that made
Kate look as though she had been flattened and crafted into an
accordion and one that widened Martha's girth so much that she
squealed and scurried off. Geoffrey stood in front of a mirror that
shaped him like an hourglass, and he laughed, filling the room
with his mirth. He motioned Kate over. They alternated between
squatting and rising up on their tiptoes, distorting their bodies.

One set of mirrors made Betsy appear thin and long in the
face, and she hovered in front of that mirror long after everyone
else had moved on. Kate stopped just inside the tunnel that led
out of the room of mirrors and called out to her. Betsy stared at
her thinner reflection. Her shoulders dropped in a heavy sigh,
and she walked away from the illusion.

In the next section, Geoffrey waited at the bottom of a spiral
staircase that disappeared into the ceiling. Red and blue strobe
lights pulsed in the room, and as Betsy and Kate moved across
the floor, sections of tile lifted and tilted, causing them to laugh
and stumble their way toward the staircase.

Betsy pitched forward and tumbled into Geoffrey, causing
him to fall backward with her on top of him. With the tilting
floor, Kate walked toward them like a drunken sailor. She helped
Betsy to her feet before grabbing Geoffrey's hands, and the three
of them laughed. Betsy's face was redder than a red moss rose,
and after apologizing to Geoffrey, she hurried up the staircase.

Geoffrey made a sweeping motion with his arm. "After you,
milady."

Kate leaped onto the bottom stair and turned to face him. The laughter warmed her cheeks and made her bold. She was nearly his exact height, so she put her hands on his cheeks and kissed him. When she pulled back, Geoffrey's amused expression excited her. She giggled and climbed the stairs.

The stairs rose into a small room with no way out except for a red slide that slipped through the floor and emptied into a pit of colorful plastic balls. The others jumped around and threw balls at one another. She glanced over her shoulder at Geoffrey before gripping the edges of the slide and launching herself forward. The wind whooshed past her cheeks, and she held her breath as she landed, her body dispersing a wave of balls in every direction. As soon as Kate stood, Charlotte tossed an armful of balls over Kate's head like a confetti parade. Geoffrey landed behind Kate and joined in the fray. Kate lurched through the pit and tossed balls at anyone she saw as she slogged toward the door.

The final room contained a bridge connecting the last platform to an enormous spinning barrel that would return them to the carnival. Kate watched the group bumble through the rotating barrel and recognized that the faster she moved, the less likely she would be to fall and flounder on the bottom like John and Ted. She waited for everyone to pass through, and once Geoffrey stood on the outside and waved to her, she ran as fast as she could. She plowed through the barrel, barely losing her step, and nearly knocked Geoffrey off the exit platform. He wrapped his arms around her to stop them from falling down the stairs, and they burst into laughter. The group waited for them at the bottom, and Kate's chest swelled with happiness at the sight of their smiling faces. Nothing could mar the sheer perfection of this night.

CHAPTER 18

AMA'S RULE TO STAY OFF THE FERRIS WHEEL HAD BEEN BROKEN. Geoffrey wanted to take Kate on the ride, and when their gently rocking bucket paused at the top of wheel, giving them an aerial lit-up view of the whole carnival, Geoffrey kissed her. While she grinned and leaned against him, he marked off *Kiss Kate on a Ferris wheel* from their imaginary list. Then he marked off kissing her behind the Tilt-A-Whirl, kissing her on the bumper cars, kissing her as the Caterpillar zoomed, and kissing her in a photo booth. Geoffrey pocketed the eight black-and-white photos for safekeeping but promised to give her half of them before they went home.

Kate's tickets were dwindling, but Geoffrey told her he had a pocketful of money. He assured her they had more rides to mark off their list. As the evening grew later, the carnival-goers shifted from young children and their parents to older youth and adults. The conversations were louder and bawdier, with some conducted in shadowy corners.

The colors in the air darkened at the edges, midnight blues and indigo with bursts of crimson. Even the carnival workers had changed shifts. The jovial, rounded faces had been replaced

with thinner, hungrier smiles.

Charlotte linked her arm through Kate's. "Isn't this the best?" Charlotte squeezed their arms together and smiled, showing nearly all of her teeth.

Kate nodded. Charlotte's cheeks were bright pink, and her glassy eyes shined. A hint of sweetness lingered around her, left behind by the mini bottles of red wine Charlotte had hidden in her purse. Matthias, Geoffrey, and Mikey stopped at the fried dough and corndog concession and waited in line so they could buy enough servings for everyone.

Charlotte leaned toward Kate, coming so close their noses almost touched. "Geoffrey seems to really like you."

Kate's eyes located Geoffrey. He joked with his brother and Mikey. "I really like him." A flush crept into her cheeks.

Martha bounced over. Her words slurred thick and syrupy when she spoke. One of her pinned-back curls had escaped and fell against her rouged cheek. "Ted heard there was someone selling alcohol to minors behind Madame Daphne's tent, so we're going for refills." She motioned toward the concession stand with her head. "I told them. You coming?"

As they weaved their way toward the fortune teller's tent, Kate's parents stepped through an opening in the crowd. Ama raised her hand in greeting, jangling an armful of colorful bracelets, and Sean lifted his striped bag of popcorn as a form of hello.

"There you are," her mama said, scanning the faces around Kate. "Hello."

The girls said hello, but Ted and John kept walking. Martha and Sally lingered behind Betsy and Charlotte, pretending to be interested in a nearby ring toss game. Kate shifted on her feet. "Hey, Mama."

"We've been looking all over for you," Ama said. "You said were going to meet up with us, but only after you left did I realize we never said where or when. We have to ride the carousel."

Martha snickered. "I haven't ridden the carousel since I was eleven."

Kate narrowed her eyes at Martha. Then she grabbed Ama's forearm and led her parents away from the group. "I'll meet up with you at the *tent*," she said, giving emphasis to the word so they would understand which tent she meant. Charlotte nodded before she herded the girls away. "Mama, I'm hanging out with friends."

Ama waited for Kate to say more. Kate glanced at Sean, but he kept shoving handfuls of popcorn into his mouth. A group of teenagers sitting on potato sacks raced down the Alpine Slide, whooping as they slid.

"Nobody else's parents are trying to get them to ride kiddie rides."

Ama frowned. "Kiddie rides? We ride the carousel every year. You love it. The horse with the rainbow mane? He's waiting for you. What is it you call him?"

"Sparkle, right?" Sean said.

Kate groaned and tried to spot the girls, but the crowds of people thickened, and her friends were already gone. Above the throngs of people, the flag emblazoned with an eye waved above Madame Daphne's tent marking where Kate would find them. "Mama, not this year, okay? I'm hanging out with friends. I can't be seen riding the kiddie ride. We're doing other stuff."

"Other stuff?" Ama's chin lifted. "You're giving up something you love because of what others think?"

"It's not that," Kate argued. But maybe it was just a little

bit. Martha would tease her relentlessly if she flitted off to ride Sparkle on the carousel.

"It's fine." Ama raised her hands in resignation. Her bracelets sparkled like jewels. "We'll see you at home." She grabbed Sean's arm and led him away.

Guilt pooled in Kate's stomach like hot turpentine. "Mama." Ama turned. "Don't be mad."

Ama's forced smile was a poor representation of the ones that lifted her cheeks and framed her lips with curved lines. "I'm not mad. Have fun, Little Blackbird."

Her parents walked away, leaving Kate standing alone in a sea of people parting around her. Ama would have to get over it because there was no way Kate was going to forfeit this night with Geoffrey and her friends. She only had so many days left before he would be leaving. Kate set off to find the group, using Madame Daphne's flapping flag as a guide.

Voices carried from the backside of the tent, and Kate slipped alongside the thick purple canvas, sliding one hand against the rough fabric. She stopped short of rounding the corner and joining her friends when she heard her name.

"What's Geoffrey doing with Kate?" Ted asked. "He can't be serious. Her brother was okay, but her? No. Kiss the Indian and get it out of your system, but tell me they aren't going steady."

No one spoke for a few breaths. Screams erupted from the Cliffhanger ride. The nearby arcade spit tickets and whirled an alarm as someone became the best sharpshooter around.

Betsy said, "I think they are going steady." She cleared her throat. "At least that's the way she described it to us, didn't she?"

"Who cares if they're dating?" Charlotte asked. "There's nothing wrong with her."

John agreed. "She's nice."

Ted laughed. "Nice isn't going to cut it with his mom. I bet Mrs. Hamilton doesn't even know he's been running around with the witch's daughter."

Kate's throat closed. She fisted her dress in her hands and swayed as though she'd just climbed off the Hurricane, still spinning, still unsure of her footing.

"Don't be stupid, Ted," Charlotte argued. "Her mama's not a witch."

More of Ted's laughter snaked around the tent and curled around Kate's feet. "You sure about that?"

Clinking bottles disrupted the conversation. "You want all these filled?" a stranger's voice asked.

Ted grunted. "Yeah, I can pay for it."

Kate stepped forward far enough so she could peek around the edge of the canvas tent yet remain hidden from their view. A young man, probably in his late twenties, knelt over a cardboard box filled with an assortment of alcohol contained in unlabeled glass bottles. He filled the group's flasks.

Martha twirled a piece of her blond hair around her finger. "You know Geoffrey. He has the attention span of a toddler. One second he's into you, and the next he wants something new. Kate is weird enough that he wanted to try her out. He'll get tired of her the way he gets tired of everyone."

Ted lit a cigarette and pulled in a long drag. He blew warped smoke rings into the night sky. "You mean the way he got tired of you last summer?"

Martha's face pinched. "He didn't get tired of me. We decided we were better off as friends. That's all."

Ted scoffed. "Friends who snuck around all last school year,

necking in closets and empty classrooms?"

Sally gasped. "You were doing that all year with him?"

Martha shrugged. "Maybe I was. So what? Don't have a cow, Sally."

Kate pressed her hands against her stomach. Her imagination created scenes of Martha and her blood-red lips kissing Geoffrey, holding on to him the way Kate did. She pictured Geoffrey's arms wrapped around Martha's waist and his hands on her curves. Geoffrey had never once mentioned that he and Martha had been together. Was Kate his newest shiny plaything, something he would toss when he left for college? She glanced down at the dwindling pen lines on her palm—seven marks—indicating when Geoffrey would leave.

Ted pointed his burning cigarette at Martha. "Why are you dressing her up like a baby doll, parading her around?"

Martha tossed her hands into the air. "If Geoffrey is going to insist on dragging her around town, the least I can do is make her look decent."

Sally snickered.

Charlotte shook her head. "Martha—"

"What?" Martha snapped, whirling around to face Charlotte. "Tell me she doesn't look like a somewhat normal person now. Tell me you wouldn't have been ashamed to be seen around town with her looking like an Indian throwaway."

Kate's stomach lurched. Wasn't Martha supposed to be her friend? Kate felt a splintering starting in her gut and cracking all the way up her chest. She couldn't breathe. She pressed her hand to her chest just so she could feel her heartbeat, but she felt nothing. Had Geoffrey already stolen it? Or had she given it to him as though it were free, as though giving her heart away were

easy and painless? Pointed blades of yellow grass sprouted from the edges of the tent, rising to nearly knee height.

"Where is everybody?"

Kate reeled around as Geoffrey, Matthias, and Mikey, laden down with paper plates, popcorn bags, and cardboard containers packed with food, stepped over ropes and cables on their way to her. Kate pointed because she couldn't speak. Geoffrey smiled at her and kept walking.

"Dinner's served," he called as he rounded the tent.

"About time," Ted said. "I'm starving."

Mikey passed by, but Matthias stopped. "You okay? You look kinda . . . seasick."

Kate's bottom lip trembled, so she pressed her lips together. She feared if she opened her mouth and said anything she'd blurt, "I want to go home" and sound like a child. But the truth was that she did want to go home and lock the window tight, hide beneath the covers, and not come out of her room again until she had forgotten about all of them. She stared as Geoffrey handed out plates of food.

The flag above Madame Daphne's tent whipped and snapped in a gust of wind that stormed through the carnival. Balloons were snatched from hands, tent openings flapped against their ropes, and dust clouds raced across the fairgrounds. Martha squealed as her dress lifted, and she pressed it against her legs, but her flirtatious laughter betrayed her. She glanced around to see who'd noticed the creamy skin on her thighs. Ted winked at her.

Matthias pressed his elbow into Kate's arm, and she moved her gaze to him.

"Hey," he said. "You okay?"

"I thought . . ." She shook her head. She thought they were her friends. "It's nothing."

Matthias motioned toward the side of the tent, a signal they should join the others, and Kate followed like an obedient child.

Powdered sugar smudged Martha's lipstick as she poked a piece of fried dough into her mouth. Ted made a joke, and Martha laughed louder than necessary, leaning against his arm, spilling sugar from her plate like a snowstorm. Sally joined in with the laughter, filling the night with her nasal, staccato laughs.

Charlotte walked over and took a bag of popcorn from Matthias's hands. Betsy stared at a fried cake hidden beneath a mound of snow-white sugar. She dipped one finger into the powder and licked it hesitantly. Then she scanned the group to see who might be watching before breaking off large chunks of cake and eating them as quickly as possible. Sally and John tapped their flasks together before testing the new drink. Ted handed a five-dollar bill to the young man who then shoved the bill into a cookie tin. Geoffrey squirted mustard on a corndog while Mikey smeared his through a blob of ketchup. They discussed riding the Scrambler.

Kate stood among them but on the outside edge of their circle. All she'd ever wanted was to fit in, to be a part of a friend group, to laugh with other girls, to be noticed by the boys. Now, having been allowed inside their group—if only for a brief few weeks—she felt more alone than when she'd had no one to call a friend. A voice whispered in her head, *They never accepted you. You could never win them over like Evan did. You're nothing like him.* Her gaze drifted to Geoffrey. He looked away from Mikey and smiled at her. In two long strides, he stood by her side.

He offered her a plate of french fries. "Hungry?"

Kate shook her head. She wanted to smile, but she felt rejected

and betrayed. Charlotte and Betsy hadn't exactly said anything awful about her. Charlotte had even attempted to argue on Kate's behalf, for which Kate knew she should feel some relief. But the shock of being on the receiving end of Martha's meanness and learning about her relationship with Geoffrey sent Kate's mind spinning.

Geoffrey leaned down toward Kate. "You okay? Did the last ride get to you?"

Kate still had Geoffrey, didn't she? It didn't matter what Martha said. Martha was wrong. Martha didn't know how Geoffrey looked at Kate or how he held her close. Martha had never seen them laughing together or sitting by the river counting fireflies.

"The last few minutes I've really felt it," Kate said.

Geoffrey nodded. "Give it a few minutes. We can ride something easy next. Maybe the Tunnel of Love?"

Kate leaned toward his grin, pulled in by the need for affirmation, the need to know he didn't reject her the way the others did. She pressed her face against his arm. His body warmth spread through her cheek, down her neck, and trickled into her chest. She inhaled slowly and exhaled. "Maybe just the two of us?" She didn't care if she and Geoffrey lost the group in the carnival. They could lose them forever.

Geoffrey kissed the top of her head. "Just the way I like it."

Martha stumbled forward, and she dropped her empty paper plate onto the ground. "Ted thinks he's the best at the milk-bottle game. Anyone up for the challenge?"

Ted draped his arm around Martha's shoulders. "It's wager time. John? Matt?"

John stepped forward. "Count me in. I have an arm for these sorts of games."

Ted laughed. "And that's about all you have an arm for."

John shoved Ted, and the two of them walked around the tent. The rest of the group followed. Geoffrey slipped his hand into Kate's and leaned to whisper in her ear. "We'll play this one game, and then we can wander off."

Martha's obnoxious snicker grated on Kate, and even looking at Martha twisted her stomach. "Would you do that for me?" Kate asked. The separation between her and the group widened with each step they took through the carnival. Fitting in with them now felt like pushing through a thicket of thorns.

Geoffrey squeezed her hand. "Losing this bunch to spend time with you? That's easy."

Kate held on to him, grabbing his words and shoving them deep into her chest where they pacified the ache, where they reassured her that Geoffrey wanted to be with her. She wasn't just some girl who was weird enough to catch Geoffrey's attention for a while like Martha claimed. Geoffrey cared about her.

They gathered around the Milk Bottle Toss. Ted and John stepped up to hurl the first balls at the wooden bottles. Ted knocked the top bottle from the stack, and two of John's bottles shot from their platform like missiles. Their next two throws missed the targets. The booth operator stacked the bottles again, and Ted asked for a new competitor. Geoffrey winked at Kate and volunteered.

Geoffrey dropped tickets into the operator's open hand. "Let's see if Ted is the better man."

Ted motioned toward the throw line. "Losers first."

Geoffrey's first toss dislodged the top milk bottle. His second toss hit the remaining two bottles but failed to knock them from the platform. His last throw missed the bottles entirely.

Ted slapped Geoffrey on the back. "Let me show you how

it's done."

Martha and Sally clapped their hands together and cheered for Ted. He pulled back his arm and launched the ball. All three bottles exploded from the platform. Martha bounced up and down, tossing her curls over her shoulder. Kate looked away. Clouds slunk across the night sky and blotted out the stars.

Geoffrey cleared his throat. "I was going to win you a bear."

Kate met his gaze. "Next time."

"Come pick a prize, Martha," Ted called.

Mikey walked over to Geoffrey. "It's going to take Martha an hour to choose her prize. Wanna ride the Scrambler now?"

Geoffrey looked at Kate, and she shrugged. "I'll be here when you're done."

"Hey, Matthias," Mikey shouted. "Come on."

Kate crossed her arms over her chest and hugged herself while she watched Geoffrey, Matthias, and Mikey amble over to stand in line for the Scrambler.

Martha's annoying voice rose above the carnival noise. "No, that one. The one with the necklace."

Sally snickered. "That necklace is plastic, Martha."

"But red is my lucky color, and I never turn down jewelry," she slurred, and both girls burst into giggles.

The man behind the booth handed Martha an oversize white bear wearing a necklace made of red beads with an octagonal ruby plastic pendant. Martha squeezed the bear and thanked Ted. Then she pulled the necklace off the bear and strung it over her own neck. She lifted the pendant and flashed a toothy smile, displaying the gap between her front teeth.

Her thick eyelashes fluttered. "I can see myself in the reflection."

"Are you in *love*, Martha?" Sally teased.

The plastic pendant caught the blinking lights around the booth and shot sparkles into the air. Kate flinched as the light flashed in her eyes. Her breath hitched. A veil dropped over her vision, obscuring the carnival, and broken images appeared in front of her eyes. *She felt herself in a dark confined space. Sticky hands pressed against her skin. Red beads dropped like hail, bouncing off her face. Panicked breaths bubbled up her throat.*

Kate staggered sideways. She bumped into a light pole and bent over, putting her hands on her knees and blinking so rapidly that it looked as though she were looking at a strobe light. A poison ivy vine pushed up out of the earth and wound around the light pole. The premonition, the car, the groping hands. Kate panicked, and her vision blurred. Whatever was coming, she had to stop it.

CHAPTER 19

THE POISON IVY LEAVES DOUBLED IN SIZE, AND KATE PUSHED herself upright. She kept one hand against the light pole for support, making sure not to touch the ivy vine. Bile rose in her throat, so she clenched her jaw. Martha propped the bear on her hip as though she held a toddler, and she slid the red plastic beads through her fingers.

"Let's get out of here and drive up to Look-Off Pointe," Ted said.

Martha sashayed toward him. The ruby pendant bounced against her chest as she moved. "I love that idea."

Sally enthusiastically clapped her hands together and momentarily lost her balance, the alcohol obviously affecting her. "Me too."

Martha surveyed the group. "How many cars do we have?"

Charlotte said, "I drove."

Ted nodded. "So did I. Geoffrey and John drove too. We can split up if we want." He leered at Martha.

Martha grinned at him with a smile that was too eager and too wide. "Definitely."

Charlotte rearranged the koala bear she had half stuffed into her purse and dug for her car keys. "We need to wait on Matthias."

Martha pointed as she spoke. "I'll ride with Ted. John, you and Charlotte can decide who takes Sally and Betsy. Geoffrey can bring the rest. Okay? Good, let's go." She slipped her arm through Ted's.

Charlotte hesitated. "How will Matthias know where we've gone?"

Martha narrowed her eyes at Kate. "Kate can tell them, can't you? Think you can manage that?"

Martha didn't wait for Kate's response. She tugged Ted away, and Betsy, Sally, and John followed. Charlotte lingered behind.

"You'll tell Matthias where we went, right? Tell him I'll—I mean, we'll all be at the Pointe waiting for him."

Kate inhaled the smoky scent of ashes. Her throat closed, and her eyes filled with tears. With unsettling clarity, she realized the girl in her premonitions hadn't been her. It was Martha.

Kate remembered the agonizing weeks leading up to Evan's death when she barely ate, barely got out of bed, barely survived. She hadn't known she could have warned Evan about his shattered windshield, the truck driver who fell asleep, or the way the radio still worked even though Evan's car was crushed.

According to Ama, altering the future was against the rules. But after talking to Aurora, Kate realized that whoever made those rules didn't care if people died or suffered. They didn't care if brothers died while sisters dreamed of them. She'd taken a risk by helping Dani at Scooper's, and *nothing* tragic had happened because of her rule breaking. Martha's nastiness infuriated Kate. Still, she couldn't let something terrible happen to Martha. But

how would she convince Martha about what she'd seen? How could she stop what was going to happen? Kate bent over and gulped air.

Charlotte touched her shoulder. "Hey, are you okay?"

Kate wiped at her tears and straightened. "I don't know." Alter the future or let Martha face her own fate? A shiver rippled over Kate's skin, and she rubbed her hands against her arms.

Charlotte worried her bottom lip. "Are you going to be sick?"

Kate shrugged. "It's okay. Just go."

The Ferris wheel spun round and round, illuminating the faces in the carts. A laugh sounded and stretched toward Kate, wrapping around her heart and squeezing. The laugh sounded like Evan. She imagined them last year on the Ferris wheel, Evan leaning forward in the cart, her gripping his shirt sleeve. Evan pointed out the people below and made up stories about them while Kate giggled and waved to their parents. He would be here now if she had broken the rules.

Charlotte nodded. "Will you tell Matthias where we've gone?"

"No."

Charlotte frowned. "No?"

"No!" Kate shouted, looking past Charlotte. She pushed away from the light pole and ran. "Martha! Martha, wait!"

Martha stopped and turned with Ted still attached to her arm. Kate gasped for air. Ted puffed on his cigarette, and the end burned like fire.

"Martha, you can't go," Kate said.

Martha laughed, but she wore a confused expression. "What are you talking about?"

Kate grabbed hold of Martha's arm and pulled her away from

Ted. She dragged Martha toward the Tilt-A-Whirl. "You can't go to the Pointe. Just go home or anywhere else, but don't go to the Pointe and don't go with Ted."

"Why not?" Her eyes narrowed. "Do you have a thing for Ted now? Geoffrey not enough?"

"What? No," Kate said, shaking her head. "You just can't go up there with him. Things happen up there."

Martha pried Kate's fingers off her forearm and smashed the bear beneath one arm. "Things happen? That's what I'm hoping. Now, if you'll excuse me, I'm going to continue my good night." Martha stalked off.

Kate rushed after her and latched onto Martha's arm, spinning her around. Martha stumbled sideways. The bear fell to the ground, staring up at them with blank glassy eyes.

"Martha, you can't. Listen to me."

Martha's face leveled with Kate's. Her breath smelled sour like rotting teeth and whiskey. "What is your problem? Let go of me."

Kate imagined hands shoving her against the car seat. She felt the sharp sting of a burning cigarette against her collarbone. "No!" Kate shouted. "I had a premonition, and Ted is going to do something awful if you go up there tonight."

Martha's mouth dropped open, revealing her lipstick-stained teeth. Then she started laughing, releasing the cold sound into the night. "A premonition? You *are* crazy. Listen, witch, I don't believe in your hocus pocus, and I don't care what you say." Martha's lip curled in disdain.

Desperation caused Kate to blurt, "I know you steal your daddy's whiskey and hide it beneath your bed."

Martha gasped so loudly that several passersby stopped to

look at them. Martha staggered sideways, staring at Kate with wild eyes. "How would you know that?"

"I know things, Martha. Please listen to me."

Martha leaned down, grabbed the dirty bear, and pressed it against her chest. "You *are* a witch. Stay away from me!" She turned and hurried away.

Panic rose in Kate's chest. She had to stop Martha. She couldn't let someone be abused like that. Kate ran to the Scrambler. She arrived just as Geoffrey, Matthias, and Mikey exited the ride. Their steps were unsteady, but their smiles were wide.

"God, that thing scrambles my brain," Geoffrey joked.

Kate bombarded him. Desperation saturated her voice. "Geoffrey, I need to talk to you."

Matthias stepped up beside her. "Everything okay?"

Kate looked at him. His pale eyes focused on her, and she couldn't look away. "Charlotte wants you to meet her at her car. Everyone is going to Look-Off Pointe."

Mikey grinned. "Sounds like Ted's idea."

Kate nodded. "She's parked in the south parking lot near the main entrance. She's waiting on both of you." It was a lie, of course, but Kate knew that Matthias and Mikey could still catch Charlotte before she left.

"And you two?" Matthias asked, not breaking eye contact with Kate.

Geoffrey slipped his arm around Kate's shoulders. "We'll be along. You two go on."

Mikey nodded and walked off, but Matthias hesitated.

"Go on, Matt. We'll be right behind you," Geoffrey assured his brother.

Matthias looked as though he wanted to argue, but he didn't. Once Mikey and Matthias disappeared into the crowd, Kate shrugged off Geoffrey's arm and looked at him. She grabbed both of his hands.

"Geoffrey, you've got to do something. Martha is going up to Look-Off Pointe with Ted. You can't let her go with him."

Geoffrey's brow furrowed, and then he chuckled. "Because he's big and smelly?"

She squeezed his fingers. "I'm serious. He's . . . he's going to hurt her."

Geoffrey straightened to his full height and squared his shoulders. "Why would you say that?"

"Because I know. You have to trust me. I wouldn't make this up."

Geoffrey pulled out of her grasp and shoved one hand through his messy dark hair. "I don't know what you're saying. Ted wouldn't hurt Martha. He's an oaf, but he's not like that."

Kate's stomach twisted. A voice begged her to tell him the truth. "I know it's going to sound crazy, but I know he's going to try to hurt her. I saw it. She can't go up there with him."

Geoffrey took a step back. A kid tripped down the Scrambler's exit stairs and stumbled to the nearest trash can where he vomited. His friends gathered around, laughing and slapping his back as though he'd won a victory.

Geoffrey's attention returned to Kate. "What do you mean, *you saw it*? You're not making sense."

She bounced on the balls of her feet. "I—I have premonitions. I see the future. Sometimes what I see comes true but not all the time. And I've been seeing this future in pieces for weeks now, and it's awful, and I just realized tonight that it's Martha because

of the red necklace that Ted won at the Milk Bottle Toss," she babbled. "She's wearing the necklace, and they're going to Look-Off Pointe. It has to be Martha."

Geoffrey held up his hands. "Whoa, whoa. What are you talking about? What do you mean premonitions?" He stepped farther away from her. "You see the future? This isn't making any sense. You . . . you sound crazy."

Those three words were all it took to sever the last threads attaching Kate to her hope, to her heart. She broke apart like a seedpod. Kate pressed her hands to her chest. She had to hold the pieces of herself together. Tears welled in her eyes. When she spoke, her voice trembled. "Geoffrey, you have to believe me. Please. I'm not crazy."

Geoffrey shook his head. "I can't deal with this right now. I can barely focus. Are you drunk?"

"Of course not."

Geoffrey exhaled. "Why don't we ride up to Look-Off Pointe with everyone else? Have a little fun?"

"Geoffrey, please, *please* believe me. I wouldn't tell you this if it weren't important."

Geoffrey shoved his hands into his pants pockets and stared off into the distance. "I don't know what to say. It all sounds so—"

"Don't say it," Kate snapped. She trembled so hard that her teeth rattled together. "Don't call me crazy."

As a balloon vendor moseyed past them, every balloon in his cloud of helium colors popped, blanketing his head in flimsy plastic. Everyone around them flinched, and Geoffrey's eyes widened. A frightened expression flitted across his face as he looked at Kate. He grabbed the back of his neck, his hazel eyes shining

in the carnival lights. "I don't know what's going on with you, but I can't do this right now. Let's talk when you're acting normal again." He turned his back on her and walked away.

"Geoffrey . . ." All the air whooshed from her lungs, and warm tears fell from her lashes onto her cheeks. "But this *is* normal."

The world around her slowed as though everyone moved through air thicker than clover honey. Kate lowered her hands from her chest. There was no use trying to hold herself together anymore. The crowd shifted to make room for Geoffrey, and Matthias's face came into view. He looked from her to Geoffrey, and as his brother passed, Matthias grabbed Geoffrey's arm. Kate couldn't hear their conversation, but Geoffrey jerked out of Matthias's grasp and stalked off. Matthias called Kate's name and pushed through the crowd toward her, but she ran.

Colors and faces streamed by her like ribbons of light. Tears streaked her face, splashing into her hair, whipping through the air like a rainstorm. She ran past the Ferris wheel, the carousel, and the bumper cars. She ran until her chest burned. As she neared the exit, she saw her mama standing beneath the lit archway, wringing her hands together, scanning faces.

When she saw Kate, Ama's eyes widened. She held out her arms, and Kate slammed into her with such force that her mama stumbled backward but held on. She crushed her arms around Kate.

"Little Blackbird," Ama said, pressing her close. Then she pulled away and cupped Kate's face in her hands. "What's wrong? Tell me. What happened?"

Kate squeezed her eyes together and choked on her heartache, on the disappointment. She leaned forward and pressed her

forehead against her mama's chest.

"Are you hurt?"

Kate swallowed. "Only on the inside," she whispered.

Ama slipped her arm around Kate's shoulders and turned her outward so they could walk side by side through the exit. "I told your dad that you were coming. He's waiting for us in the car."

Kate blinked up at Ama. More tears dripped from her dark lashes. Her bottom lip quivered. "How did you know I needed you?"

"Oh, Little Blackbird," she said, "what have they done to you?"

Kate allowed herself to be bundled into the backseat as though she were a toddler. She didn't want to cry in front of her parents, but too many emotions crowded inside her, and they leaked from every pore. She covered her face in her hands and crumpled forward.

The radio station stopped working. Someone turned off the static. A streetlight cracked and burst overhead and rained sparks onto the car as they passed by. Was this why it was forbidden to try and alter the truth? Would no one believe the truth anyway? Would they reject and mock you?

When she felt them nearing the house, Kate stared out the window as her daddy pulled into the driveway. The silhouette of the magnolia tree down by the river loomed in the darkness. The tree reminded her of Geoffrey. She could almost imagine his thin form standing there, waiting for her. She saw the boulders where she'd sat with him, the reeds where they'd kissed for the first time. None of those moments would ever happen again. They'd never laugh and skip pebbles across the water. They'd never race

to the top of the next hill. They'd never be so close that not even a sliver of pine straw could come between them.

The fire in her spirit had been snuffed, leaving a hollow behind, causing her breath to rattle. Her tears were dry, but her eyes burned. She climbed out of the car and dragged her feet to the front door. Once inside her room, she sat on the edge of the bed and stared at the window. She imagined Geoffrey on the other side with his crooked grin, his long fingers resting on the windowsill. She squeezed her eyes closed, trying to erase the vision.

Raindrops splattered against the panes, light at first but soon pelting the house with fast rain moving in sheets blown in by easterly gusts of wind. Kate thought of all the people still enjoying the carnival, none of them suspecting a summer storm.

"Want to talk about it?" Ama stood in the doorway with her black hair spilling over her shoulders.

Kate wilted beneath her gaze and sagged forward. "He didn't want me." The truth closed her throat and squeezed her chest so tight she could barely inhale. Hearing the words aloud brought another onslaught of tears. Not only had he not believed her or wanted her just as she was, but he also called her *crazy*.

Ama sat beside Kate on the bed. "Who didn't?"

Kate stared at her hands. The wind howled. "Don't be mad, okay?" She glanced up at her mama, whose expression was difficult to read. "Promise?"

"I can't promise anything other than I'll listen. Now, who are we talking about?"

Kate sighed. To say anything about him now would mean she had to surrender the secret she'd been guarding for weeks. "Geoffrey Hamilton." Saying his name created an ache for him, a longing she couldn't shove aside. Thunder rattled the books on

Kate's shelves.

"Based on your reaction, I'm going to assume that Geoffrey is more than your friend. Although I can't imagine *how* since you've never once mentioned his name in any sort of serious conversation."

Kate closed her eyes. "I've lied. I've been seeing him all summer. In the park. We've been meeting there."

Ama stiffened beside her. Kate stood and walked to the window. When she turned, her mama's hands were clenched in her lap, and her full lips were reduced to a thin slash.

"Mama, please, don't be mad," Kate begged. "I know it was wrong, but I really cared—*care*—about him. I wanted to tell you, but I was afraid. I didn't want you to take him away. But none of it matters now." She faced the window again and wiped at her tears.

"Why doesn't it matter?"

"Because I'm me." Kate covered her face and spoke into her hands. "I hate being me. Why can't I be someone else, someone better, someone who's enough, who's not crazy?" Kate whirled around, gripping Martha's borrowed dress in her hands. "Why, Mama?"

Ama exhaled. "Did he tell you there was something wrong with you?"

"No. But look at me—"

"I'm looking at you, Kate."

"But you don't see what they see," Kate cried. A terrible emotion unleased inside her, clawing, ripping her apart. Self-loathing nearly choked her where she stood.

Ama's voice was calm, but unexpected tears shined in her eyes. "I see a beautiful girl in a dress. What do they see?"

"An Indian in someone else's clothes. A crazy witch." Kate

sobbed. Her knees buckled, and she slumped against the window, sliding down to the floor where she covered her face.

She felt Ama kneel beside her. "That's not what they see, Little Blackbird. That's what *you* see." Her mama stroked her head. "Yes, you're wearing someone else's dress, but that doesn't make it any less beautiful on you."

Kate dropped her hands. "Geoffrey thought I looked pretty. He said so, but he still doesn't want me. He wants a version of me." Kate's voice trembled. "I could do all that. I could change for him. I could pretend I'm not different, that I don't have the curse, couldn't I? Then maybe he'd want me."

"Is that what you want? To pretend you're not *you*."

Kate shrugged, but Aurora's voice reminded her about the path her great-grandmother had taken, the path *away* from who she truly was, and how it had destroyed her.

Ama pulled Kate to her feet. She hugged her tight before letting go. "You won't find all the answers tonight. Wash your face and change your clothes. I'll make peppermint tea. Would you like that?"

Kate nodded. "Thanks for not being mad."

"Oh, I'm mad, Little Blackbird, but I'm saving it for another time. I'm not going to tell your dad that you've been sneaking around with a boy. He would go ape, you know that. He still thinks you're ten, but don't think I'm happy with it. You should have been honest."

Kate wiped at her cheeks and nodded. "I'm sorry."

Kate grabbed her pajamas from the drawer and went into the bathroom. She scrubbed her face and pulled the brush through her hair. Her red-rimmed eyes stared back at her in the mirror. She changed into her pajamas and considered tossing the dress into the trash can, but instead she dropped it into the laundry

basket.

Kate sat on her bed and watched the rain hammer against the window. Ama moved around in the kitchen, probably boiling water for their tea. Kate closed her eyes, but as soon as she did, images formed in her mind. *A shoe kicked against the window. A knee pressed into the steering wheel. Hot tears. Red beads scattered across the car floor.* Kate jerked her eyes open. Her heart pounded. Even if Martha and Geoffrey didn't believe her, that didn't mean that something awful wasn't going to happen.

Kate looked at the photograph she kept on her bookcase. The picture had been taken by the river the year before Evan died. His arm looped around her shoulder, and he smiled at the camera while she leaned into him, laughing at something he'd said. "I can't just sit here and do nothing. I can't let Martha get hurt. Do you think I should do something?" Kate's eyes burned with tears. "You think I should help her?" She knew what Evan would say.

Kate slipped off her bed and stood in her bedroom doorway. She heard her mama still in the kitchen, and her daddy called from the living room, his voice muffled by the wind and rain. Would her parents believe her if she told them the truth? She and her mama had been keeping the truth from her daddy for so long, what fractures would revealing it now cause in their relationships? If Ama believed her, would she tell Kate that altering the future was forbidden? Or would she drive Kate to Look-Off Pointe so she could help Martha? Thunder rumbled the floorboards.

Kate snatched a sheet of paper from a notebook and scribbled, *I'm sorry. There's something I have to do. I'll be back, I promise.* She placed the note on her bed, changed out of her pajamas, and yanked on a T-shirt and jeans. Then she slipped on an old pair of tennis shoes. She ran to the window, unlatched it, and pushed

up the sash. Slanted rain slashed through the opening and wet the front of her shirt. Kate hesitated for only a moment before she slipped one leg out the window and then the other. Rain soaked her clothes in seconds.

Before she could close the window, Ama appeared in the doorway holding a tray with two cups of tea. Steam rose from the cups. "Kate . . . what are you doing?"

Kate's wide eyes were wild and panicked. "I have to, Mama. I'm sorry." Kate slammed the window shut.

CHAPTER 20

AMA RUSHED TO THE WINDOW AND LIFTED IT. SHE SHOUTED Kate's name into the rain as Kate sprinted toward the forest. As she neared the trees, Kate heard her daddy's voice shouting from the back door just before the rain and wind swallowed everything.

Rain poured through the tree canopy, saturating the ground. Kate splashed through ankle-deep puddles, inhaling half air and half water into her burning lungs. If she hadn't taken this path so often this summer to see Geoffrey, she never would have been able to navigate the forest in the darkness.

In less than ten minutes, she hustled up the last hill that flattened on top to create Look-Off Pointe. Half a dozen cars were parked twenty yards or more from the edge of the drop-off. A Chevrolet Bel Air was parked to the far right, backed against the tree line in the distance. Kate heard voices, and her eyes found the covered picnic shelter. Through the rain, she saw the tiny flare of a lighter and the glow of a cigarette. The feeble light illuminated John's face and a girl standing near him. Charlotte.

Car tires had created deep muddy ruts in the soggy earth,

and Kate stumbled across the grooved ground as she ran, her shoes squelching through the mud. She slowed as she approached the shelter. Thunder rolled across the valley and rumbled in Kate's chest.

Once on the concrete slab, she recognized the other shadows in the darkness. Charlotte sat on one side of the picnic table between John and Matthias. Geoffrey leaned against one of the wooden posts that held up the roof, and Mikey sat on the opposite side of the picnic table with Martha.

Kate gasped. "Martha?"

As a collective, the group looked stunned to see her. Geoffrey pushed off the post and gaped at her.

Matthias slid off the end of the bench and stood. "Kate?"

Someone switched on a flashlight and shined it right onto Kate's face. She squinted in the harsh light and lifted her hand to shield her eyes. The flashlight lowered and created a halo of light around Kate's feet.

"Lord have mercy," Martha said, "you look like a pig in a sty. What are you doing here?"

Kate frowned. "No," she mumbled. "This isn't what I saw happen." Her gaze darted across the faces in the group. "Where's Ted?"

Martha scoffed. "Still hoping to neck with Ted?" She glanced over at Geoffrey. "I told you Kate was no good for you. She's already moving on to your friends."

"Where's Ted?" Kate demanded. Lightning split the stormy sky in half before striking a tree and shooting sparks into the air.

Geoffrey crossed to her. "He went to his car for more cigarettes. What are you doing here, Kate?"

Had her premonitions about Martha been wrong? Were Martha and Geoffrey right to think she was crazy? Charlotte placed the flashlight on the table, and the beam spotlighted Martha.

Kate pointed. "Martha, where's your necklace? The plastic one you got at the carnival."

Martha reached her hand up to her neck. "What's it to you?"

Kate pushed Geoffrey out of the way and grabbed Martha's arm. "Where is it?"

Martha's blue eyes widened, and she glanced nervously around at the others. "I—I gave it to Sally."

Kate's stomach fell toward the concrete. "Where is she?"

Geoffrey grabbed Kate and pulled her away from Martha. "What's this about, Kate? What are you doing here? Why are you acting so—"

Kate jerked out of Geoffrey's grasp, giving him a withering glance. "Where is Sally?" Kate knew she sounded irrational. She felt wild and cracked open. Her insides were vibrating so badly that she shook the ground beneath her feet. Rain pounded against the shelter's tin roof.

Matthias stepped toward them. "She went with Ted."

No. Kate could barely see the cars through the lashing rain. "Where is his car?"

Matthias pointed to the only car backed against the trees a few hundred yards away. "It's the Bel Air. Kate, what's going on—"

Kate dashed from the shelter. Someone shouted her name. Her body reacted faster than her mind could think. She approached the Bel Air too quickly, and when she tried to stop, she slid through the mud like a runner stealing second base.

She scrambled to her feet and wrenched open the driver's side door. The dome light on the car's ceiling turned on.

Kate saw a man's back hovering over someone. Between his legs she saw a pair of saddle shoes and snatches of green fabric—the same color dress Sally had been wearing at the carnival. The girl in the car shouted for help at the sight of the dome light, and her feet kicked with new fervor. Kate grabbed one of the man's legs and yanked. With her adrenaline pumping, she continued to yank until she'd pulled him from the car. He landed in the mud and rolled onto his back. Ted's belt was undone, and his pants were unbuttoned and halfway down his legs. He stared up at Kate, cursing and trying to shield his face from the rain.

Kate leaped over him and leaned through the open door. Sally had pressed herself against the passenger-side door. Mascara streaked her pale skin with black tears on her cheeks. Her nose ran onto her swollen top lip. Rosy lipstick smeared up one cheek like an angry scar. Sally trembled so hard that the car rocked. Kate climbed inside and held out her muddy hand.

"It's okay, Sally. You're going to be okay."

At the sight of Kate's outstretched hand and the realization that she was saved, Sally sobbed. A round cigarette had burned through the top of Sally's dress and seared the skin beneath. Red plastic beads were scattered all over the front seat and in both floorboards. Kate slid closer to Sally and gently pulled the skirt of Sally's dress down over her knees.

"It's going to be okay now, I promise," Kate said gently.

Sally looked at a point over Kate's shoulder and gasped. Before Kate could turn around, she was snatched out of the car and thrown onto the ground.

A shadowed silhouette leaned over her. "Who do you think you are, witch?" Ted reached down and lifted Kate by both shoulders and slammed her against the side of the car. The rear door handle buried itself in Kate's back. Sally screamed. Four shadows appeared through the sheets of rain.

"Let her go, Ted. You're drunk, and you don't know what you're doing."

"Get out of here, Geoffrey. I can handle this," Ted said.

Geoffrey jerked Ted off Kate, and she slumped against the car. Ted fought back like a man thrown into a boxing ring, but he couldn't defend himself against Geoffrey, Matthias, John, and Mikey. John and Mikey pinned Ted's arms behind his back, and when he wouldn't stop fighting them, Geoffrey punched Ted in the jaw, and Ted collapsed.

Kate shivered and wiped her muddy hands down the front of her soiled clothes. She climbed back into the driver's seat. "It's okay, Sally. They have him. There's a picnic shelter where Martha and Charlotte are. Do you want to go there?"

Sally slid across the seat toward Kate and gripped Kate's hand and didn't let go even as they hurried through the rain toward the shelter. Charlotte and Martha stood on the edge of the concrete slab, out of the rain, but waiting. They reached for Sally and pulled her out of the storm.

Charlotte grabbed Sally's hand and sat her down on the bench. "Are you okay? What happened?"

A pool of water formed beneath Sally. Kate stood beneath the shelter, dripping mud and rainwater. Sally shook her head and started crying again.

Martha narrowed her eyes at Kate. "You knew this was going to happen." Martha sat down and put her arm around

Sally's shoulders. "You really are a witch."

Sally looked at Martha, and then she glanced at Kate. "You knew? How did you know he was trying to—" Sally closed her eyes but continued. "How did you know what was happening? We left you at the carnival. How did you end up here?"

"She had a premonition." Martha said the word *premonition* as though it were synonymous with Satan or witchcraft.

Charlotte laughed. "What? That's ridiculous."

Martha's lip curled. "How do you think she knew to look for Sally and Ted?"

Charlotte's laughter stopped abruptly.

Kate exhaled and used the back of her hand to wipe mud from her cheek. What did it matter now if they all knew? "I thought it was going to be Martha and Ted. I tried to warn Martha, but she didn't believe me."

Charlotte's forehead wrinkled. "Warn her of what?"

"Of what Ted was going to do. Because I saw the red necklace in my vision, and I thought it was Martha because she was wearing it at the carnival."

Sally's face scrunched in confusion. "Your vision? You mean, you do have premonitions? You see the future? You saw what was going to happen to me?" She shuddered, and the three girls huddled together. "That gives me the creeps."

Kate's fists clenched at her sides. A tiny spark of anger flared inside her. "But . . . but I helped you. I ran all the way from my house to stop it."

Thunder shook the ground, and the girls flinched. Sally cowered against Charlotte.

Geoffrey and John stepped onto the slab out of the rain. Their clothes were mud splattered and drenched. Matthias and

Mikey dragged Ted between them like a knocked-out boxer who needed to be carted from the ring.

Mikey grunted and adjusted his grip. "Where are we going to put him?"

"Throw me your keys," Matthias said to Geoffrey.

Geoffrey's body stiffened. "No way are you putting that mess in my car."

Matthias grunted and leveled his gaze at Geoffrey. "Give them to me."

Geoffrey shoved his dirty hand into his pocket and pulled out the keys. Two sets of black-and-white photographs fell onto the concrete, and Kate stared down at their smiling faces, now ruined with mud and water. Geoffrey's knuckles were bloody, and his eyes strayed to the pictures from the photo booth. He glanced at Kate. Neither one of them made a move to pick up the photographs. Geoffrey threw the keys at Matthias, and they bounced off Matthias's chest and landed in the mud.

Matthias propped Ted against Mikey and searched for the keys. "I was going to help you clean the car afterward, but you can forget that. You'll be lucky if he doesn't puke."

Matthias lifted the keys from the sludge and shook them around to free most of the muck from the metal. Together, he and Mikey dragged Ted toward Geoffrey's car near the cliff. John walked over and knelt in front of Sally. He asked her if she was okay and if Ted had hurt her in any way.

Geoffrey looked at Kate, but he didn't approach her. Martha stood abruptly and marched over, planting her shoes on the photographs. She wrung her hands together. "You can't be with her, Geoffrey."

Kate stared at Martha with her clean dress and perfect

makeup. In comparison, Kate knew she looked like the creature from the black lagoon while Martha could have been a high-class store-window mannequin. Never were there two girls who were more different, and yet Geoffrey had been interested in both of them. How was that even possible? Why would anyone choose the outcast over the homecoming queen? But a small part of her heart held out hope that Geoffrey was different too. He could still choose Kate, couldn't he?

Martha latched onto Geoffrey's arm with both hands and spoke to him as if Kate weren't even there. "You just can't. She's not . . . normal. Somehow she knows things, things nobody should know. She'll hurt you, and I don't want that."

Kate's hands fell open at her sides. "I'd never hurt you, Geoffrey."

Geoffrey glanced between Martha and Kate. "But you knew this was going to happen."

Kate nodded.

Martha pointed at her. "See, she admits it. She's evil."

"I'm not evil!" Kate argued.

Thunder shook the entire hill, and the pine trees trembled. Winds whipped across Look-Off Pointe, and rain slammed the ground more furiously than before. The group staggered beneath the quaking ground. Martha stared open-mouthed at Kate. Charlotte and Sally clutched onto each other, and John stood protectively beside them.

Martha's voice came out as a whisper. "She's doing this."

Kate tossed up her hands in exasperation. "I can't control the weather! Geoffrey, please believe me."

Geoffrey watched the rain pummel the earth. A car door slammed.

Kate's eyes filled with tears. "Geoffrey, you know me. I would never hurt you. I came here to help." She moved toward him, but he stepped backward. "Please. It's me. You *know* me."

He wouldn't even look at her. In his silent rejection, she crumpled like a fragile leaf. Kate stepped off the concrete into the storm. Geoffrey watched her. Martha pressed herself against Geoffrey's side. Rain pelted Kate's face, washing away her tears as soon as they fell. She turned and stumbled into the darkness with the wind and the rain wailing for her.

CHAPTER 21

RAIN FELL FROM THE SKY FOR THE NEXT TWO DAYS, AND
through her tears, Kate watched the world drown from her bedroom window. Mystic Water flooded, or so her parents told her.
Kate wasn't allowed out of her room unless it was to use the bathroom. At all other times, her bedroom was her prison, and that
was fine with her. Everything outside—the trees, the flowers,
the river—reminded her of Geoffrey. Her chest ached where her
heart used to beat; her swollen eyes drooped.

Kate's parents hadn't asked for specifics on why she had
decided to sneak out of the house the night of the carnival. Ama
assumed she'd run off to see Geoffrey, which is what she'd told
Sean. To say her daddy went ape was an understatement. Kate
had never seen him so angry, and it was only after she promised
on his mother's grave that *nothing* inappropriate had happened
between her and Geoffrey that his fury relented.

Kate was tempted to confess the truth to Ama, to tell her
mama that she'd altered the truth and helped someone, but the
results of Kate's "help" had destroyed the last threads holding
her friendships together. It had also ruined any chance that she

and Geoffrey could stay together. Kate didn't want to relive the heartbreak by telling her mama what really happened, so she let her parents believe the lie instead.

Every day during her banishment Ama updated her about town when she brought Kate food. While she ate a grilled cheese with tomato soup, Kate learned everything around Jordan Pond had flooded. Over a plate of baked chicken and potatoes, Ama told her that people were traveling around in boats and Mystic Water had become the Venice of the South.

"Did gondoliers sing to their patrons?" Kate had asked.

"With banjos and mason jars," Ama said, attempting a joke.

At the end of the week, Kate stopped crying, and the sun returned. Slowly the swollen river receded, the puddles evaporated, and the town dried. Ama brought in a tray filled with fluffy pancakes, fresh fruit, and a cup of lavender tea.

She placed the tray on Kate's desk and sat on the edge of the bed. Kate thanked her mama and sliced into the pancakes.

Ama cleared her throat. "Dogwood Lane didn't flood."

Kate lowered the fork in her hand. "Okay."

"The Hamiltons did a lot to help the people around town. They have a couple of fishing boats, you know."

Kate didn't dare look at her mama. "I didn't know that."

"Well, they do. Dr. Hamilton takes them up to the lake now and again to fish. He's invited your dad a few times." Ama slid her bracelets up and down her arm. "They've been very generous with their time, especially those boys, helping get people out of their homes and back to their families."

Kate slid the tray away. Out of all the people on the planet Ama could talk about, why was she reminding Kate about the one boy who had crushed her spirits? "That's good of them." Kate

glared at the sunshine streaming through her window.

"I agree. In fact, one of them is here to see if you've survived the storm okay."

Kate's heart slammed against her ribcage. "What?" She stood as rigid as a wooden soldier. "When? Here?"

Ama stood and straightened her skirt. "Breathe, Little Blackbird."

The books on the shelves trembled; two hopped free, slapping against the floor and popping open.

Ama rested her hands on Kate's shoulders. "Breathe."

Kate inhaled and exhaled. "Are you going to let me see him?"

Ama picked up the fallen books and returned them to the shelf. "How could I not? He came all this way, and he has excellent manners."

Kate glanced toward her bedroom door. Was Geoffrey in the living room right now? Was he going to apologize?

Kate combed her fingers through her hair. "What about Daddy?"

"Your dad is in town, and he'll be there for a few more hours. This will be between you and me."

Kate rushed to her closet. "Should I change? Do I look all right?"

Ama walked over and shut the closet door. "You should go just as you are. That's who he came here to see. *You.*"

Kate closed her eyes. Then she squared her shoulders and walked up the short hallway to the living room. The room smelled of peppermint and maple syrup. He stood at the back door, staring out at the yard.

Kate's eyebrows knit together. "Matthias?"

He turned to look at her. His hands were shoved into his

pockets, and his smile was slow but genuine. "You're alive."

"If you call this alive." Kate heard Ama step into the room. "What are you doing here?"

Matthias motioned toward the back door with his head. "Can we take a walk?" His eyes strayed to her mama.

Ama nodded. "Of course. This is the first sun we've seen in days. You two enjoy it."

Matthias opened the door and motioned for Kate to step outside first, but she couldn't move. She stared at him. One question looped through her mind: Where was Geoffrey?

Matthias's blue eyes were the exact color of his collared shirt. He held his hand out toward her. "Please."

That single word caused her foot to take a step and then another and another until she passed right by him and stepped outside into the sunlight. Kate blinked in the light. The long grass softened her bare footsteps, and she surveyed the waterlogged yard. Most of the flowers looked abused, but in the sunlight, they were drying and waving hello to her. She almost smiled.

Matthias stood beside her. "Let's walk to the river."

"I'd rather not."

Matthias chuckled. "Why not?"

Kate glared at the boulders nearest the river. "Because I used to go there with Geoffrey."

"Now you'll go there with me," Matthias said as he made his way to the river.

Kate watched him walk away until her curiosity couldn't be contained. She hustled to catch him. The river had stretched past its usual boundaries during the storm, and it left behind mud and displaced stones closer to the house. Kate hopped her way through the mess until she caught up with him.

Matthias found the bench that Kate's daddy had built by the river for Evan and her. It was as though Matthias knew the one spot Kate and Geoffrey had never shared together. The sun poured down its warmth onto the bench seat, and Matthias waited for Kate to sit before he did.

They sat for a few minutes watching the rippling water travel downstream before Matthias spoke. "So, you're okay?"

Kate sighed. "Depends on your definition of *okay.*"

"Breathing, still a part of the world."

Kate heard the smile in his voice, and she turned to look at him. His pupils constricted in the sunlight, and his blue irises reflected an image of her. "Then, yes. But by any other definition, no." She lowered her gaze to the space in between them on the seat. "Where's Geoffrey?" His name felt raw in her throat.

Matthias pulled an envelope from his shirt pocket. "This is for you."

Kate took the offering and held it for a few seconds before opening it. Her fingers trembled. She slid the letter from the unsealed envelope and stopped breathing. Kate recognized Geoffrey's handwriting as soon as she unfolded the letter.

Kate,

I've written this at least a half dozen times. This attempt will have to do. Although I'm hopeful this letter will help somehow, I'm not sure it can. I have no excuses to offer for the other night. To say I was shocked isn't accurate. It was more than shock. Even now I find your abilities difficult to believe. I do know you helped Sally, and that is admirable.

I wanted you to know that I have enjoyed spending these last few weeks of summer with you, but as you know, I'll be

leaving for college in two days. It would be unwise for us to continue our relationship. I wish you all the best, Kate. You are really special.

Geoffrey

Kate turned the letter over to look at the back, to see if he'd written some secret message to counter the truth that he didn't want her. The paper trembled in her hand.

Matthias cleared his throat. "There's nothing more. I checked too."

Kate rested the letter in her lap and lowered her head. She squeezed her eyes shut, but tears leaked from the edges anyway. She clenched her jaw because she refused to sob in front of Matthias. After what happened at the carnival and at Look-Off Pointe, what had Kate hoped for? That he'd profess his love for her? That he'd admit he was wrong and shallow and he could accept her just the way she was? Yes.

Matthias shifted on the bench. "I'm sorry."

"For what?" she croaked.

"For him. That he didn't even have the decency to apologize. That's not the way you treat people."

Kate lifted her head and swiped at the tears before looking at Matthias. "What about people like me?"

Matthias frowned. "What kind of people are you?"

Kate shrugged and crumpled the letter in her hands. "Different. Weird. Crazy. Unnatural."

Matthias lifted his eyebrows. "I hardly think you're unnatural. I see a person with legs and arms and ears. You look natural to me. And would you look at those angry eyes?" Matthias smiled.

Kate huffed and glanced away. She smoothed the letter out against her thighs. When she spoke, her voice was almost lost in the breeze. "I could change. I could be more like them."

"Why would you want to?"

Kate's bottom lip trembled. "Because Geoffrey wouldn't have written this letter," she waved the paper in the air, "because he would have come here himself. If I were more like him, he would love me." She covered her mouth with her hand to stop from saying any more.

Matthias leaned forward and propped his elbows on his thighs. He watched the current carry away a fallen log. "Do you love him?"

Kate's body tensed. She'd never been in love with anyone before Geoffrey. She had no idea what love should feel like, but her longing for him and the way her heart had responded to him felt like what she had always imagined love to be. The way he was capable of still hurting her had to mean she loved him. "Yes."

Matthias turned his face toward her. "But you were only together a few weeks."

Kate shrugged and folded the letter. "How much time needs to pass before someone is allowed to love someone else? I didn't realize there was a time requirement." But what did she know? She was just a girl who had fallen in love with the impossible. She slouched against the back of the bench. "But I'm not going to do it."

"Do what?"

"Change." She shrugged. "This is me. All of it. The weird, the Indian, the girl who sees the future. It might not be what Geoffrey wanted," she said as her chest tightened, "but that's okay. I mean, it *will* be okay. Right now, it feels awful, but Mama

says it won't always." Kate stared out at the river. "And I have to trust that."

Matthias nodded. "That's good to know you're going to keep being you. Evan would want you to be just who you are."

Kate sighed. "He would. He always liked my weirdness."

Matthias's mouth lifted in one corner. "I wouldn't want you to be like them, Kate. Be you."

Kate made a scoffing noise in her throat. She swiped at her tears. "Oh sure, because you think *being me* is working so well?"

Matthias laughed, and the sound startled Kate. His laughter swooped across the river, and two cardinals took flight from the trees on the other side and flew straight toward them, landing in the magnolia nearby. Kate's shoulders relaxed, and her mouth tugged into an almost smile. She caught herself appreciating the way his cheek dimpled when he grinned.

Matthias's expression changed, and she saw the seriousness in his eyes when he spoke. "I'm returning to college in two days as well. Classes start at the end of the week. Now that it seems Mystic Water will bounce back after the flood, I feel okay leaving. I won't be able to come home as often this term because my classes will be more demanding. But . . . well, I'd like to know if I could write to you."

Kate tucked the letter beneath her thigh. "Write to me? What do you mean?"

Matthias grinned. "You know, letters. I'd like to see how you are, check in with you, that sort of thing."

"Like a pen pal?"

Matthias chuckled. "Exactly."

Kate shrugged. "I don't see why not. But I'll be fine, Matthias. It isn't your responsibility to clean up your brother's mess. You

shouldn't feel bad. I'll be okay."

Matthias shifted on the bench and propped one knee on the seat so he could face Kate. "You misunderstand. I *want* to write to you."

"Why?"

Matthias's grin widened. "Why would anyone *not* want to write to you?"

Kate motioned to herself, sweeping her hands from her head down to her feet. "Is that a trick question?" When Matthias laughed again, the sound of it warmed her, and she allowed herself to smile at him—the first true smile she'd had in days. "It might be like having a friend. A real friend."

Matthias stretched out his legs in front of him. "Something like that, yes."

What had been ultimately snatched away during the rainstorm when her friends and Geoffrey had snubbed her had been quietly and ever so gently returned by Matthias: hope.

EPILOGUE

THE SATURDAY KATE TURNED EIGHTEEN SHE SPENT THE MORN-
ing in the garden with her mama. They'd pruned the spring
flowering bushes, tied up the tomatoes, and harvested radishes,
heads of lettuce, and early potatoes. Kate planted strawberry
plants in a sunny, sheltered section of the backyard. She used
the back of her trowel to pat down the earth around the new
additions.

A truck rumbled up the road. Her pulse quickened, and she
turned to look at Ama. Across the yard, her mama gazed at her
over the tops of basil and sage. They shared a smile before Kate
jumped to her feet and sprinted around the house toward the
front yard. She ran up the driveway and arrived at the mailbox
just as the mailman parked.

"Good afternoon, Miss Muir."

Kate pulled air into her lungs. "Hey, Mr. Thomas. Anything
good today?"

He smiled at her. "I think I may have seen something for
you." He handed a bundle of mail to her, and Kate wished him
a good day.

She shuffled through the envelopes, holding her breath as

she walked. She stopped when she saw a letter addressed to her in familiar handwriting. She smiled so brightly that the sunflowers in the front yard turned their faces toward her.

Kate rushed through the front door, tossed the rest of the mail on the kitchen table, and flew out the back door with the envelope in her hand. "I'm taking a break for a little bit. Going for a walk."

Ama nodded, and her gaze drifted down to the ivory envelope in Kate's hand. "Make sure you're back for dinner. Your dad had Mrs. Beatrice make a special cake for you today."

"Yes, ma'am," she said as she hurried into the trees.

Kate wanted to rip open the letter as soon as it arrived, but she forced herself to wait. She always carried his letters to the clearing, where she sat down and read his words over and over again. Taking his letters into the forest started with Kate's need years ago to read in private without Ama hovering around, and then reading them in the clearing became a habit. Now, she didn't feel right unless she opened the envelopes among the trees and the birds and the flowers.

Kate jogged toward the clearing where the trees thinned, and she noticed a small lavender plant had grown near the center of the grassy area. Monarch butterflies, flapping their orange-and-black wings, darted in and out of the tiny purple blooms. Kate tilted her head. "Where did you come from? Here to keep me company?"

She dropped down cross-legged on the soft, spring grass beside the plant. She wiggled her finger beneath the envelope's fold and slit it open. She slid out the letter. A single daisy had been pressed into the folds. Kate held the stem between her fingers and smiled on a sigh.

Happy Birthday, Little Blackbird!

I am hoping this letter arrives to you on your birthday—
at least that is what I requested of the letter as I dropped it
into the postbox. I'm sending one flower to start the festivities
with the promise that I will have more the next time I see you.

My final term at college is finished at last. I passed all
of my classes, and graduation will happen next week. But
the best news of all came just this morning in the post. I've
been accepted into medical school. What a relief! It wasn't as
though I doubted my ability to meet their standards (especially not with your constant encouragement), but there is
always the possibility that life will throw a curve ball when
you least expect it. I couldn't wait to share the good news with
you, and I'll tell my parents the next time I come home.

It's your eighteenth birthday! How are you going to spend
it? Do you have big plans? I'm hoping you will agree to spend
the day (or at least part of it) with me because I don't want to
miss your special day. Your parents know I'm coming into
town, so I'll see you at your birthday dinner.

Miss you,
Matthias

Kate gasped and pressed the letter to her chest. Then she
reread the last paragraph. "He's coming here?" she squealed and
startled a robin pecking the ground nearby.

Kate placed the daisy inside the letter and refolded it. Then
she slipped the parchment back into its envelope. She brushed
her fingers across the leaves of the lavender plant, and the

butterflies fluttered around her hands. "Matthias is coming here." Their wings beat faster against the summer air, sending whispers of a breeze across her cheeks.

She held out one hand, and a butterfly landed in her palm. A hazy veil lowered over Kate's vision. The butterfly took flight, and Kate lay in the grass, breathing in the scents of lavender, peppermint, and birthday cake before the premonition cast images into her mind.

Four pieces of vanilla cake filled with colorful sprinkles. Laughter. A kaleidoscope of colors dancing across the floor. A dozen daises. Blue eyes. Love as constant and as warming as a summer sunrise. Matthias's hand in hers as candles blow out and wishes are made.

AUTHOR'S NOTE

THIS STORY CAME ABOUT BECAUSE READERS OF *The Baker's Man* (book 1 in the Mystic Water series) kept asking, "What happens next? What else is going on in Mystic Water?" This novel was originally titled *Little Blackbird*, and the previous dedication was to those same readers: for everyone who wanted to know more about Mystic Water and the enchanting people who call it home.

As you know, Little Blackbird is the nickname given to our heroine, Kate, and it made sense for the title to represent the main character. But as all things advance—me, my life, and my art— Kate's story and the characters filling her world also evolved. With the relaunch of *The Baker's Man* by my fabulous publisher Harper Muse, I knew that the whole series needed to be given the same kind of care, refreshment, and new breaths of life.

So *Little Blackbird* transitioned into *The Necessity of Lavender Tea*. And not only did the title change, but so did the cover, now with a gorgeous new design created by one of my longtime best friends, Julianne. The story grew longer and more refined too. If you read *Little Blackbird*, thank you, and you'll find all of your favorite people and moments are still intact, perhaps a bit shinier and with more depth.

Kate's character is inspired by my mama, who was part Cherokee. While she didn't experience the same kind of discrimination that Kate did, she was wildly beautiful, kind-hearted, resilient, and loving. She was also a bit unconventional, which is only one of the myriad reasons why she was infinitely special and loved.

I hope Kate's story not only whisks you away into the magical Southern town of Mystic Water but that it also gives you the courage to *be you* no matter what, no exceptions, at all costs, for all time. If you know me, you know I love literary quotes, so I'll leave you with this one by Oscar Wilde: Be yourself because everyone else is already taken.

IN MEMORY OF PATRICIA RENEE HEISLER MOORMAN 1952–1988

ACKNOWLEDGMENTS

A GAZILLION THANK-YOUS TO ALL MY READERS WHO WANTED TO know what else happens in Mystic Water time and time again. Without you I might have never started book 2 in the series. Thank you for loving our magical Southern town, its lively characters, and their loveable whimsical stories. You make Mystic Water feel like a place we share together.

Karissa Taylor—you are the most rockstar editor an author could ever have. Your attention to detail, your thoughtful questions, your sense of humor, along with a million other reasons, make me so incredibly grateful to have you as part of my team. Thank you for loving Mystic Water from the very beginning and for making my voice stronger, clearer, and shine brighter.

Julianne St. Clair—your designs have always blown my mind, and your talents make the world a more beautiful, more magical place. Your enduring friendship through more than twenty years has often been a life raft, a place of refuge, and a dance party. Thank you to the moon and back and back and back again.

Marisa Gothie—you are steady, supportive, creative, and

passionate, and I'm so thankful that a deep love of books connected us. You are a tremendous gift and encouragement to me. Thank you for writing brilliant discussion questions for this edition. You add such richness to the reading experience, and you're one of the most supportive readers and author advocates I know. Find Marissa on Instagram @Marisagbooks at Bookends and Friends.

People often say that writing is a lonely journey, but that's not been my experience. Although I spend many hours alone, I also have dear friends who coach me, listen to my endless babbles, bolster me when I'm wobbly, and celebrate with me. Natalie Banks, Jeanne Arnold, and Tia Lee—there aren't enough thank-yous to sufficiently show my gratitude for your years of friendship, but I'll keep trying. Thank you, thank you, thank you!

RECIPES

LAVENDER COOKIES

These light, buttery cookies have a subtle floral aroma. One bite will settle any restless heart and open the door for peace and calm. Paired with a cup of tea, these are perfect for a cozy day.

Prep Time: 20 minutes
Baking Time: 10 minutes
Chilling Time: 30 minutes
Total: 1 hour
Yield: 20 cookies

Ingredients

2 cups all-purpose flour
½ cup (1 stick) salted butter, cold
½ cup granulated sugar
1 teaspoon salt
1 teaspoon dried food-grade lavender buds

Instructions

1. Crush the dried lavender into smaller bits.
2. In the bowl of stand mixer fitted with a paddle attachment, beat the sugar and butter until pale and fluffy, about two minutes. Add the crushed lavender and salt and mix for another minute.
3. Sift the flour into the butter-sugar mixture. Add 1 to 2 tablespoons of ice-cold water, and mix on low until just incorporated.
4. Turn out dough onto parchment paper, and knead for just a few seconds to combine all the crumbles into the dough. The dough should be soft but not sticky. If the dough seems too sticky, add 1 tablespoon flour at a time until it just starts to come together.
5. Transfer the dough to a piece of plastic wrap. Shape the dough into a log about 2 inches in diameter and 8 inches long.
6. Wrap up the log in plastic wrap, and put it into the freezer for 30 minutes to 1 hour.
7. Line two cookie sheets with parchment paper, and preheat the oven to 325°F.
8. Remove the dough from freezer and unwrap. Using a sharp knife, slice thin rounds off the log, and place them on the baking sheet, spacing the cookies 2 inches apart.
9. Bake for 10 to 12 minutes. Watch the cookies closely while baking so they don't overbake. It's okay if the cookies look soft and underbaked. They continue to cook as they cool.
10. Let cookies cool on the cookie sheet for 10 to 15 minutes or until they are set enough to be handled. Transfer the cookies to a wire rack, and cool completely.

DOUBLE CHOCOLATE CHUNK BROWNIES

These chewy, chocolately brownies are baked up in Bea's Bakery every week. For chocolate lovers and those who are falling in love and need to calm their nerves.

Prep Time: 20 minutes
Baking Time: 22 minutes
Cooling Time: 15 minutes
Total: 1 hour
Yield: 12 large brownies

Ingredients

1 cup plus 2 tablespoons all-purpose flour

¾ teaspoon salt

¼ teaspoon kosher salt

½ teaspoon baking powder

4 large eggs at room temperature

1 ½ cups granulated sugar

½ cup packed brown sugar

½ cup canola oil

2 teaspoons pure vanilla extract

½ cup (1 stick) unsalted butter

8 ounces dark chocolate chunks

¼ cup cocoa powder

Instructions

1. Preheat oven to 350°F. Spray with cooking spray a 9 x 13-inch baking pan, and line with a parchment paper sling.

2. In a large bowl, whisk together the eggs, granulated and brown sugars, canola oil, and vanilla.

3. Place the butter in a small microwave-safe bowl, and microwave in 15-second increments until melted. Add cocoa powder, and whisk until completely combined.

4. Add the butter-cocoa mixture to the sugar-egg mixture, and whisk until smooth.

5. Add the flour mixture, and stir until just combined. Fold in the chocolate chunks.

6. Pour the batter into prepared baking dish, and bake for 22–27 minutes, or until the edges are set and the top looks crackled.

7. Transfer pan to a wire rack, and let cool completely. Cut the brownies into squares and serve. Store brownies in an airtight container at room temperature for up to 2 days.

DISCUSSION QUESTIONS

1. In this coming-of-age this story, Kate feels as though she is outgrowing some of the rules her parents have given her. She wants to assert her independence but is also weary of changes. How do you feel she approaches these shifts? Do you think she would have felt better about some of the situations if she had been honest? Why or why not?

2. Kate doesn't fit in because of her upbringing, her skin color, and the way she responds to certain situations. One way she tries to fit in is by allowing the girls to give her a makeover and change her style. Have you ever changed yourself for someone else? What was the result?

3. Kate desperately wants to conform to what Geoffrey wants. What do you think of their relationship? Do you think Geoffrey's feelings for Kate were sincere? Why or why not?

4. Kate's mama calls her visions "a curse." Ama teaches Kate how to control and suppress her visions. Yet the

elder, Aurora Catawnee, in the Cherokee village and Kate's brother, Evan, refer to Kate's visions as a gift. Would you describe Kate's talent as a curse or a gift?

5. Matthias seems to see Kate for who she really is. Do you think Matthias has more-than-friendly feelings for Kate early in the story? If so, why do you think he doesn't say anything about Geoffrey dating her?

6. Kate had a special bond with her brother, Evan. How do you think this relationship guides her in the way she responds to life, people, and even to herself? Do you have a sibling? If so, does your sibling relationship affect how you see the world and the people around you?

7. Kate's mama warns that she can't change the future regardless of what visions she sees. How do you think this burdens her? Do you believe that if she told people about her visions, it would change the course of the future or do you believe in fate?

8. If you had visions of the future, would you tell your friends, even if you knew they might respond negatively? How would you respond if someone approached you and told you they'd had a vision about you? Would you want to hear it? Why or why not?

9. This is the second book in the Mystic Water series, but it is more of an origin story, taking you back to the 1950s. What makes you want to return to Mystic Water? What do you think will happen to some of the characters?

10. Who would you cast if a TV show or movie was made of this novel? What songs would you use for a soundtrack?

ABOUT THE AUTHOR

Photo by Matt Andrews

BORN AND RAISED IN SOUTHERN Georgia, where honeysuckle grows wild and the whippoorwills sing, Jennifer Moorman is the bestselling author of the magical realism Mystic Water series. Jennifer started writing in elementary school, crafting epic tales of adventure and love and magic. She wrote stories in Mead notebooks, on printer paper, on napkins, on the soles of her shoes. Her blog is full of dishes inspired by fiction, and she hosts baking classes showcasing these recipes. Jennifer considers herself a traveler, a baker, and a dreamer. She can always be won over with chocolate, unicorns, or rainbows. She believes in love—everlasting and forever.

Connect with Jennifer at jennifermoorman.com
Instagram: @jenniferrmoorman
Facebook: @jennifermoormanbooks
TikTok: @jennifermoormanbooks
BookBub: @JenniferMoorman

LOOKING FOR MORE MYSTIC WATER ADVENTURES? LOOK NO FURTHER!

Mystic Water Series

Delight in a town where anything can happen—and usually does.

The Baker's Man
The Necessity of Lavender Tea
A Slice of Courage Quiche

Visit online to learn more:
jennifermoorman.com

From the Publisher

Sharing Is Caring!

Loved this book?
Help other readers find it:

- Post a review at your favorite online bookseller

- Post a picture on a social media account and share why you enjoyed it

- Send a note to a friend who would also love it—or better yet, give them a copy

Thank you for reading!

Printed in the USA
CPSIA information can be obtained
at www.ICGtesting.com
LVHW070737180923
758461LV00003B/272

9 781734 739510